TAMING A WILD SCOT

"Get ready for a rich, exciting new voice in Scottish historical romance! Rowan Keats captures all the passion and heart of the Highlands as she expertly weaves a wonderful tale of passion, intrigue, and love that you won't want to put down. I'm already looking forward to the next book in what is sure to be a must-read series."
—Monica McCarty, *New York Times* bestselling author of *The Hunter*

"A rising star of medieval romance . . . [Keats] seamlessly weaves an unusual romance with the intrigues and power plays associated with the era, greatly enhancing the story's emotional power."
—*RT Book Reviews*

ALSO BY ROWAN KEATS

The Claimed by the Highlander Series
Taming a Wild Scot

WHEN A LAIRD TAKES A LADY

A CLAIMED BY THE HIGHLANDER NOVEL

ROWAN KEATS

A SIGNET ECLIPSE BOOK

SIGNET ECLIPSE
Published by the Penguin Group
Penguin Group (USA) LLC, 375 Hudson Street,
New York, New York 10014

USA | Canada | UK | Ireland | Australia | New Zealand | India | South Africa | China
penguin.com
A Penguin Random House Company

First published by Signet Eclipse, an imprint of New American Library,
a division of Penguin Group (USA) LLC

First Printing, May 2014

ISBN 978-0-451-41608-7

Printed in the United States of America
10 9 8 7 6 5 4 3 2 1

Chapter 1

Perched atop a huge black-and-white warhorse, Isabail had an unimpeded view of the destruction. Six of her guards, including the valiant Sir Robert, lay lifeless on the moonlit trail. The others had been forced to their knees and tightly bound like cattle. A pair of chests, packed with her belongings, had been rifled and the contents scattered. The men who had attacked her party had gathered only a few items, mostly simple gowns and practical shoes. The more expensive items—those intended for her sojourn in the king's court—lay in careless heaps, trampled in the snow and mud.

Isabail had no sympathy to spare her fine clothes, however. Fear had cinched her chest so tight there was no room for anything else.

Amazingly, the attackers numbered only three.

How such a small group had succeeded in defeating the dozen guards that accompanied her carriage, she could not fathom. But defeat them, they had. What they lacked in count, they made up for in size—the fur-cloaked Highland raiders were a mouth-souring blur of towering heights, broad shoulders, and powerful limbs.

Their leader, the dark-haired warrior who had demanded her surrender, wore a scowl so thunderous that her belly quailed each time she spied him. Which was often—to her chagrin, his clean-shaven face and neatly trimmed hair drew her eyes again and again.

The raiders worked swiftly, their movements spare and deliberate. No pack was left unopened, no chest left unturned. They concluded their pillage in no time and were soon mounted and ready to depart.

Except for the leader.

He scooped a colorful selection of clothing into a pile, removed a flint from the pouch at his belt, and crouched with his back to the wind. With experienced ease, he soon had the pile in flames. Isabail's fingers clenched in her horse's rough mane, as a sizable portion of her fine wool gowns, white linen sarks, and beaded slippers went up in fiery pyre.

Had she been alone, she would have burst into tears. But her maid's pale, plump face was turned to her, the older woman's eyes a silent plea for hope and guidance. Isabail could not give in to the waves of despair pummeling her body. Not now. Not when Muirne needed her to be strong.

The leader eyed the plume of gray smoke drifting its way into the sky, then grabbed the reins of Isabail's horse and, in a single fluid bound, leapt up behind her. His steely arm slipped around her waist and hauled her into his lap. A short shriek escaped her lips before she could tame it. Instinct urged her to fight for release, to wriggle free and run, but fear held her fast. The man was huge. He could kill her with a solitary blow from one of those massive fists.

Better that she wait for rescue.

She swallowed the lump in her throat. Surely their intent was to ransom her. To sell her back to her cousin for a hefty sum of coin. If she but braved this brute's inappropriate touch for a short while, Cousin Archibald would pay the ransom, and she would be freed. There was no need to risk life or limb to flee.

Her captor urged the horse forward, leading his small group toward the narrow opening at the end of the ravine. Isabail glanced at the fallen bodies and bound figures of her men, and words spilled from her lips before she could stop them.

"You cannot mean to leave them like this."

"I do." His terse response rumbled through his chest, vibrating against her back.

"But large packs of wolves roam these hills."

He said nothing, just urged the horse into a trot. The winding path up the mountain slope was narrow, but they took it at a relentless pace. Higher and higher they climbed, the horse picking its way around boulders and thick patches of heather.

As they traversed a steep ledge, she got a clear view of the moonlit glen and the mist-shrouded castle that was her home.

The folk in the stone fortress below were no doubt going about their usual evening chores, oblivious to the tragedy that had struck her party. How long would it be before the remaining guards were found? Helpless as they were, would they not starve to death, or be torn apart by wild animals?

Isabail chewed her lip.

One of the bearded outlaws riding alongside her caught her eye. "You fret for naught," he said. "The smoke will draw notice from the castle. Unless the earl's soldiers are asleep at their posts, your guards will be home by morn."

Her captor released a derisive snort.

Isabail breathed a sigh of relief, but did not relax. She was struggling to retain her dignity. The upward climb made it extremely difficult to hold herself aloof from the warrior at her back. She did her best to maintain a stiff, ladylike poise, but every time the massive warhorse surged up a steep incline, she collided with her captor's very solid chest.

It was bad enough that their hips were so intimately connected. She refused to give up any more of her self-respect than was necessary. But as the air thinned and grew colder, the steady warmth he exuded held more and more appeal. Determined to resist, she clutched her beaver cloak about her shoulders and buried her hands in the soft fur. Still, the hours in the saddle and the frigid air began to take their toll. She slipped farther and farther back in the saddle. Several times, she stiffened abruptly when she realized her body had slumped wearily toward the wall of male flesh behind her.

Fortunately, her captor did not seem to notice her lapses. His attention was focused on carving a trail through the bleak wilderness that was the Highlands in January. Perhaps fearing pursuit, he kept their pace as hard and as fast as the terrain would allow.

Isabail was just beginning to wonder how far he intended to drag her from her home when he drew the massive destrier to a halt and barked out an order to his men. "Make camp here."

As he leapt down, causing icy air to swirl around her in his absence, she took stock of his chosen campsite. She considered herself born of much hardier stock than her English cousins, but even to her seasoned Scot's eye, the spot looked anything but hospitable. Barren rock, blanketed by a thin layer of ice and snow. The only break to the north wind was a large boulder and, in the distance, a tall standing stone erected by the ancient Picts.

But the lack of obvious comfort did not dismay his men. They helped Isabail and Muirne to dismount, then immediately set about making a fire. Once the peat bricks were generating some heat, they tethered the horses and passed around meager portions of bread and cheese. The meal was too late to be supper and too early to be breakfast, but it tasted wonderful just the same.

Isabail and Muirne were left alone as the men went about their tasks. The ground was icy beneath their boots, discouraging movement, so they simply stood and ate. Muirne's thoughts had not eased on the long ride up the mountain. Her eyes were bright with unshed tears. "They mean to rape and kill us," she whispered.

"How can you know that?" asked Isabail. "They've not made any such threats."

"You need only to look at the dark face on that one"—she pointed to the towering shape of the leader as he unsaddled the horses—"to know that we are doomed."

Isabail's stomach knotted. Muirne's assessment had merit. Everything about the man was terrifying, from the daunting width of his shoulders to the grim set of his chiseled jaw. And her maid was correct—the scowl on his face did not bode well. But to admit the bend of her thoughts to Muirne would stir the maid's fears.

"The only sane reason for them to accost a noble-woman is to ransom her," she said firmly. "They will not harm us for fear of losing their reward."

"That may protect you, my lady, but it'll no protect me," muttered Muirne. "I'll no see my Fearghus again. I can feel it in my bones."

"You are spying a badger where there is only a skunk," chided Isabail. "The possibility of rescue yet remains. We are still on Grant land."

Muirne frowned. "How can you be certain? We've journeyed several hours beyond sight of the castle."

Isabail nodded toward the standing stone in the distance. It was too dark to see the Pictish symbols engraved on its surface, but the shape was very familiar. "I recognize that stone. We are but a short distance from the bothy my brother used as a respite stop during lengthier hunts."

Her maid's face lit up. "Och! We are saved. We can escape there and await the earl's men."

"Nay," Isabail said sharply. "I will not risk the wrath of these men by attempting an escape. Our best option is simply to wait. They will ransom us soon enough."

Her harsh tone drew the attention of one of the reivers—the heavy-set fellow with the wiry dark beard. He stopped brushing the horses for a moment and stared at them. Neither woman dared to speak another word until he resumed his task.

"See?" hissed Isabail. "They watch us too closely. Escape is not possible."

Muirne nodded and sat silent for a time, chewing on her bread and cheese. Although morn was surely only an hour or two away, the reivers laid bedrolls near the fire and offered two of them to the women. Isabail claimed her spot with trepidation. Passing a night under the stars without a tent overhead was disturbing enough, but in the presence of three dangerous men . . . Impossible. Especially with their leader staring at her across the campfire. The flickers of the firelight added bleak shadows to an already stern countenance. His expression left her with the distinct impression that he resented her, though heaven only knew why.

She'd seen him for the first time just two days ago, in the orchard. At the time, unaware that he was a villain and a cad, she had silently admired his physical form. Few men of her acquaintance sported such a blatantly muscular body, and he possessed a rather handsome visage for a heathen brute—the sort of sharply masculine features a woman does not soon forget.

He stood suddenly, and Isabail's breath caught in her chest. By God, he was huge. Dark and powerful, a veritable thunderstorm of a man. He tossed back one side of his fur cloak, revealing a long, lethal sword strapped to his side. Beneath the cloak, she spied a leather jerkin atop a dark lèine and rough leather boots that hugged his calves. His clothing was common enough, but there was something decidedly uncommon about the man.

Perhaps it was the intensity of his glacial blue stare—neither of the other two held her gaze for more than a glance. Or perhaps it was the way he held himself, shoulders loose but firm, like he was a direct descendant of Kenneth MacAlpin himself. Lord of all he surveyed.

He glared at her and drew his sword.

Muirne shrieked, and Isabail's heart skipped a beat.

But the brute did not advance. With his gaze still locked on Isabail, he returned to his seat before the fire and began to clean his weapon.

It took long moments for Isabail's heart to resume its regular rhythm. Not one word had been exchanged, but she had felt the weight of his blame as surely as if he'd unleashed a furious diatribe. In his mind, it would seem, she was the cause of his troubles.

Perhaps Muirne was right. Perhaps he had no intention of ransoming her. Perhaps escape was a wiser option after all.

Isabail dove beneath the blankets provided by his men and lay on her side with her back to the fire. The bedroll provided little comfort—the frozen ground dug into her hip and shoulder, and the fire only warmed one side of her body. Her nose and fingers were chilled, but rolling to the other side was not an option. Her nape already tingled under the cold gaze of her captor. Facing him would be unbearable.

"The women are slowing us down," one of the men muttered. "At this pace, it'll take another full day to reach Dunstoras."

Isabail froze. *Dunstoras?*

"That assumes the earl's men don't catch us first," retorted another.

"You worry for naught," said their leader crisply. "The earl's men are a league behind us. They think we're headed south. We'll lose them when we turn west and descend into Strath Nethy."

Nausea rolled in Isabail's belly. Dunstoras was home to the MacCurrans—the clan whose chief had robbed the king and murdered her brother. The same chief who had escaped Lochurkie's dungeon and absconded to parts unknown. If the man seated across the fire was Aiden MacCurran, she was in far more dire straits than she had thought. A murderous traitor to the Crown would hardly follow the unwritten rules of hostage taking.

She lay stiff and silent, unable to sleep.

MacCurran deserved to pay for his crimes. John had been a fine man and a good earl—far more noble and worthy than her father had been. If only she could escape, she could ensure MacCurran was brought to justice. From the standing stone, she could find her way to the hunt bothy with ease—she and John had stopped there a dozen times over the years.

The challenge was getting away from MacCurran and his men. It might be possible for one of the women to sneak away, but two? Unlikely. Yet she could hardly leave Muirne behind. No, if an escape was to be made, it would be both of them or neither of them.

Worrying her bottom lip between her teeth, Isabail reviewed her options—discarding most ideas as foolhardy. Eventually, she settled on one. She waited until MacCurran and the other guard had bedded for the night and uneven snores were rising into the dark sky. Then she nudged Muirne.

"I've a need to visit the privy," she whispered.

It took a raised eyebrow and an exaggerated wink to sweep the sleepy look from her maid's face. "Och, of course you do. Let's away, then."

They donned their boots and cloaks, then crossed the camp to where the eldest of the reivers stood watch—a grizzled warrior with a patch of gray hair braided at each temple. Isabail pointed to the standing stone, which was a vague shape in the darkness. "I must see to my needs. My maid will accompany me to the privy."

He followed her finger, frowning. "Nay, that's too far. See to your business behind this boulder. I'll not pry."

Isabail straightened her shoulders and favored him with her most imperious stare. "That will not do at all. Women are not men. We do not simply open a door and piss into the wind. Privacy is an absolute requirement for a lady."

His lips thinned with annoyance. "Fine."

Isabail fought to contain a grin of satisfaction. She had won. "We'll return shortly."

"That you will." He strode across the camp and nudged one of the other men with his boot. "Graeme, wake up," he whispered. "The ladies need to visit the privy."

"What?"

"Just get up."

Isabail's heart sank as Graeme rolled out of his pallet and reluctantly got to his feet. So much for their grand escape. Even with his eyes groggy from sleep, the beefy warrior would not miss them scurrying through the heather. Her plan was dashed before it even started.

She sighed heavily.

She and Muirne made quick work of seeing to their needs and returned to the warmth of the fire. Graeme replaced the older warrior on watch, giving his cohort leave to bury himself in the blankets and close his eyes. As Isabail should do. But the tantalizing thought of escape refused to die. Mac-Curran was a madman. He would slay her just as surely as he'd slain her brother—no doubt in some far-fetched notion of justice. But the ruin of his clan was his own fault, not hers or her brother's. He'd dared to covet the ruby necklace King Alexander had commissioned for his new bride and had murdered a dozen people to get it. He was touched in the head to blame the Grants for his imprisonment.

She shivered. Unfortunately, having right on her side wouldn't save her. She was at MacCurran's mercy. He could exact whatever revenge he wanted. And with huge fists made for beating, he could do it with ease.

She must make another attempt. Dawn would soon be upon them, and this might be her last opportunity to reach safety.

"Muirne," she whispered.

"Aye?"

"Make the lad a spot of tea."

Her maid frowned. "You want me to show him kindness, after what they've done?"

"The man is no doubt chilled. Chat with him for a moment; ease his lot."

Muirne tossed her a rebellious glare but got to her feet and put a small pot on the fire. The men's supplies had been bolstered by their raid on Isabail's party, and the copper pot was one of hers.

Isabail tried not to resent that as she peered around the camp area for a suitable rock. It had to be small enough for her to lift but large enough to knock the man out. Problem was, she had no clue how large a rock it would take. Denting a man's skull was not one of the skills she had acquired while acting as chatelaine of Lochurkie. And even if it had been, she'd have been out of practice by now. Her cousin Archibald's wife had taken over her duties after John's death, leaving Isabail at a loss for purpose.

Aha. There was a rock that might do.

The guard was watching Muirne. Isabail waited until the maid had approached him with the tea; then, taking care not to wake the sleeping men around her, she eased from her pallet. Snowflakes had begun to drift down from the night sky. Moving as swiftly as her long woolen skirts would allow, she snatched up the rock with both hands and ran for the large boulder at the guard's back. But the icy ground beneath her fine leather boots proved perilous. One moment she was darting for the boulder, the next she was flat in the snow. Her hip and elbow took the brunt of the fall. She bit back a squeal of pain, but feared the thump of her fall had alerted the guard. She held her breath and listened.

Muirne and the guard were talking.

"And what do they call you?" she asked him.

"Graeme."

"Is there a lass waiting on your return, Graeme?"

They had not heard her fall. Isabail released her breath, slowly and carefully. Then she scrambled to her feet and rounded the boulder, slipping up behind Graeme. Apparently, Muirne's conversation had him thoroughly engrossed. Only when she was within striking distance did he pivot to face her. But by then it was too late. The rock was already on its descent. She slammed it against his skull, and he went down fast and hard, collapsing against her and sliding to the ground at her boots. A trickle of blood oozed from beneath his hair, and Isabail felt a bitter pang.

"Did I kill him?" she whispered.

Muirne bent over him. "Nay. He's still breathing."

Relief made her dizzy. "Thank the Lord. We must hurry now. Who knows when the others will awake."

Muirne looked back at the fire. "Can we take the blankets? And perhaps some of the food?"

Isabail's gaze locked on the large sleeping shape of MacCurran. Falling snow had accumulated in the folds of his blanket, farthest from the fire. "We dare not. If either of the other two awakens, we are doomed."

"But it might be days before the earl's men find us."

"My brother kept the bothy well stocked. There's bound to be some food there. We must move swiftly." She wrapped her cloak and fur tightly about her body. She was already missing the heat of the fire.

They set off for the standing stone once more, and when they reached it, turned sharply south. If memory served her correctly, the bothy was at the base of this hill, tucked into the woods. There was a small circle of stones about a hundred paces from the front door, and this taller, solitary stone pointed directly toward it. All they had to do was stay straight and true.

They marched forward, Muirne following Isabail's lead. The older woman struggled over the rocky terrain and stumbled several times. As they traversed the hill, Isabail looked back at the standing stone several times to keep her bearing, but darkness and a thickening veil of snow soon blocked the stone from sight.

In some ways, the snow was a godsend.

Any evidence of their passage was obliterated by a sea of white. If Graeme roused or one of the other men awoke, they would not know in which direction the women had set off. They would surely assume they would head back the way they'd come—east, not south. But the snow was also a serious hindrance. It was thick and wet, and it accumulated with surprising speed, making walking much more difficult.

"Ah!"

Isabail spun around.

Muirne lay sprawled on the ground, pain etched on her face. "My foot. I've twisted my foot."

Isabail waded back to her maid's side. "It's not much farther. I'm certain of it. Can you stand?"

"I don't know."

"Let's give it a go." Determined to get to the bothy and out of the blowing snow, Isabail offered Muirne her arm. "Up we get."

The older woman clutched her arm and pushed

to one foot. Then she gingerly tested her injured limb, wincing the instant she placed weight on it. "Nay, my lady. I cannot walk. You'll have to get on without me."

"Don't be daft. I'll not leave you here." Isabail studied the snow-blurred tree line at the bottom of the hill. Where was the circle of stones? Should she not be able to see them by now? The snow was thick and drifting, but it hardly seemed possible that they would be completely buried. Yet there was no sign of them.

Without a guidepost, the wisest option was to head straight for the trees. At least there they would enjoy some protection from the wind.

"One step at a time," she encouraged Muirne as they set off.

Between the snow, the uneven rocks beneath, and the shivers beginning to rack the older woman's body, they made very slow progress. The weather was unforgiving. Few people dared to cross the Red Mountains in the winter, and Isabail got a bleak taste of why. Although the sky began to lighten with the impending day, the winds picked up and the snow changed from soft flakes to hard pellets. It stung their faces and snatched their breaths away. Unable to bury her hands in her cloak because of her hold on Muirne, Isabail's fingers first reddened and then turned white. She could no longer feel her fingers or her toes.

Yet she fared better than Muirne.

Her maid's cloak was woven of much thinner wool than Isabail's, and she had no fur bundled about her shoulders. By the time they made it to the tree line, Muirne's lips were blue and her usually rosy cheeks were pale as parchment.

"I cannot go on," she murmured, sinking to her knees in the snow.

Isabail prodded the other woman. "You must. If you stop here, you will surely die." She glanced around, hoping to spot the stone circle, but saw only a glaring sea of white. Had she wandered from the path to the bothy? "It's only a few more feet," she lied.

Muirne shook her head. "I cannot do it."

Exhausted and thoroughly disheartened by the way the fates had played with her attempt to escape, Isabail flopped into the snow next to her maid and huddled against the wind. "Seems rather unfair, doesn't it? To escape one death only to meet another?"

Tears sprang to Muirne's eyes. "I'll never see my Fearghus again."

A pang rippled through Isabail's chest. Muirne's bitterest regret at this dire moment was failing to see her beloved husband one last time. Isabail had no similar yearning to latch onto. Her brother was dead; her parents, too. And she'd outlived her husband, who'd died of a festered wound only a year after they'd been wed.

Aye, she lived with her cousin Archibald, but they were not close. He would pay for her ransom, but more out of duty than fondness. He'd allowed her to remain at Lochurkie when he assumed the earldom in November, and they sat next to each other at the high table for meals, but she could not have named his favorite food, nor he hers.

Strangely, though, Isabail had never thought her life lacking until this very moment.

She pushed to her feet again and held out her hand. "Come on, then. Another hundred paces for Fearghus."

Muirne shook her head. "I'm too cold."

"Is that how you intend to meet him in the afterlife? By telling him you could not return to him because you were too cold?" Isabail grabbed her maid's hand and tugged hard. "Actions speak louder than words, Muirne. If you truly love him, you will strive until the your last breath to be with him. To your feet now."

The other woman rocked to her feet, her face a reflection of utter misery. "Every part of me is numb."

Isabail was exhausted and cold as well, but she suspected her fur shoulder wrap offered protection the other woman's woolen brat did not. The fur was her just due as a noblewoman, but the stark hopelessness on Muirne's face called for uncommon action. A practical act, not one based on right. All that mattered was encouraging Muirne to move again.

Isabail unpinned the beaver fur, wrapped it around her maid's shoulders, and fastened it at her throat. "The bothy is just ahead," she lied again. "You can make it."

The other woman's face eased noticeably as the

heat from Isabail's fur seeped through her clothes. "Another hundred paces."

"Aye."

They set off again, hobbling through the drifts. The wind tore at Isabail's cloak, sapping what little warmth she had left. She supported Muirne's weight, and they made slow and steady progress, right up to the moment they ran into a snow-plastered standing stone. Wet snow had encased the stone's gray facade completely, making it impossible to see against the background of white drifts.

Isabail's heart thumped with excited fervor. They were indeed close to the bothy. A little to the left and through the trees and they would be there. Her legs strengthened. "I can see the door, Muirne. Don't falter now."

They pressed on.

It look longer than Isabail could've imagined to bridge the gap, but they eventually arrived at the door. Isabail unlatched it, and they fell inside. The bothy was a primitive one-room abode with a dirt floor and no bed, but Isabail viewed the open chamber with a huge grin. Against all the odds, they had made it.

But the struggle had sapped Muirne's last reserves. She collapsed just inside the door, sinking to the floor without uttering another word.

Isabail shut the door against the blowing snow and checked to make sure Muirne still breathed. To her relief, the woman was alive, just bone weary. Brushing the snow from her clothes, she tried to make her maid as comfortable as possible. Then she took stock of their surroundings.

A table, two chairs, and a fieldstone hearth. Some blankets and an iron kettle, but no food and no kindling. When her brother had been earl, the bothy had been well provisioned because he had enjoyed the hunt and had spent every spare moment in the saddle. Archibald took more interest in political affairs and spent much of his time in Edinburgh. A fact Isabail regretted at that moment.

No fire, no food, no water. The sorry truth was, although they had succeeded in reaching their goal, they were as likely to die here as they were in the snow. Only more slowly.

Isabail gathered the blankets and a small pile of rabbit pelts. She covered Muirne with most of them, but kept two for herself. Unfortunately, the snow had left her clothing damp, and the chill in her flesh remained in spite of the extra layers. In desperate hope that she would find some forgotten tidbit, Isabail searched every corner of the bothy, every box and every tin.

Nothing. Not even a crumb.

She sat on a chair and glared at the empty hearth. A cruel twist of fate to be so tantalizingly close to safety. A few logs and a piece of flint would have worked a miracle.

Muirne murmured something unintelligible, shifting beneath the blankets. Some color had returned to the older woman's cheeks, but the tip of her nose remained bone white. Isabail was familiar with basic healing remedies, such as willow bark tea for pain and mint for nausea, but her skills did not extend to treating severe cold. She had a sense she ought to do something more for her maid. But what? A sense of helplessness tugged at her shoulders. Not a common feeling for a woman who typically had three dozen gillies at her service.

She was chewing her bottom lip, contemplating her very limited options, when the door to the bothy burst open. A very large, snow-covered figure stepped across the threshold, nearly filling the room with his broad shoulders. He shoved back his hood and stared silently at Isabail.

She swallowed.

Dear God. It was MacCurran. And judging by the dark glitter in his eyes, cold and hunger were the least of her problems.

Chapter 2

Aiden stared at Isabail Grant, torn between berating her and hugging her with joy. She was alive and seemingly in good health. But, damn it, the story could so easily have had a bitter ending. He glanced down at the maid. Frostbite had gripped the woman's fingers and nose and likely her toes.

They needed a fire.

He crossed to the hearth, pulling several peat bricks from his pouch. Breaking one of the bricks into small pieces, he crouched to light them with his flint. "Remove her boots and any wet clothing."

When Isabail just stared at him, wide-eyed, he barked, "Now."

She scrambled to the other woman's side.

"Put your hands on any flesh that is white. Do not rub; just hold her."

The peat came to fiery life with gratifying ease, and he layered on more bricks, taking care not to smother the flames. Then he snatched the rabbit furs from the pile atop the maid and shaped them into a thick pallet before the fire. When he was satisfied the bed would triumph over the cold of the dirt floor, he crossed the room to the unconscious woman.

He scooped her up, blankets and all, and carried her to the fire. The color had returned to her nose, a good sign. When she was settled, he turned back to Isabail.

"You next."

She blinked. "If you think I'm going to disrobe in front of you, you are—"

He grabbed her and forced her onto a chair. "Boots first."

"My feet are fine."

The leather was soaked, which suggested her stockings were also wet. "I'll be the judge of that." He untied her boots and tugged them off. Her stockings quickly followed. The tops of her feet glowed a healthy pink, but the soles were a bloodless white. Unceremoniously, he opened the lacings on his lèine, took a foot in each hand, and planted her soles on his chest.

Her cheeks flushed a furious shade of red, but she said nothing.

He studied her face. A collection of delicate features, very feminine—except for her eyebrows, which were strong arcs above her smoky blue eyes. A contradiction not unlike the lady herself. Who would have guessed she'd make a bold bid for escape? With a rock, no less. "You're a fool."

"Because I dared to escape?"

"Because you very near killed your maid."

Her gaze dropped. "Were it not for the winter storm, we would have traveled much swifter. I cannot be blamed for the snow."

"Had you looked at the clouds, you'd have known."

Her eyes lifted. "You knew it would snow?"

He said nothing, believing the answer obvious. *Why else would we have built the camp in such an open area?* He checked the soles of her feet. Still pale, but no longer colorless. "Warm your maid's feet while I fetch some wood from the log pile."

"How do you know there's wood? The food stores are empty."

"I've passed this bothy many a time in the summer."

She frowned. "If you knew it was here, why did you make camp in the hills?"

He tossed her a cold, pointed stare. "I do not willingly take solace from my enemies."

Aiden yanked his brat over his head and braved the blizzard once more. Isabail Grant was his enemy. He had to remember that. John Grant had robbed him of all he held dear—his reputation, his home, and his kin. The justiciar could have chosen to believe Aiden's version of the events—in fact, for a brief time Aiden thought he had won the man over—but he had not. The earl had ruled against him. And he hadn't stopped there. In the days that followed, he'd brutally tortured Aiden and outlawed all who carried the MacCurran name. Every hardship his people currently endured could be laid at feet of the Grants. Seeing Isabail as a gentlewoman in need of protection was a mistake.

She could restore his life, or she could destroy it. *And it was up to him to decide which it would be.* Isabail possessed information that could redeem him in the eyes of the king and return his clan to their rightful prominence. She knew the identity of the man in black—the man who was behind all of the misfortunes that had befallen him.

Gaining that information was all that mattered.

Aiden trudged around the bothy to the wood-pile, which was buried under several thick inches of snow and ice. He swept aside the layer of snow; then, with a clenched fist, he hammered the ice. With one mighty blow, the ice cracked and fell away. The smaller pieces of kindling were at the top, the larger split logs at the bottom. Aiden scooped up some of both, then returned to the bothy.

Inside, he stomped his feet to rid his boots of clinging snow. Isabail was bent over her maid, binding her sprained ankle, but the moment his gaze fell upon her, she shrank against the back wall of the hut. *Saints above.* He'd never struck a woman in his life, and he wasn't about to start now. He'd lost enough. He refused to give up his principles, no matter how justified his anger might be.

The peat bricks were still burning nicely, so he stacked the wood near the flames to dry it out. Wet wood would create more smoke, and in a bothy with no chimney and a winter storm preventing open shutters, smoke was a hazard.

All the while, Isabail hugged the daub and wattle wall, watching him warily.

"Are you hungry?" he asked.

Hope brightened in her eyes for a moment, but she tempered it and then shook her head. "I don't willingly take solace from my enemies."

He shrugged. "The key word there is *willing*, lass. If you don't eat, you won't be strong enough to make another attempt to escape." He dug into his pouch and pulled out two large strips of dried venison. One, he chewed on. The other he broke in half and offered to Isabail.

She resisted for several heartbeats.

Then she darted forward, snatched the meat from his hands, and retreated to her corner of the hut.

"You'll not benefit from the fire over there," he said, with a shake of his head.

"I'm fine."

"Nay, you're not." The woman still wore her damp clothes. If she did not dry out, he'd be tending to two invalids, not one. Aiden crossed the room in an easy stride, grabbed her about her slender waist, and hauled her over to the fire. He forced her down onto a blanket before the flames. "Eat, then sleep."

Then he stepped away, seeking his own pallet.

Isabail stared at him, her face pale. But she remained where she was, her feet almost instinctively reaching toward the fire. The room was quiet for a while, with only the crackle of the fire and the chew of dried meat.

Then, with a hesitant voice, Isabail asked, "Is he all right? The man I hit?"

"Graeme? Aye."

"I feared I might have killed him."

Aiden snorted. A rock wielded by a sturdy milkmaid, perhaps. But not one hefted by a will-o'-the-wisp like Isabail Grant. Graeme would face a great deal of ribbing over being felled by the likes of her.

"Sneer if you'd like," she said quietly, "but I am not like you. I do not murder people with an easy conscience."

Aiden tossed her a hard look. "Be careful, lass. You know naught of what you speak."

"You deny you killed my brother?"

"I do."

She shook her head lightly. "Do you deny slaying the king's courier, too? My brother said they found the necklace in your chamber." How easily those accusations spilled from her lips. Like they were an absolute truth.

All the rage he'd contained for months suddenly poured through Aiden's veins like molten steel, sending him to his feet. Isabail cringed, and he swiveled to avoid the fear on her face. He was too angry to be kind. "The accusations made against me are sheer madness. Why would I poison my own kin? Why would I steal from a king while his courier was feasting under my own roof? Only a fool would do such a thing, and I assure you, I am no fool."

Crossing the room to a wall hung with antlers

from bygone hunts, he did his best to contain the fury that burned in his chest . . . and failed. He punched the wall with a heavy fist, sending antlers crashing to the floor.

"Eight of my kin died that night, including the wife of my cousin Wulf and her wee son, Hugh. No necklace, no matter how grand, could be worth the loss of those lives." He closed his eyes, picturing the faces of those who were lost that night, one by one. Most of the dead had been very young or very old. The healthier sorts had sickened, but survived. Except for Elen and Henry de Coleville, both very fond of eel soup—they'd consumed two bowls.

He opened his eyes and stared at the dent his fist had left in the wattle and daub wall. "'Twas your brother who caused their deaths."

"Nay," she said vehemently. "That's not possible. If you knew my brother, you would never say such a thing."

Aiden pivoted. "One of the men who accompanied Henry de Coleville to Dunstoras was also at Lochurkie the next morning. I saw him when your brother arrested me."

She frowned. "Of what relevance is that? All of the king's men came to Lochurkie after the murder of de Coleville."

"I spied this one in the corridor leading to my chamber. He hid the necklace there."

Her lips thinned. "A rather far-fetched tale. Why would anyone go to such lengths?"

"To discredit the MacCurrans."

Her eyebrows lifted. "Your clan is small, and your land is mostly mountains. What could they possibly gain?"

A very good question. One Aiden had given much thought to in the months since the necklace was stolen. But he was still no closer to an answer. His father had been a staunch supporter of the king, even from the early days of his minority, and he had spent a fair amount of time at the king's side—but more as a warrior than a political ally. Compared to the Comyns, the Balliols, and the Bruces, the MacCurrans had little influence. They were renowned for their battle skills, but these were peaceful days in Scotland—the Norse had been conquered and England had ceased to play their wicked games of control, at least for a time.

But some sort of treachery was afoot. "You know the name of the man I seek."

A genuinely puzzled look stole over her face. "You cannot believe that I remember the names of all the king's men."

"Not all, just this one."

"And why him?"

"He was standing next to your brother when I was dragged into the great hall and accused of my crimes."

She adjusted her skirts, fanning the pale blue material out to dry the folds that were still wet. "I was not there, but if you describe him, perhaps I can name him."

"He wore black from tip to toe, including a black wolf cloak."

"And his face?"

"I did not see it."

"The color of his hair, then?"

Aiden said nothing. He had no more to offer. The black wolf cloak was his best clue.

Isabail shook her head. "I cannot identify a man simply by his clothing."

"Surely you would remember a man who garbed himself entirely in black? A man of enough consequence to wear a wolf pelt?"

"You ask too much. That night is several months in the past, and my brother took ill and died shortly thereafter." A shadow passed over her face.

He empathized with her loss. But *his* memories of that night were clear as spring rain, and the safety of his clan hung on her ability to remember. "Name all the men of consequence who were guests of your brother, then."

"And have you accuse them falsely of murder? Nay, I will not."

Aiden stalked across the room. This woman was his only hope of identifying the poisoner. He needed those names. "You will tell me."

Isabail shot to her feet and darted back to her corner of the hut, flattening herself against the wall like a tapestry of some enacted Greek tragedy.

Aiden followed, determined. "I will have the truth." Placing his hands on the wall on either side of her, he caged her in. Then he leaned closer, his gaze pinning hers. "Give me the names."

Aiden fully expected Isabail to maintain her dignified refusal, but she did something quite unexpected—she fainted. He was so surprised, he almost neglected to catch her as she fell. English ladies fainted all the time, especially when confronted with large, fierce Highlanders, but Scottish noblewomen tended to be made of sterner stuff.

He adjusted the unconscious woman in his arms. Light as thistledown.

Perhaps she was overly weary, exhausted from her trek through the snow. Surely, she hadn't collapsed due to his anger. As chatelaine of Lochurkie, she would have regularly dealt with soldiers and laborers, many of them clad much as he was. Of course, he was larger than many and built of sturdy MacCurran stock. Raised as a warrior first and a chief second.

Aiden laid the woman gently on her pallet and covered her with a blanket. Almost without thinking, he picked up her heavy braid of hair. The strands glistened like silk, the hue so blond, it was almost white. Gazing at her this close, it was hard to imagine she was John Grant's sister. The earl had been a large dark-haired man, perhaps a little too fond of ale and fine foods. Quite an imposing fellow, especially with a sword strapped to his side.

Perhaps they were born of different mothers.

The earl he knew reasonably well; John Grant had been the justiciar of Glen Avon, and as such held court for the judgments of serious crimes in the region. But all Aiden knew of his sister was that she'd been wed to the ill-fated young Macintosh heir who'd died of a festered knife wound shortly after a faire in honor of his name day.

He stepped back, frowning.

She was also deeply frightened of him. To her mind, he was a savage stranger who had attacked her carriage, slain her guards, and kidnapped her person. In truth, she'd been remarkably brave thus far. He doubted his mother would have endured such an attack without weeping or wailing.

Isabail's fear could cause him serious grief, however.

In little more than a week, the king would grant Dunstoras to a new lord. The MacCurran keep had been reclaimed by the king when Aiden was arrested in November, and only Alexander mac Alexander's infatuation with his new bride had seen it linger without a lord this long. Aiden had only a brief window of time to prove his innocence before the land was lost. And it wasn't just the land he would lose. Outlawed after their chief's disgrace and routed by soldiers, much of his clan had scattered. Only a handful of loyal kin remained, and those had withdrawn to a stone ruin deep in the forest. If Dunstoras were given to a new lord, it would not be long before those kin, too, were gone.

Aiden's hands fisted at his sides.

If he gained the identity of the man in black, he might have a chance to save Dunstoras and re-build his fractured clan. But to gain the names of John Grant's guests, he would have to conquer

Isabail's fear and gain her trust. In less than a sennight.

No so great a challenge, surely?

When Isabail woke, the bothy was dark and shuttered. The howl of the winter storm had quieted, but she had no sense how long she had been unconscious. Her last memory—the fierce face of the MacCurran swooping down upon her—was still vivid enough to make her heart pound, and she wondered if she'd taken a beating. Biting her lip in anticipation of pain, she shifted in her pallet. To her relief, there was almost none. Her hip was sore from lying in the dirt floor—the blankets beneath her couldn't compare to the feather-stuffed mattress she was accustomed to—but save for that, she felt perfectly fine.

Isabail looked around.

The fire was merrily blazing, having recently received a fresh log, and she lifted her head to find the person who had fed it. Her heart stumbled. Aiden MacCurran sat on the other side of the flames, sleeves rolled up, carefully tending to his sword. He seemed unaware of her, so she watched him for a moment.

Unlike his two henchmen, the MacCurran chief's chin was clean-shaven, and his hair appeared to have been recently washed. Not a typical Highlander, then, despite the warring nature of his clan. His forearms rippled with sinews as he worked, the hairs on his arms golden in the firelight. Isabail was woman enough to admit she found him attractive—from a distance. Broad shoulders and tapered hips were attractive in a man, no matter who that man might be. But it was also strangely comforting to watch him hone his sword—his hands were strong and sure as they worked, displaying a level of care and control over his weapon that belied the bestiality of his large fists.

"There's more venison, if you've a hunger," he said quietly.

Isabel swallowed dryly and sat up. "I've more a need for something to wet my mouth."

He pointed to the door of the hut. "Fetch some snow."

Isabail flushed. Why hadn't she thought of that? Of course she could eat some snow. She scrambled to her feet and headed for the door.

"I've beat a good path to the woodpile," he added. "If you must see to your needs, it'll provide a measure of privacy."

Her flush deepened, though she couldn't quite pinpoint why. A visit to the privy was a common enough event, and he was hardly giving the delicate topic excessive attention. But just the knowledge that he'd thought about her needs made her cheeks heat. Isabail escaped quickly.

Outside the bothy, the snowfall had ceased, but the sky was still sullen with cloud. The sun was little more than a smudge of brightness above the trees, but a pair of crossbills flitting through the branches thought it was well worth chirping about. For the briefest of moments, the notion of fleeing took hold, but she couldn't leave without Muirne. Besides, where would she go?

Nay. As much as he frightened her, the MacCurran was her best hope of survival.

She ate her fill of cold wet snow, completed her ablutions, and returned to the cozy warmth of the hut. MacCurran had not moved—he was still polishing the fine steel of his blade with a purposeful attention to detail. For some reason, that eased Isabail's tremulous thoughts. Surely a man capable of such focus could keep his temper under tight rein.

"Rouse your maid," he said.

She knelt beside Muirne and checked her fingers and toes—save for the woman's right small toe, all were a healthy shade of pink.

"We'll set off as soon as she is ready."

Isabail nodded. With a gentle shake and a firm voice, she encouraged Muirne to rise. The older woman was still clearly exhausted, but she sat up when Isabail offered her food and water. "Nay, my lady. It should be I who sees to your welfare, not you to mine."

But she took the food and consumed it with a very unladylike haste.

MacCurran handed her a pair of dry stockings. "Your boots are dry, but they likely won't remain that way. If you lose feeling in your feet as we walk, let me know immediately."

When they were once again bundled against the winter chill, MacCurran doused the fire and led them back up the mountain. It took them half the time to return to camp as it had to find the bothy. Due in part, no doubt, to the powerful way MacCurran cut a swath through the snowdrifts, but also because the route he took was more direct.

She caught his eye as they spied the billowing gray blankets that served as a tent for his two men. He shrugged. "You lost your way as you traversed the hill."

"So, it was a miracle we found the bothy?"

He grimaced. "Aye."

Isabail flinched at the return of the fierce visage. He clearly thought her a fool, but could he not understand her desire to be free? Would he not have done the same in her boots?

The other two men greeted MacCurran with subdued respect. Graeme, in particular, wore a pained expression that had nothing to do with the lump on his head. They were ashamed to have let down their chief. They packed up the camp and saddled the horses with spare movements and little chatter. By the time the sun had fully broken free of the horizon, they were plowing through the snow in a westerly direction, the white-capped cone of Ben Avon reaching into the sky to the south.

Isabail was no happier to be sharing a mount with MacCurran this time than she was the last, but she had a new appreciation for the horse's long-legged ability to cut through drifts. She kept as much distance from her companion as their close proximity would allow, grateful for the extra padding provided by the blankets. Making a mental note to restock the hunt bothy, she snuggled deeper into the wool.

MacCurran and his men kept an aggressive pace, their horses agilely navigating the rocky mountain paths. The leagues passed uneventfully. Despite the improvement in the weather, there was no sign of any soldiers from Lochurkie. Either they'd fallen significantly behind, or they had given up.

As the sun reached its zenith in the sky, the air warmed, and Isabail's breath no longer made a foggy exit from her lips. There was a certain monotony to the journey—the rolling gait of the horse, the thud of hooves on the frozen ground, the gentle heat on her face and at her back. And she felt remarkably secure with MacCurran's unyielding arm wrapped around her waist. Perhaps because she could not see his grim face.

He said nothing as they rode, leading the group over the rough terrain without a hint of uncertainty or indecision. The only sound that left his lips was an occasional series of clicks to encourage their horse when the terrain was especially challenging. Isabail actually managed to forget that she was the prisoner of a Highland barbarian . . . at least briefly.

Exhaustion crept up on her. It grew harder and harder to keep her eyes open and her back stiff. Especially during those moments when the path led straight up the mountain. Isabail struggled against her drooping eyelids . . . and lost. The last thing she remembered as her eyes slid shut was a gruffly worded, "Sleep."

Aiden felt Isabail go limp in his arms and knew she had finally succumbed to the rigor of her snowbound adventure. She surprised him with the extent of her endurance—she'd slept no more than a wink during the night. Her timing was unfortunate, though.

He reined his horse in at the edge of the cliff and looked out over the wide glen below. Forest stretched as far as the eye could see in all directions, the trees a mix of barren winter branches and green needled firs. Approaching Dunstoras from the east always made his heart soar. Wrapped in leafless winter vines, the pale gray stones of the castle's tower were clearly visible against the afternoon sky. They stood above the trees like a beacon calling him home.

"Now, there's a sight for sore eyes," Graeme said, drawing alongside him.

Aiden nodded, but his gaze had already moved south of the tower, settling on a rocky rise at the base of the mountains—the site of their current camp, a ruined palace built by the Picts more than five hundred years ago. Or so said the legends. For the past several months, he and his clan had camped amid the rubble, hidden from view by the harsh landscape. Using remnants of the old stone walls as a foundation, they had laid new thatch roofs and wooden floors, creating a primitive but livable abode. The stone castle designed by his fa-

ther and raised with the blood and sweat of his
MacCurran kin might lie under the temporary
stewardship of Tormod MacPherson, but he could
still go home.

At least, for now.

Aiden turned his mount away from all that had
once been his and made his way down the slope
to the glen. The woman in his arms was not to
blame for his plight, but he still felt the twist of a
knife in his gut when he looked at her. John Grant
had stolen his future. Living in the Pictish ruin
was bearable only because it held the promise of
returning to their true home. Once that was gone,
it would be only a matter of time before all else
was gone, too.

MacPherson had been ruthless in ridding the
land of his outlawed kin. Many had died in the
siege of the castle, but many more had simply
been run off. Men, women, and even children had
been dispossessed. The king's man had shown no
mercy. Those who had not made haste to leave
Dunstoras land had been run through or tossed in
the cramped dungeons beneath the keep.

The bitter taste of gall rose in Aiden's throat.

He'd sworn an oath to protect his kin, and he'd
failed them. The clan elders, the learned men
who'd appointed him chief upon his father's
death, were all dead. Two of them had fallen victim to the poison, the remaining three to the siege
and the trials of a cold winter. All he had left was
a small band of skilled warriors and a solitary clue
to who had wreaked havoc upon his clan.

Reaching the bottom of the hill, Aiden urged his mount into a canter. In the glen, amid the trees, the snow cover was thin and easily navigated. Proving his innocence would save his kin. He had nine days left to succeed, and by God, he would do it or die trying.

The leafless boughs of the woodland gave Aiden a sweeping view of the land as he rode. Having hunted almost every inch of the glen over the years, he was very familiar with the trail—and he knew immediately that a broken twig on a nearby hazelnut thicket was cause for alarm. A quick glance at the frozen ground confirmed his suspicions. There was almost no snow here, but in the occasional patches of white, he made out the faint curve of hoofprints. Somewhere up ahead, there were riders.

Raising a hand, he drew his party to a swift halt.

With two women among them, they were at a serious disadvantage. They could ill afford to engage any soldiers over a sharp blade, else they'd put the women at risk. He signaled to Duncan to dismount and take responsibility for the ladies. Aiden put a hand over Isabail's mouth, then shook her awake.

Her eyes widened in alarm, and he removed the hand from her lips.

"Go with Duncan," he told her quietly. "Do exactly as he says." Then he lowered her gently to the ground and drew his sword.

Chapter 3

Watching MacCurran leap to the ground and hand off his horse, Isabail felt a surge of hope. Had the soldiers from Lochurkie finally caught them up? Was freedom only moments away?

"If you release me peacefully," she said quickly, "my cousin will show you mercy."

"These are not your cousin's men. They are MacPhersons."

Was that supposed to frighten her? If so, it failed. Tormod MacPherson was a personal acquaintance—he'd been to Lochurkie on several occasions to meet with her brother. He had been tasked with holding Dunstoras until the king pledged it to a new lord. If his patrol had chanced upon them, Dunstoras must be close.

Almost as if he read her thoughts, MacCurran tossed her a hard look. "Before you open your mouth to alert them, you should be aware that MacPherson's men are mostly hired sword arms. They believe raping and pillaging are their just

dues. I've buried several women who did not survive their attentions."

Isabail's stomach turned.

Whether the story was real or not, it had the
desired impact. Isabail lost her urge to shout into
the forest. She allowed the MacCurran chief to disappear through the trees without uttering a single
syllable. But she wasn't willing to let her dream of
freedom die without a fight. With their leader
gone, this was her best opportunity to escape.

Her gaze turned to his men. In theory, a younger
man would be less set in his beliefs and easier to
sway than an older man. But Graeme's pride had
been wounded during her attempted escape. Now
almost as grim faced as their leader, the tall, black-
haired warrior had taken to strapping four blades
to his body—a broadsword, two dirks, and a small
ax—all honed to a razor's edge. Earlier in the day,
she'd seen him fell a rabbit with the ax and then
gut and skin the poor creature in a matter of minutes.

Aye, Graeme was too great a risk. She'd have
better luck with Duncan. The older man, a sturdy
fellow with a hint of gray in his sandy beard, had
a gentle eye, especially when he looked at Muirne.
Even as she studied him, the burly warrior helped
Muirne dismount and offered her a round of bread
and some cheese. Isabail slipped down from the
big black-and-white destrier and joined them,
leaving Graeme with the horses. Muirne offered
Isabail food, which she accepted with thanks.

Isabail spoke quickly and quietly. "Duncan, you

are a good and kind man. Anyone can see that. And it's clear you understand the hardship this event has presented for myself and Muirne."

The warrior stiffened, but said nothing.

She pressed on. "A woman shouldn't be the pawn in a political game. We have a chance, right this minute, to ride off to Dunstoras and make our way to safety. Will you turn your back for just a moment and let us go free? Let us reach safety?"

His brows knitted together. "Do you know what you're asking?"

"I'm asking you to show two innocent women some leniency."

"Nay," he snarled, stepping back from Muirne. "You're asking me to betray my chief and allow the sister of John Grant to escape. The sister of the man who saw our clan outlawed and cleared from these lands. The lands that have been our home for three hundred years. Because of him, the MacCurrans were slain, arrested, or scattered hither and yon. Homeless. My brother and his wife are gone—I know not where—and I may never see them again."

He spat in the snow at Isabail's feet. "Aid my enemy in making an escape? I think not."

Then he snatched the food from Isabail's hands and stomped away.

Muirne gripped Isabail's arm. "Och, they hate us, they do. It's a miracle their chief didn't murder us in our sleep at the bothy."

Isabail shook her head. "He was more interested in information than revenge. He pestered me with questions about visitors to the keep."

"Well, one thing's for certain," Muirne said. "Had you given them the information they seek, we'd be lying in the sod, not standing here shivering and hungry in the cold."

Isabail would have disputed that assessment a few minutes ago, but the depth of Duncan's hatred had come through in his words. He'd not even given her the chance to remind him that it was the MacCurrans' actions that had caused their grief, not John's. John had merely done his duty as justiciar of Glen Avon. The MacCurran had murdered his kin and stolen a necklace from the king. How did they expect John to react? His duty had been to uphold the law.

But Muirne was right. They weren't safe here.

Aiden crouched and picked up a small rock loosened in the dirt.

The glimmer of metal flash on one surface told him the horses he was following were shod, which confirmed it was soldiers from the castle. MacPherson regularly combed the woods for souls still loyal to the MacCurrans, although it was unusual for a patrol to venture this far south. Aiden would prefer not to stir the hornet's nest by alerting the patrol to his presence, but he could not risk the lives of his captives either—and MacPherson's men had a tendency to choose weapons over diplomacy.

He slipped between the trees, taking care to leave the ground unturned and branches unbent. In the past few months, he had learned a great deal about stealth from his half brother, Niall. Niall had grown to a man in these woods and could pass unnoticed through the trees in broad daylight. Aiden was not so skilled. His expertise lay in the blade.

Still, he was a far better woodsman than MacPherson's lot. They left a trail so clear that even a bairn could follow it. Even before he spotted them, he knew they were six men mounted on bronze-shoed horses. He also heard them long before he gained sight of them. Not their voices— they were professional soldiers, not given to idle chatter—but the clink of their mail and the jingle of their horse trappings.

Cutting through the trees at an angle, he caught up to the patrol. One sergeant and five armed soldiers plodding along on sturdy Highland ponies. They scanned the barren wood left and right as they passed, hoping to spot a movement, be it man or deer.

The path leading to the old Pictish palace lay just ahead, and Aiden's hand tightened on the hilt of his sword. Was that their destination? Were they under orders to investigate that section of the glen? Hidden among the rocks, the old broch was not easy to spot, but a determined search would almost assuredly lead to its discovery. They'd been lucky so far; soldiers who'd passed by had given the terrain only a cursory look.

He peered through the trees. Was his clan alerted to the impending danger? It was impossible to tell. Niall's Black Warriors, the clan's most seasoned men, were all formidable woodsmen. If they were watching the advancing patrol, there was no sign.

The patrol moved deeper into the woods, until they were only twenty paces from the moss-covered fallen tree that marked the path to the broch. At any moment one of MacPherson's men might spot a clue that more than fifty men, women, and children were secreted in the rocky terrain ahead.

Having been absent for several weeks, Aiden could only pray that his kin were prepared—that they had gathered the evidence of their existence and taken shelter. Else the arrival of a patrol would result in disaster—crying children, terrorized women, and slain men. A flare of anger burned in his chest. This was what John Grant had wrought with his false accusations. The torture of innocents. A life for his clansmen that had danger and fear hanging constantly over their heads.

Protecting the clan was paramount.

He was about to step out in the open and draw the patrol's attention when the leader of the small group of soldiers tugged his reins and turned his horse west. Still eyeing the shadows between the trees with a piercing stare, the fellow led the patrol slowly and steadily away from the broch.

Aiden watched them until the beat of his heart had returned to its usual pace; then he spun on his heel and slipped back through the trees.

Isabail wrung her hands. Time was short. She had to make another bid for escape. But how? Steal a horse? She eyed the horses. Graeme held two of them behind a large holly bush, murmuring an occasional soothing word to keep them quiet and still. His hand was loose on the reins, but his focus was entirely on the beasts. It was unlikely she'd be able to snatch one.

Graeme lifted his gaze and caught her staring at him.

Isabail flushed and lowered her eyes.

Without a horse, she'd not have a hope of outrunning Aiden MacCurran. A man who could track them through a blinding snowstorm would have no trouble locating them in a winter woodland. There wasn't enough brush to hide behind. So, it had to be Duncan's horse. The chestnut gelding with one white stocking. But if stealing a horse from Graeme was a challenge, taking one from Duncan was doubly difficult. He hadn't stopped glaring at her.

Fortunately, Isabail had a secret weapon, and her name was Muirne. She turned and said, "Whatever I say, nod and look forlorn."

The maid blinked, a little confused.

Isabail bent to Muirne's leg, lifted her skirt a bit, and peered at her foot. "The toes are paining you, are they? It must be remnants of the severe chill you took." She flung an arm around Muirne's waist and pretended to take some of her weight. "We should get you off that foot. Back in the saddle, I think."

Hobbling forward, Isabail glanced at Duncan. Sure enough, the sandy-haired warrior had exchanged his glower for a look of concern.

"Help her into the saddle," she requested. "Then we'll remove her boot and have a look."

Duncan gently spanned Muirne's waist with his hands and swung her up on the horse. "Poor wee lass," he said as he settled her in the saddle.

"I think I saw some salve in Graeme's bag," Isabail said. "If you fetch it, I'll rub some onto her toes."

"Duncan," came a dark voice from behind her. "If you fetch it, I'll be embarrassed to call you kin. She's playing you for a fool."

At his chief's cold words, Duncan's scowl returned in a furious rush.

Isabail spun to face her nemesis. Although she was growing accustomed to his large size, his towering form still stole her breath away. Or was it the fierce male beauty of his face? Really, the devil must have had a hand in shaping the man— he had it all: a powerful body other men would envy, an easy grace that made the sword in his hand seem like an extension of his arm, and the face of an angel. An *avenging* angel.

She swallowed. "She complained of pain."

"Liar."

The faint heat in Isabail's cheeks became a bonfire. "I beg your pardon?"

"I was watching the two of you as I approached. Your maid was not favoring her foot; nor did she wince with pain. You are a liar."

His voice was cold and hard, not loud and angry, so Isabail was able to hold her ground, even though her instincts were clamoring at her to flee.

He could kill her with that sword. One mighty swing and her life would be over in a flash. Like her mother's had been.

But he wouldn't kill her.

Not until he had the information he desired. At least, she prayed that was so.

"Please," she begged. "Release us. It was my brother with whom you had a grievance, not me."

He stared back at her, seemingly unmoved by the tears that had sprung into her eyes. "Tell me what I need to know, and I'll have no need to hold you."

Isabail heard Muirne gasp at his words and knew what the other woman was thinking. *Tell him and we're as good as dead*. There was a fair chance she was right. Especially as she suspected his clan was camped somewhere at this end of the glen—the tension in the men's shoulders had eased in that way that suggested they were home. He would not risk releasing her and having MacPherson discover his kin.

"I do not recall any names. It is too long in the past."

He sheathed his sword. "Then face the consequences."

Two huge hands reached for her, and Isabail crammed her eyes shut. It was an instinctive reaction, but a woefully inadequate defense. Shutting out the world never made the punishment more bearable. Indeed, it had often made it worse— even that small rebellion had infuriated her father. But it was all she could do against the might of a man's anger. She steeled herself for the blows.

But they never came. MacCurran simply tied something soft about her head, blinding her view. Then he grabbed her by the shoulders and prodded her forward. When her outstretched hands met the warm, silky coat of his huge steed, he thrust her unceremoniously into the saddle and leapt up behind her.

"For your lies," he growled, "you'll miss the evening meal. You'd best hope the pinch of hunger in your belly stirs your memories."

Aiden wasn't certain what made him angrier—the woman's continued attempts to throw herself into danger or the look of frozen terror that took over her face each time he lifted a hand. What cause had she to believe he would strike her? Aye, she had annoyed him. But there was a huge leap between feeling anger and using one's fists.

A warrior was only as good as his self-discipline, after all.

He shackled her tight to his chest with one arm and guided his mount around a huge oak with the other. Her fear was understandable, given what she knew of him. But it still rankled.

If she would simply confess the names of her brother's guests that night, they could part ways. She would be free to seek solace from Tormod MacPherson, and he could hunt down the filthy cur who'd actually done the evil deeds he'd been accused of. Oh, to have the satisfaction of running that bastard through.

"You went off into the woods in search of miscreants. Did you slay anyone?" Isabail asked, a note of faint disapproval in her voice.

"Not today."

She grimaced at his response and turned her head away.

Aiden refused to feel guilty for reminding her that he'd slain several of her men the day before. He blamed her for that necessity. She had incited the head of her guard, Sir Robert, to a lovelorn devotion. He'd seen her speaking with the man in the orchard two days before, her cheeks flushed, her hand on his sleeve. The man had been given ample opportunity to surrender, but he had refused, insisting on fighting to the death. Had he surrendered, all of his men would have surrendered as well. Bloodshed could have been avoided.

With her head slightly bowed, she asked, "Where are you taking me?"

"Does it matter?"

Her shoulders sagged. "Perhaps not."

Aiden frowned. She made him feel like a cad and a brute, all with a simple sigh. Yet he was the one who had been wronged; he was the one who had lost everything. She'd lost nothing thus far but a few hours.

They reached the mossy stump and swung left. Moments later, they exited the forest and came upon an overgrown circle of stones three feet high—a small broch, even older than the one that housed his clan. Useful, in that it distracted casual observers. Most never bothered to study the surrounding rocks, and none had thus far discovered the barely discernible path snaking up into the mountain. There was a plateau above them, but it wasn't visible from this level. Large rocks that had broken from the mountain a thousand years past hid it from view.

Aiden led the climb up. The slope was littered with shards of fallen shale, but nimble as the horses were, they gained the top of the foothill in short order. Only after he navigated the shattered shale was he rewarded with the sight he yearned for.

There, amid the snow and boulders, lay a much larger broch. A fortress, really. Compared to others Aiden had seen, it was a detailed structure— double stone walls that were in some places six feet tall. The outer wall was built into the existing rock and took advantage of large sections of mountain stone that provided a natural defense. The inner wall was a man-made oval that stretched more than sixty feet wide. A dozen roundhouses were scattered inside the enclosure, each with a new thatch roof laid by Aiden's men.

He slipped Isabail's blindfold from her head and signaled Duncan to do the same for her maid. Then he dismounted.

At first glance, the broch appeared deserted. But he knew better.

"Give the signal," he said brusquely to Graeme. Niall's men communicated via a series of clicks and whistles that resembled noises of the native wildlife. Aiden had never mastered them. As the eldest son, all his spare hours had been spent with his father, learning to manage Dunstoras and play

the political games required of a Highland chief—
identifying which clans he could count on and
which were his enemies. Aiden glanced at the
lovely woman seated on his horse. Of course, his
father would have counted the Grants among his
allies.

And look how that turned out.

Graeme trilled a short series of whistles and
then waited for a response. The wait was not long.
No sooner had the sounds been carried away on
the breeze than a man stepped out from behind a
large rock, sword and targe at the ready.

He offered Aiden a deep nod of his head. "A
fine sight you are, Chief."

"Udard," Aiden acknowledged. "Is all well?"

The guard frowned. "MacPherson's men have
been more active of late, and they've caused us
grief. You'll want to speak with Niall about it."

"My brother has returned?"

Udard nodded. "Last eve. Quite the adventure
he had, but I'll let him be the one to tell you the
tale."

The guard led them forward, and as they
breached the outer wall, members of his clan came
out of hiding, greeting him with smiles, waves,
and hailed good tidings. As pleased as he was to
be home, Aiden was struck by the obvious signs
of hardship and poverty. The past few weeks had
not been kind to his clan—clothes were threadbare, bodies were gaunt, and faces were etched
with weariness. This life as hunted outlaws was
taking a cruel toll.

In the open space between the two walls, the men had set up quintains to practice their sword craft and straw targets to hone their bowmanship, while the lads maintained the horses. Inside the inner wall, women and children worked and played with the subdued enthusiasm of those in hiding. Fires were small to contain any smoke to mere wisps, and voices were low and calm. The roundhouses with rebuilt roofs served as homes, though they were primitive compared to the blackhouses built in the lee of Dunstoras castle.

A group of men were gathered in the center of the ruin, and as Aiden led his party into the close, one of the men broke away from the group and trotted toward Aiden.

Niall.

Aiden helped Isabail dismount, then turned to face his half brother. As he expected, Niall's face was a mask of cool blandness. Reading his thoughts had always been a challenge. Yet he must have been surprised to see Aiden's two guests.

"What news?" Niall asked, as if Isabail Grant wasn't standing in front of him.

Equally dispassionate, Aiden responded, "Nothing yet. And you?"

"I returned from Duthes yestereve. Upon my arrival, I was informed that one of our hunting parties was lost to a MacPherson patrol. Three days ago. Hamish, Conal, and four others were taken."

Aiden grimaced. "Were they caught with game in hand?"

"Aye."

"He'll see them hang for poaching."

His brother nodded grimly. "The rest of the men are understandably unhappy. The deer are ours, in their minds. They want to fetch our kin back."

"I'll think on it. Udard says you've a tale to tell."

Niall nodded. "The how and the wherefore are a wee complicated, but we found the queen's necklace."

A slow grin crept across Aiden's face. "Truly?"

"Aye."

"Bloody hell." Aiden gave his brother a heartfelt pound on the back. "By God, I should never have doubted you."

Niall threw him a grim look. "The news is not so fair as you would believe. Although I gained some sense of the path the necklace took to Duthes, I was unable to find evidence that would prove our innocence in its theft. All I know is that a traveling merchant delivered the necklace to Duthes a fortnight before Yule. Alas, without the name of the man who sold it to the merchant, we are no further ahead."

Aiden let his hand drop. "And the merchant?"

"I've sent Bran and Conal in search of him." Niall cocked his head at the woman standing beside him. "You've a tale of your own to tell, it would seem."

Aiden tugged Isabail forward. "Lady Isabail Grant, my brother, Sir Niall MacCurran."

"Lady Macintosh," she corrected mildly. "I am

the widow of Andrew Macintosh. And I believe this man's knighthood was stripped from him after it was ascertained that he freed you from my brother's dungeon."

Niall shrugged. "A knighthood is of little consequence in the Highlands. All that matters here is my clan and the strength of my sword arm."

"Aye, I can see how honor and fealty to your king would be inconvenient qualities."

Aiden's brother tossed her one of his icy stares. "Our loyalty to the king is unwavering."

"Killing his courier and his justiciar and stealing his gift to his new bride are not disloyal? My, I must have been taught a different measure of trueness."

Aiden yanked Isabail against his chest to silence her virulent words. It annoyed him that she was so easily able to speak her mind with his brother while he was treated to terrified silences. "I'll settle her with Beathag. Then you can tell me the whole of your complicated tale."

Beathag turned out to be a rather formidable woman. She reminded Isabail of the wife of Lochurkie's seneschal—same big bosom, same deep laugh, same tendency to get right to the point.

"The MacCurran tells me you're to get no supper," Beathag said as she led Isabail and Muirne toward one of the thatch-roofed huts. "He didn't say you couldn't drink, though, so I'll make you a spot of tea. This place is as damp and drafty as a dungeon."

Isabail studied the six-foot-high wall that surrounded the camp. "What is this place?"

"According to legend, it's the palace of an ancient Pictish king." She swept aside a draped boar skin and ushered them into the roundhouse. "This will be your room. Your maid will sleep here with you, of course."

A plump straw mattress sat directly on the hard-packed dirt floor, a woolen blanket folded near the bottom. It was better than sleeping in the mud, but only just. Isabail frowned. "Where's the pallet for my maid?"

Beathag laughed, a great booming chuckle. "You'll share that one and be happy about it. Many here have no pallet at all." She pointed to a bucket of water. "We've drawn some water for you, but from now on, you'll need to fetch your own from the stream."

Isabail wrinkled her nose at that notion, but said nothing. "I will need the services of the laundress. I've been wearing these same clothes for two days."

The big woman laughed again. She pointed a finger at Muirne and then at Isabail. "Meet the laundresses." Still chuckling, she ducked under the lintel beam again and disappeared.

"This is ridiculous," Isabail said.

"Have no fear, my lady," Muirne said. "I'll take care of things."

Isabail took stock of the room. There wasn't much to look at. Windowless walls of lichen-spotted stone, a heather roof, and the mattress. No chair, no chest, no table for a taper. Had she offered such accommodation to a guest at Lochurkie, she'd have squirmed with embarrassment.

"First things first. Let me check your ankle." Isabail encouraged Muirne to sit on the mattress and unwrapped the linen strips that bound her maid's foot. The flesh had turned a nasty shade of purple, but the swelling had subsided. She rewound the linen, ensured a snug fit, and sat back on her heels. "So long as you walk with care, it should be fine. MacCurran's men gathered some of my belongings from the carriage. Go see if you can find them. And have someone fetch me a broom. I'll not sleep under a cobweb that size, else I'll be swallowing spiders in my dreams."

Her ankle now neatly bound, Muirne hobbled out of the room to do as she was bade.

The blanket on the bed was actually three blankets of a good size. The weaving was of excellent quality, and the colors of the wool were vivid and bright. A weaver among the MacCurrans had a true talent.

Isabail dipped her hand into the bucket. The water was so cold, it sent a shiver up her arm, but she splashed a little on her face anyway. It felt good to wipe the grime of two days' travel from her skin.

Muirne returned a few moments later with the broom and a bright spot of color on each cheek. "A problem, my lady."

"What is it?"

"There's none of your belongings to be had," the maid said, not meeting her gaze.

"That's not possible. I saw that man Graeme pick up several of my gowns and my tortoiseshell comb."

Muirne sighed. "Aye, but they've been given to other women in the camp. MacCurran women."

Isabail felt as if she'd been punched in the gut. "My serge blue cotehardie? And the chemise with pink lilies embroidered on the sleeves?" Two of her favorite items.

"Aye," the other woman verified, her voice little more than a whisper.

"And what am I expected to wear?" wailed Isabail. The pale blue gown she had chosen as a travel dress had not fared well. The soft wool had wrinkled badly, especially at the elbows and underarms. Mud had stained the hem a permanent shade of brown, and a large smear of soot had sullied the cord-trimmed bodice. That was in addition to the general wear caused by her primitive travel conditions.

"Beathag says that's what the extra blanket is for. To wear while you wait for your dress to dry."

Isabail's legs went numb. She sank onto the mattress, absolutely shocked. She couldn't even imagine letting the scratchy wool touch her bare skin. Who knew where those blankets had last been? They could be home to vermin.

"What did I do to cause God to punish me so?" she asked. "I don't think I can endure this."

Muirne bustled into the room, sweeping the cobwebs from the corners. "Of course you can. You survived all those years with your da, didn't you? This is not nearly as challenging."

Isabail blinked away the tears in her eyes. She'd never spoken about her father with anyone except her brother, John. "What do you know of my father?"

Muirne stopped sweeping and met her gaze. "What everyone knew. That he was a drunken abuser of women."

Isabail's jaw dropped. "Who told you that?"

"We're not fools. His drunken rages may have taken place behind closed doors, but sounds carry very well inside a castle."

"But no one said anything."

Muirne shrugged. "He was the earl. What was there to say?"

"Did you know—" Nay, she couldn't ask about her mother. Not out loud. Doing so would make that horrible night a reality . . . and she preferred to pretend that it wasn't. She'd never even shared the truth with John. He'd had suspicions and had made broad hints that he knew what their father had done, but the words were never spoken. And it was better that way. "Never mind. This is hardly the same situation."

Muirne arched a brow. "Are we not at the mercy of an angry madman?"

That coaxed a faint smile to Isabail's lips. "True enough."

"Then there is no one better suited to dealing

with this MacCurran fiend than you." Muirne pointed the twig end of the broom at Isabail. "So, how did you handle your da?"

"Well," said Isabail dryly, "the first thing was to stay out of his way as much as possible. Unfortunately, I have little control over that here."

"What else?"

"Ensured the castle ran as smoothly as possible, so he had less reason to be angry." Isabail shook her head. "Plenty of things here to anger a man."

Muirne nodded. "That's where you begin, then."

"This place is in shambles," Isabel agreed. "If no one else will see to my comforts, then I suppose I'll have to arrange it myself."

"There's a lass," Muirne said encouragingly.

"Let's start here," Isabail said. "Give me that broom."

Chapter 4

Aiden strode across the inner close toward the central fire pit. Every weary face he passed tightened the knot in his gut. His people deserved better. Bringing Isabail Macintosh here was an additional risk to their welfare, and the weight of that decision sat heavily on his shoulders. He'd done his best to obscure their trail, but if luck went against him and the earl's men succeeded in tracking her here . . . By all that was holy, why couldn't the woman simply have given him the names?

The group gathered in front of the central fire parted to let him pass, and Aiden stopped abruptly. In their midst was a lovely redheaded woman—a woman he had last seen in the market square at Duthes. Ana Bisset. The healer who had been tried and convicted of killing John Grant, the earl of Lochurkie. Isabail's brother.

"Bloody hell," he said. "What is *she* doing here?"

Niall flung an arm around the woman's shoulders and tucked her close—a protective stance that said far more than his next words did. "Hold off, brother. She's no more guilty of killing the justiciar than you are. We're all victims of the same plot."

Aiden grimaced. "By God, I never thought to see the day when you'd be gulled by a beautiful woman."

"She aided me at great personal risk," Niall argued.

"To prevent you from apprising the constable of her dubious history, no doubt." How dare Niall bring a murderess home to live among his kin? "She cannot stay."

The woman slipped out of Niall's embrace. She smiled sadly at his brother. "I feared as much. This isn't meant to be, Niall. I'll find my own way."

"You'll go nowhere. Not without me." Then his brother turned to him. "Do you trust me?"

"You, aye. Her, nay."

"If you trust me, then you must trust my judgment. I know this woman through and through. She is no murderess. She stays, or I go. It's as simple as that."

Aiden ignored Niall's threat. "Why are you so sure she's not capable of murder? Beneath many a sweet lamb hide beats the heart of a wolf."

"Because she saved my life, not once, but twice. When it would have been easier to simply let me die," Niall said quietly. "She could have walked away, with none the wiser about her past. Instead she cured me and, in so doing, drew the attention of the constable."

The woman met Aiden's gaze easily, no hint of guile. Was it possible? Had she been falsely accused of killing the earl, just as he'd been falsely accused of killing the king's courier? It seemed a stretch. Or perhaps he was just angry because she'd managed to further tarnish his honor? When Niall had rescued Aiden from Lochurkie's dungeon, he'd rescued this woman, too. Unfortunately, in so doing, he'd linked the murder of Earl Lochurkie to Aiden. He'd been accused of masterminding all of it—the murder of the king's courier, the theft of the queen's necklace, and the murder of the earl.

Which, of course, led to the loss of Dunstoras and the outlawing of all MacCurrans.

Damn the man in black. If his objective had been to torment the clan MacCurran, the wretch had certainly been successful.

Aiden favored Niall with a long, hard stare. His brother could be quite stubborn when he chose. If he said he'd leave with the lass, then he'd leave. "Fine. She can stay. But any hint of trouble, and you'll both feel the weight of my boot on your arse. Now, come. We have much to discuss."

His half brother nodded and followed him.

As they toured the camp, inspecting the defenses, Aiden said, "Tell me the whole tale of your adventure. Leave nothing out."

Niall proceeded to share a madcap tale involving a fire, a traitor, and a harried race for freedom. "Great mystery still surrounds the theft of the queen's necklace, but Baron Duthes is not the man in black. I know that much. He was unaware of the necklace's history. I believe his seneschal knows more, but I was unable to query the man while I was there, and I cannot easily return to do so now. Our best hope lies with the merchant."

"Then we'll pray he is swiftly found."

Niall nodded. "What of the Lochurkie lass? I trust you had good reason to kidnap her? The earl's men will expend considerable effort to look for her."

"It was a risky decision," Aiden acknowledged "But she knows the name of the man in black, and she'll give it to me or face my wrath."

Niall shrugged. "Well, you'd best work quickly. MacPherson has stepped up his patrols this past sennight, reaching farther and farther up the glen. It's only a matter of time before they find us."

"And only a few short days before the king announces a new lord of Dunstoras."

His brother grimaced. "I hope to God it's not MacPherson. The man is a layabout. Not once has he been spied sharpening his skills in the lists or even walking the ramparts. He sits in the castle and eats. Nothing more. Dunstoras deserves better."

Aiden glared at the other man. "None but a MacCurran will rule Dunstoras. If necessary, we'll retake the keep by force."

Niall said nothing.

Both men were well aware that they had less than three dozen trained men at their disposal, compared to MacPherson's two hundred. The castle had been taken while Aiden was locked in Lo-churkie's dungeon and Niall had been preparing to set him free. Numerous good men had died defending the keep, including the seneschal and the castle's senior man-at-arms.

Taking it back would likely be a vain cause.

Still, Aiden could not let Dunstoras go without a serious fight. His father had built that castle stone by stone, some days with his own hands. Aiden had been born inside those walls, his father had died inside those walls, and his mother had—

"Where is my mother?" he asked, glancing about.

Niall grimaced. "Why ask me?"

"Because you know everything that happens in this camp," Aiden pointed out.

"I've given my oath to protect all who dwell here," Niall said, with a short nod. "But that doesn't include putting myself in range of Lady Elisaid's venomous barbs."

Aiden's mother had a longstanding grievance with Niall—he was the baseborn son of her husband, brought by him to live under her roof. Aiden's father had also praised Niall's prowess as a warrior to her face several times while implying that *her* son was a weak-willed incompetent. Untrue, of course, but Aiden's father believed that strong competition would make both his sons better men.

But Niall's troubles with Lady Elisaid would never interfere with his duty. Aiden was confident he kept tabs on his mother . . . if only to know where *not* to wander.

"Where is she?" he asked again.

"Down by the burn with Master Tam."

Aiden left the camp enclosure, descended the rocky slope, and crossed the rock-studded field to the edge of the burn, wet snow accumulating on the toes of his boots.

His mother was enjoying a leisurely stroll in the late-afternoon sunshine. Refusing to give up any of the amenities of her station, despite their current outlawed state, she insisted on a full entourage as she walked about—Master Tam held her arm and engaged her in conversation, two maids followed behind carrying the hem of her cloak, and two young pages brought up the rear, carting a flagon of wine and some refreshments.

"Aiden," his mother exclaimed with a smile. "You've returned. Have you secured the ownership of Dunstoras? May we now return to our rightful place?"

He took her proffered hand and brushed a kiss over her knuckles. "Nay. We are still outlaws."

She pouted. "This abode is unacceptable. Your father built me a stone castle; I expect no less of you."

"You waited years for that stone castle," he reminded her. "You must be equally patient now. How do we fare for stores and supplies? Are we running short?"

"Why ask me?" His mother waved a hand. "The seneschal is taking care of those details."

Aiden frowned. "The seneschal died during the

siege, Mother. You were going to appoint a new one. Have you done that?"

"No," she said, "Nor will I, not until we are settled once more in the castle. When can we return?"

"Perhaps never," he told her honestly. "Manage this camp like it is our true holding. If we are to survive the remains of winter, we must carefully oversee the distribution of our supplies."

A melancholy look stole across her face, and she sighed heavily. "I miss your father."

"You must make the best of the current situation."

"Nonsense. If I settle for what we currently have, there's no incentive for you to produce better. You are the chief. Reclaim our castle."

He loved his mother dearly, but she either did not understand how dire the situation was, or she purposely chose not to acknowledge it. He was an outlaw with a price on his head. If he were caught, his head would be publicly displayed on a pike in front of the very castle she wanted him to reclaim. His priority had to be clearing their name. And keeping his people alive.

"My plans are my own," he told her brusquely. "Do not presume to make them for me. I will see you anon."

He nodded sharply to Master Tam and left the stream. By God, women were difficult. His life would be a good sight less complicated without them.

When Isabail was satisfied her chamber was as clean as she could make it, she went in search of someone who could add to her comforts. A pillow or two, a small chest, and a brazier. Surely that was not too much to ask.

"Where is the seneschal?" she asked Beathag, who stood next to the cook, peering into a huge iron cauldron.

"There is no seneschal," the big woman said without looking up. She scooped several handfuls of dried peas from the bowl in which they were soaking and tossed them into the pot. The cook stirred.

"Who is in charge of the stores, then?"

Beathag thought for a moment, her head cocked to one side, her finger tapping her chin. "Lady Elisaid, I suppose."

"The chief's wife?"

The other woman shook her head. "His mother. The chief has never taken a wife. He was to wed the daughter of Rory MacDonald, a chief from the western isles, but she ran off with a Campbell lad instead."

"Oh." Faced with wedding such a fierce man, Isabail might well have done the same. "Where will I find Lady Elisaid?"

"A fine question," Beathag said. Taking the ladle from the cook, she sampled the steaming liquid from the pot. "When you find her, let me know. She has the key to the spice cabinet, and I'm in need of some flavoring."

Isabail released a frustrated huff of breath. "What does she look like?"

"You'll know her when you find her."

Beathag was being decidedly unhelpful, but Isabail could not take her to task. She had no authority in the MacCurran's household. "What are you cooking?"

"Venison broth."

"May I taste?"

The big woman turned to her, a sneer curling her upper lip. "Never had a simple bree, my lady?"

"Of course I have," Isabail said. "Many times. A well-prepared broth is a staple in the kitchen. You said you were missing some spice. I'd like to taste what you've prepared so far."

The cook took no offense at her request. He ladled a small portion into a wooden cup and gave it to her. Isabail sniffed it first, inhaling the rich scent of boiled venison. Then she sipped. It was satisfactory, but as Beathag suggested, a little bland. "If you are unable to get the spice of your choice, you could consider adding some leek and parsnip." As Beathag's eyebrows soared, she added, "Just a suggestion, of course. Good day."

Isabail scanned the inner close, seeking some sign of the MacCurran's mother. He was a very large man, so surely the woman who birthed him was also large. Perhaps of a similar size to Beathag. She saw no one who might fit that description.

Marching toward the outer wall, she scanned the people assembled in the outer close. A group of men was laying siege to one another with wooden swords. She recognized the man MacCurran had hailed as Niall among them, seemingly the one in charge. But no women at all.

Down the rocky slope beyond the perimeter wall, she could see a field and, cutting through the field, an icy burn. Next to the water, she spied a party led by a small, slender woman wearing a blue serge gown and a white headdress. From this distance, Isabail could not be certain, but the gown looked painfully similar to the one she'd lost. Unable to help herself, she picked her way down the slope and then marched across the field toward the woman, determined to see if it was truly hers.

As she got closer, it became clear that the woman was at least a score of years older than Isabail. Her hair was hidden beneath a linen wimple, but her skin was thin and pale, her bones sharply defined in her face. Still, it was not her age that sapped Isabail's anger away; it was the elegant way the woman carried herself—like she'd been born to privilege and expected no less.

"Lady Elisaid?" Isabail guessed.

The elderly woman ceased her stroll along the burn bank. "Aye?"

It was indeed Isabail's gown draped over the other woman's body—the size, especially in the bosom area, was a trifle large. But as Lady Elisaid's faded blue eyes turned to her, any demand she might have uttered for its return died on her lips.

"I am Lady Macintosh, cousin to Archibald, Earl Lochurkie," she said instead. "Your son has seized my person in hopes of ransoming me for political gain."

Actually, she doubted he intended to ransom

her, but accusing him of more villainous goals at this moment hardly seemed polite.

"He neglected to mention your presence to me, Lady Macintosh. You are John Grant's sister, are you not?"

"Indeed."

The lady waved her over. She kindly said nothing about the obvious stains upon Isabail's gown, for which Isabail was grateful—if pressed she was not sure she could refrain from pointing out the lady wore stolen clothing. "Walk with me awhile."

Isabail gave the invitation some thought. She was fully prepared to dislike Lady Elisaid—for the simple fact that she was the MacCurran's mother—but she was not above using any and all methods at her disposal to win her freedom. Perhaps a mother could influence the man where a sense of fair play could not.

Isabail fell into a step alongside Elisaid Mac-Curran.

"Were you wed to young Andrew Macintosh?" the older woman asked.

"Aye."

"An unfortunate death that was, to be felled by a wound gained at a faire. How long had you been married?"

A twinge of sadness pinched her just beneath her breast. She hadn't thought of Andrew for several months. "A year and a month."

"And there were no children?"

"Nay," said Isabail softly. "We had not been blessed."

The older woman shot her a curious look. "It upsets you to speak of him. My apologies. I assumed it was an arrangement, not a love match. Your father gained a powerful ally in the Macintoshes."

"It was an arrangement," Isabail confirmed, "but we were well suited."

Although Andrew had been dead for four years, every moment of their time together was a treasured memory. The handsome, capable man had swept her off her feet, professing his love from the moment they met and treating her with an honor and respect she'd been unaccustomed to. The year she had spent with Andrew had changed her irrevocably—for the better. She'd gone into the marriage a shy, tentative girl and left it a confident, sure woman.

"You're young to be a widow. Have you considered another marriage?"

Isabail shrugged. "I'm in no hurry to wed again. My dower estates were given to me to hold, and they more than pay for my keep. Playing chatelaine to my brother kept me busy."

Lady Elisaid's expression was shrewd. "Your cousin has a wife and you no longer have a household to run. Surely that suggests you are open to new arrangement."

Isabail frowned. "Such thoughts are premature. Although I have recently put aside the colors of loss, I still mourn my brother's passing."

"My son needs a good wife."

Isabail stopped short and stared at the older woman. Was she truly suggesting . . . ? *Surely not.*

"Your son stands accused of murdering my brother, Lady MacCurran."

"A false charge."

"Any mother would say the same," said Isabail coolly. "But the law disagrees. You insult me to even hint of an arrangement between our families."

"Nonsense," the other woman dismissed. "I am merely seeking a peaceful resolution to our troubles. How can that be insulting?"

"My brother was a good man. He deserves justice, not to be forgotten the instant his memory becomes inconvenient." Isabail felt her grief rise in her throat, nearly choking her. "Good day, madam."

Turning on her heel, Isabail lifted her skirts and prepared to stomp off.

"Did you approach me for a particular reason, Lady Macintosh?"

She froze, her heart pounding a mournful dirge in her chest. She'd completely forgotten her mission. Pivoting slowly, she did her best to wrestle her emotions under control. "Aye. A ransom prisoner is due every courtesy while held by her captors. I wish to examine the stores for items that might ease my ordeal. I understand you hold all the keys."

Lady Elisaid frowned. "Do I?"

The man standing just behind Lady MacCurran bent toward her and whispered in her ear. The frown eased. "Apparently, I do. Master Tam will give them to you. Take whatever you like, but I assure you, comfort is a scarce commodity in this ancient pile of rocks."

Master Tam, slowly and with obvious reluctance, handed Isabail a small iron ring hung with four rust-spattered keys.

Isabail nodded sharply to Lady MacCurran. "I will return them presently."

Then she departed, her stomach knotted so tight she could barely breathe. The gall of the woman, suggesting an alliance between their families. Her fiendish son had stolen away the one true friend she had in this world, felling him in his bed. John was dead.

Tears blurred Isabail's vision. And Lady Elisaid thought she could simply brush those horrid memories aside. Impossible.

She wiped her eyes with her sleeve and marched up to Beathag. "I have Lady Elisaid's permission to examine the stores. Show me where they are." Determination added weight to her demand. "Now."

Once he was confident that the defenses of the hill fort were as strong as they could be and that Niall's men were diligently keeping an eye out for MacPherson's patrols, Aiden returned to the keep. Although he knew Isabail was weary from her journey, he could not afford to give her a lengthy respite. The names she held in her head were all that stood between his clan and safety.

The inner close of the ruined palace echoed with his boot steps. Crumbling stone walls and the towering crags of the mountainside gave rise to eerie sounds.

He knocked on the lintel of the roundhouse assigned to Isabail, then ducked inside. The room was empty, save for a neatly covered pallet and a bucket of water. There was no sign of Isabail or her maid.

"Beathag," he roared.

The large woman arrived at the door with surprising speed. "Aye?"

"Where in the bloody hell is Lady Macintosh?"

A family retainer since before he was born, Beathag simply folded her arms over her ample bosom and stared at him for a moment, waiting for him to re-collect his composure.

"Where is she?" he asked, quieter.

"In the cave."

Aiden blinked. "Doing what?"

"Counting."

"By the gods, woman!" The cave was their secret refuge, their last hope if MacPherson's men discovered the hill fort. Divulging its whereabouts to their enemy, even if the lovely lady lacked a dangerous air, was a grievous mistake. "What possessed you to reveal the whereabouts of the cave?"

Beathag gulped. "Lady Elisaid gave her the keys."

His mother had simply handed off the keys? To a stranger? Unable to wrap his thoughts around that tidbit of information and frustrated by his lack of understanding, Aiden simply glared at the good woman. Then he headed for the cave.

The entrance to the tunnels beneath the ruin lay at the very back of the inner close, where the stone wall met the rock face. It was hidden in a small chamber that had once been a storeroom. Or so they guessed, based on the fragments of old wooden chests and shards of pottery found on the floor. He slipped behind a slab of granite that to the undiscerning eye appeared to be just the back wall, and entered. The stairs were narrow and steep, carved directly into the rock of the mountain. Aiden took them two at a time, his familiarity with the old ruin dating back to his childhood.

Torches were seated in iron wall brackets every thirty feet or so, providing scant but welcome light. At the far end of the long tunnel, the narrow confines opened into a small cave that housed the chests and sacks and bits of furniture they'd managed to remove from the castle before it was overrun by MacPhersons. Lids were open, doors swung wide, and the contents of every chest revealed—including the rather small chest that housed his coin.

In the center of the room, Isabail stood holding a torch, a sheet of parchment, and a thin piece of charcoal. Muirne and Brother Orick, the friar, were counting sacks of grain and calling numbers.

"Seven bags of wheat flour," Orick said, dusting off his hands.

"Twelve of oats," Muirne said.

Isabail recorded the numbers on her parchment with a heavy frown. "Are you certain? That may not be enough to last until first harvest."

Muirne lifted her head, caught sight of Aiden, and gave a short signal of alarm.

Isabail spun around and flinched. "Oh."

"What are you about?" he asked, annoyed at her reaction.

Isabail's hand trembled as she held out the parchment. Aiden did not take it. Was he truly that frightening? Most women found him attractive. "Answer me, please."

"You've no seneschal," she said. "No one seems to be tracking the use of your stores."

"And why," he asked, "did you feel the need to do so?"

She lowered the parchment. "Only a handful of your people can count past twelve."

Which explained her role in the inventorying, but not her need to see it done. He stared at her, waiting.

His silence prompted a further reply, "All right. If you must know, I found my accommodations unsatisfactory. By right I should be treated like a noble guest, not a servant. A straw pallet and threadbare blanket are hardly appropriate. I merely sought some additional comforts."

His eyebrow lifted. "And how does knowing how many sacks of flour I possess enhance your comfort?"

Even in the dim light, he saw her cheeks redden. The disadvantage of possessing such fair and flawless skin. "Mistress Beathag and the cook suggested that while I was down here, and since I had the keys, they would benefit from knowing exactly what they had at their disposal." Her gaze dropped to her feet. "You really ought to appoint a new seneschal."

"How did you acquire the keys?"

Another flush, this one accompanied by a straightening of her spine and a fisting of her hand around the charcoal. "Your mother made them available to me."

"You mean you coerced her."

"I had no need. She is a woman. She sympathized with my plight."

Incredible. She'd been in the camp for only a few hours and she'd already befriended his mother, unearthed their biggest secret, and begun an assessment of his belongings. A very talented spy. "Cease what you are doing and return to your chamber immediately. You are not to be wandering the camp on your own. You are not a guest; you are a prisoner. Any comforts you receive will be those I choose to offer, not those you claim for yourself."

"And what am I to do in my empty chamber? Count cobwebs?" She stood there for a long moment, mutiny in the stiff cant of her shoulders.

"Dwell on the names of those men who visited Lochurkie last autumn. Revealing them is your only path to freedom." Aiden pointed down the tunnel. "Go."

She stood her ground, but with less surety.

"Now!" he barked.

Isabail took off at a run, the parchment flying into the air, the charcoal rolling across the dirt floor. Muirne hesitated only a moment before scurrying off after her lady.

Aiden eyed Brother Orick. "Find a few more helpers and finish what she started."

Chapter 5

Magnus chopped wood until every muscle in his arms ached with the effort. A cool winter wind swept across the loch and snatched away his breath, but no matter how hard he worked, nothing could rid him of the nagging sense that he should be somewhere else.

When the wood was split and neatly piled shoulder high behind the bothy, he paused.

Only then did Morag approach him. "Remain angry if you wish," she said, "but accept this water. Spiting your body to get back at me is childish."

He faced her squarely. "Tell me the truth, and we'll have no more quarrel."

"Nay," she said, her long black hair floating loosely on the breeze. "You are not completely healed. I will not risk your life by sending you back into danger unprepared."

"My memory has not returned in three long months. More rest is not the answer. I must seek out those who might know me."

She laid a gentle hand on his left side, just below the ribs. "You were nigh on dead when I found you, and your injury was caused by a sword. If you leave now, while your body is not fully mended, you'll meet an unfortunate fate."

Magnus brushed aside her hand. The wound she spoke of had healed. It was his leg—and his lost memories—that still troubled him. "My injuries may never heal completely. I cannot hide forever."

She said nothing, her silence an answer of its own.

"If you will not tell me what you witnessed the day you found me, then we've nothing more to say." Magnus snatched up his bow and a quiver of arrows and limped toward the edge of the forest. "I'll fetch something to eat for supper."

She watched him until he disappeared into the depths of the trees—as she always did. Most days, he enjoyed the feel of her eyes upon him, but today it only fueled his frustration. Being coddled like a bairn did not sit well with him. He was no longer badly injured. He was as healthy as he might ever be. It was time for him to go, to seek out his past—no matter how ugly that past might be.

And it might indeed be ugly. Only nobles and soldiers carried swords. If he'd been injured by a blade, he had almost assuredly stood on the wrong side of the law. A worry that was upheld by Morag's fear for his safety. Although she refused to reveal the details of that night, the pallor of her face when she spoke of it suggested she had witnessed the attack, not simply found him lying in a pool of blood.

Magnus lifted his gaze to the stone tower in the distance.

Castle guards had felled him, most likely. Which made him at best a thief, a spy, or a poacher. At worst, a murderer and a knave.

Not that he wanted to believe he was any of those. His gut insisted he was an honorable man with a fine purpose. But with no memories of his past, how could he be certain? His only clues were the vague feelings that assailed him—like the one that insisted that somewhere, in some place he couldn't envision, someone was waiting for him to come home. Or the bone-chilling sense of dread that always followed his attempts to recall who that someone might be.

Magnus slipped behind the wide trunk of an ancient oak tree. Up ahead, through the thin winter brush, he could see the telltale dark brown coat of a hind. His mouth watered at the thought of eating venison, but Magnus did not lift his bow. Downing a deer would set the castle huntsman on his tail—deer were reserved for the nobles. In truth, all the animals of the forest belonged to the laird, but hiding the carcass of a dead rabbit was a great deal easier than hiding a deer.

A branch cracked to his right.

The hind took fright and bolted into the trees. Magnus flattened himself against the trunk of the oak and slowed his breaths to a silent draw of air. Deep and even. From the corner of his eye, he spotted a flash of movement. A solitary man. Someone on foot, accompanied by a large hound.

Magnus stared as the stranger and his dog made their way through the forest. Quite possibly, it was someone from the castle. Not a huntsman— his trek through the brush was far too noisy and untrained for that. A noble, then.

A person who might recognize Magnus.

He glanced over his shoulder in the direction of the bothy. This was an opportunity that carried little risk. He could easily overpower one man and a dog, if it came to that. And if the man could name him, he'd learn much about the life he'd led before he had awakened in Morag's bed.

But it might also lead to trouble for Morag. Although she traded with the castle, selling her colorful weaves to the inhabitants on market day, she was an admitted outcast. The moment he explained where he had been living for the last three months, she would be subjected to unwelcome scrutiny. Possibly even sanctions. And after all she had done for him, he couldn't allow that. Even if she drove him to the brink of madness with her refusal to tell him what she knew, he could never betray her.

Magnus stood silent and still and watched the man and his hound march out of sight.

"You found her in the cave?" Niall asked with a frown, as he accepted a tankard of ale from the alewife. Snowflakes drifted down from the open sky above their heads, but the walls of the ruin kept the winter breeze at bay. "Did she see the other tunnel?"

"I can't be certain." Aiden took a sip of ale, washing down the rather tasteless oatcake that accompanied his venison broth. At least the soup had been tasty. "But that's hardly the point. The woman has gained a troubling knowledge of our encampment in a very short period of time. And at some point I'll be forced to let her go."

"If she shares the dismal state of our affairs with MacPherson, he'll be even more inclined to root us out."

"Indeed."

His brother shrugged. "So, don't let her go."

"I've given her my word," Aiden said. "If she tells me the names, she can leave."

"Then you've no choice. You need to sway her to our cause."

"Easier said than done," Aiden said dryly. "She believes I murdered her brother, and she's terrified of me."

"Aye, well, you *have* acquired a rather angry mien of late." Niall stood up as Ana Bisset joined them at the table. He gave her a slow smile that was easy to interpret. "Rightly so, of course. But sharing your ill humor with Lady Isabail will not gain you her trust."

Aiden didn't begrudge Niall his happiness—his brother's trials had been near as difficult as his—but it underscored the emptiness of his own life, and at this moment it was more than he could endure. He grunted a noncommittal response and pushed away from the table.

His time was better spent charming the lady. Or

at least attempting to. Pocketing an oatcake, he left the great hall in search of her. Not that her location was any great mystery—he'd confined her to her hut. And even if he hadn't already known which house was hers, the flicker of candles and the sound of voices raised in lively discussion would have led him there unerringly.

He entered without knocking.

Inside, the cook, the friar, and Beathag had gathered around Isabail. She held court on a small wooden stool used for milking goats. Anyone else would have looked ridiculous seated a few inches from the floor. Isabail looked quite the opposite. Wearing only a multihued blanket atop her white chemise, her back straight and tall, she managed to look positively regal. The frothy white folds of her diaphanous shift floated about her feet, and a tiny hint of it peeked from beneath the heavy wool at her neck—just enough to draw his attention to the pale pink flesh beneath her chin. A tantalizing glimpse that for a brief moment sent his imagination spinning into inappropriate realms.

The group was discussing the menu for the next day's meals. Cook was reciting the dishes he knew how to make, the friar was interspersing that list with an account of the ingredients they had available, while Beathag reminded everyone how many mouths they had to feed. A very needful conversation—but naught to do with the task he'd set for Isabail.

There was no effort being made to detail the visitors to Lochurkie. Time was passing, and he was no closer to finding the man in black. He'd given very explicit instructions and had left her alone to perform the task. He'd even renewed his promise to free her should she give him the names.

Aiden surged across the wooden planking. "Out," he barked.

Her entourage took one look at his face and scattered into the night.

Isabail scrambled to her feet, knocking the three-legged stool to its side. "I did not seek them out; they sought me."

"Why?"

She backed up several steps. "Th-they lack guidance."

The tremble in her voice registered, and he bit back the snarled response that leapt to his lips. He had no idea what expression lay on his face, but clearly it frightened her. Mindful of his brother's advice, he attempted to soften his features. Her gaze darted away, and he had the distinct impression his efforts hadn't entirely been successful.

Still, she persevered. "Guidance that is typically given by the lady of the keep."

"My mother is grieving. Her attention is justly scattered."

Isabail nodded. "I understand. But a castle runs more smoothly when all within are assigned specific duties and are held accountable."

He frowned. "My people have served the clan for many a year. They know their tasks."

"Would your soldiers be well organized if their captain had been slain in battle?"

"A new captain would be appointed."

She smiled tremulously. "Exactly. The seneschal is the captain of the household. Without him, even your seasoned staff feel lost and at cross-purpose."

"It's my mother's duty to appoint a new seneschal." He shrugged. "She'll take care of it in due time."

"And while she grieves, your caretakers struggle to work together and keep food on the table."

The note of disapproval in her voice did not sit well. "We are surviving," he said coldly.

"Aye," she said, "and you will continue to survive . . . until you do not. But how much longer do you have? A week? A month? Without someone regularly counting the supplies and visiting the menus, how can you know?"

Aiden crossed his arms over his chest. Her words were an echo of his own concerns. And the conversation he'd just had with his men had only heightened those concerns: Food was becoming a problem. According to Udard, the reason the hunting party had been captured by MacPherson was that they were venturing farther north in search of game. The forest around the hill fort had been hunted out. Still, Aiden wasn't willing to cede the point. Not to Lady Isabail. "My household is none of your concern."

"Of course it is," she insisted. "I am your prisoner. My safety is at stake. A brave warrior can hold off an attacking army indefinitely. A starving warrior has only days before he must bow in defeat."

Her brazen challenge drew Aiden forward. "Now you impugn my ability to keep you safe? By God, woman, you are too much."

She took a hasty step back, a rapid pulse fluttering in her long, elegant neck.

A very obvious sign of fear, which twisted his guts. She believed he would harm her. Good sense told him to back away, to let her run. But he did not. Instead, he gave in to impulse and closed the gap between them to mere inches. Her eyes widened, and one trembling hand flew to her throat.

Aiden grasped that hand in his.

It was cool and delightfully soft-skinned. The temptation to press a kiss to her knuckles came and went as he stared into her eyes. This was not the time for such an indulgence. He placed her hand on his chest, just above his heart. "Know this. Never, no matter how angry my words or how furious my stance, will I do harm to a woman," he said. "If ever you need to know that you are safe in my presence, simply place your hand here and push. You have my word that I will back away."

He let his hand drop. Hers remained on his chest.

With their gazes locked, he pressed lightly forward, encouraging her to test his vow.

And she did. She pushed.

Aiden stepped back. "I am a passionate man, lass. I've been known to shake the rafters with the sounds of my fury. But I've never lifted a hand to a woman, and I'll not start now. You possess information that I am determined to get, but I can assure you that my methods will never include beating it out of you. Understand?"

She nodded, her eyes meeting his more easily.

With her fear contained and her trembles calmed, Isabail's pale face regained its ethereal beauty. Smooth skin the color of milk, long-lashed eyes that rivaled the woodland bluebell, and rosy lips that begged to be kissed. What was not to admire? The desire that sang through his veins came as natural as breathing.

He took her chin lightly in hand, rubbing his thumb over the silky softness of her flesh.

"Lovely," he said.

She flushed but did not draw back. Nor did she attempt to push him away.

"I've traveled the length and breadth of Scotland and met many a lass, but none as bonny as you," he admitted. One or two had come close, including his once-betrothed, Fiona MacDonald. But Isabail's silvery blond hair and blue eyes charmed him in a way none of the others had. Of course, those other lasses had not given him near as much trouble, either.

He shifted the path of his thumb upward, across the velvet texture of her lips.

As he tugged on her bottom lip, a gentle sigh escaped her mouth. The sound made his pulse pound and his head spin. Up until that moment, he'd fully intended to pull away, to let the tension between them ebb and the passage of time add strength to her trust in him. But that sigh was so full of promise, so sweetly encouraging, he could only bow to it.

With excruciating slowness, giving her every opportunity to halt him, he lowered his mouth toward hers. A hairbreadth away, he stopped, needing to be certain. Breathing deep of her sweetly feminine scent, he found her hand and placed it upon his chest once more. One push and he would be gone. She had to know that.

To his relief, she did not push. Her hand slipped up and around his neck. It was an invitation he could not refuse—on an indrawn breath, he captured the petal-soft curve of her lips.

Sweet. So unbelievably sweet.

A deep groan rose in his throat as he leaned in to her body. Soft flesh met his hard grind, and it was enough to send his blood searing through his veins in a glorious burn of desire. After all the hours she'd spent in his arms on the long journey to Dunstoras, there was a sense of familiarity—of rightness—that came over him as he gathered her close.

She responded by tipping her head to accept his kisses.

And as swiftly as that, all resentment toward her died. What her brother had done to him was not Isabail's doing. She might be a tad arrogant and finer than an Englishwoman in her linen smallclothes, but she was also intelligent, persevering, and loyal. Despite all the challenges he'd thrown her way, she'd proven herself a stalwart champion of her maid, her brother, and even herself. She was incredible.

He deepened the kiss, burying his fingers in the silken strands of her blond hair and taking all that she had to offer.

For the moment, the lady was his.

Chapter 6

His kisses were neither sweet nor gentle. They were a fierce attack on Isabail's senses. Every press of his body against hers sent a thousand tiny tremors racing through her. The fear she'd felt only moments ago was gone—banished by the knowledge that he would stop if she but commanded. In its place lay excitement. And anticipation. And delightful ripples of pleasure.

His hands, which she had once envisioned as brutal, began to wander the curves of her body with the experience of a man born to sin. Kneading, mapping, caressing. Her mind was not so easily won as her body, and for a moment, two images of him warred within her thoughts—one, the dark warrior who had attacked her caravan, brimming with wrath and vengeance; the other, the purposeful leader, warming her toes against his bared chest and greeting his kin with subdued but obvious joy.

Which was the real MacCurran?

She let her eyes drift shut, and immediately one image triumphed over the other.

A shiver of delight ripped through her body as his hand found her breast and squeezed. At this moment she wasn't sure it mattered. Her body craved his touch, wanton traitor that it was. Four years of loneliness. Four years without a husband to warm her bed. Until this moment, she had not seen those years as hardship—but now she ached for an intimate touch. *His* intimate touch.

Isabail's hands, one of which had been clutching the blanket around her shoulders, suddenly found themselves roaming the steely expanse of his chest. The blanket slid to the floor at their feet, leaving only the thin barrier of her chemise between his hands and her skin—and even that felt like too much. The fine linen rasped against her eager flesh.

His hands stilled for a moment.

Isabail shuddered under the loss of sweet friction, torn between the urge to recover the blanket and her modesty, or to press herself wantonly against his hands in an effort to recapture the heavenly sensations of moments before.

He took the decision away from her.

A low growl escaped his lips.

Cupping both hands beneath her buttocks, he lifted her up his body, slammed her against the stone wall, and stole her breath away.

Despite the roughness of his actions, there was no fear in Isabail's heart. There was too much restraint and too little brutality in his assault. Aye, it

was fierce—but there was also the barest suggestion of a tremble in his arms. The tremble of a
muscle primed with raw need but couched by reason.

MacCurran was doing his best to be gentle.

As gentle as a large, sensual marauder could be.

His lips crushed hers, his tongue demanding
entry to her mouth. Aware that it was as much a
symbolic gesture as one born of need, Isabail gave
in to the heated promise and opened herself to
him.

Their tongues tangled in a sensual duel.

"Oh!" Muirne's voice came from the door.

MacCurran broke off the kiss and gently lowered her to the floor. Both of them were breathing
hard, their eyes now open. The reality of Isabail's
surroundings slowly sank in.

"Shall I return in a wee moment, my lady?"
Muirne asked carefully.

MacCurran's arms dropped. He stepped back,
scooped up her blanket, and handed it to her, all
the while keeping her shielded from Muirne's
view. The look in his eyes was unreadable. Was he
as disappointed as she? Or relieved by the inter-
ruption?

"Nay." Isabail wrapped the blanket about her
shoulders, her cheeks flushed. "Were you able to
get the stains from my gown?"

"Not all." Muirne laid the wet dress on the bed
and smoothed out the worst of the wrinkles. "But
most."

Isabail knew she would face Muirne's curious

questions later, but she was grateful that for the moment her maid ignored the scene she had just witnessed.

MacCurran cupped Isabail's chin and forced her to meet his gaze. "Take up needlecraft or something equally innocuous. Cease your interference in my affairs."

Then he dropped his hand and departed.

Aiden was ten feet beyond Isabail's door before he realized that he'd completely forgotten his reason for visiting her in the first place—the names of her guests. He tipped his head to the moon visible beneath a thin layer of cloud and released a frustrated howl. By the Holy Maker, the woman drove him completely senseless.

Another day had passed—a day he could ill afford to lose. His inability to put name to the man in black was a risk to his clan—if MacPherson discovered the hill fort, all his efforts to recoup his good name would be for naught. His kin would be rounded up and tossed in Dunstoras's very cramped dungeons. Men, women, and children. MacPherson had shown no leniency thus far, so it would be foolish to hope for any. Only the tunnels below the ancient ruin would save them if the wretch found his way up the rocky slope to the broch. Aiden's people kept minimal belongings on the surface to ensure they could quickly hide— but even that last resort was dependent on the ability of the Black Warriors to give them notice.

Aiden descended the narrow stairs to the tunnels and made his way to the storeroom.

Behind a short stack of flour sacks was a very old but still useable winch. Verifying that it had already been wound and locked open, he left the storeroom and traveled deeper into the tunnel. Some twenty paces past the storeroom, he reached a dead end—a flat wall of rock decorated with a half dozen Pictish symbols similar to those carved on the stones scattered all over northern Scotland. Aiden placed the flat of his hand on the symbol of a boar with bristles along its back and pushed . . . hard.

The stone mechanism was an amazing feat—a huge granite slab that pivoted on a small round rock at the base. It required only a determined push to move it. It hadn't always been so easy to move—a hundred years of wear and tear on the pivot had once made it nearly impossible to open. Aiden's father had tasked an elderly but talented stonemason with repairing the door a number of years ago.

The slab slid sideways, creating a gap wide enough for a single man to pass through. Aiden entered the narrow chasm and then carefully pivoted the slab back into place. Familiar with the dark confines, he stood for a moment and allowed his eyes to adjust to the dimness. An enticing light flickered beyond a curve in the passageway ahead, but he knew better than to rush forward. His second step was a large, exaggerated pace, calculated to avoid the stone tile inset in the floor—a trap intended for an unsuspecting thief.

Around the curve, he found a small room lit by a single torch. The room had only one major feature—a great basalt tomb built upon a raised dais. His brother, Niall, stood before the tomb, staring into the silk-lined display box that fronted it, with his head bowed.

"Sometimes I wonder if doing our duty is the best thing for Scotland," Niall said softly.

Aiden understood the sentiment, but disagreed with it. "King Alexander has his own history. He has no need to wear the crown of the last king of the Picts to make his claim on the throne of Scotland."

"But should these not be part of the royal jewels?" Niall said, pointing to the items in the display. "They were hidden away when our history was turbulent, when it was less clear who the true king of Scotland should be. But King Alexander is a strong monarch, and the threat of an English king claiming the land has faded."

Aiden joined Niall in front of the tomb.

The long silk-lined rectangular box served as a bed for a double-edged, silver-hilted broadsword, a tall willow staff topped with a silver boar head, and a simple crown crafted from a flat band of silver and set with a brilliant blue sapphire.

"There are always men who would make false claim to the throne had they the means within their grasp," Aiden said. "We've sworn an oath to protect this treasure, so protect it we shall. Do you have the necklace?"

Niall handed Aiden a velvet drawstring bag.

Aiden opened it and peered inside. A glint of gold and red winked back at him, and unbidden, the burn of anger seared his veins. This necklace had cost him everything. Such a small thing to carry such power over his existence . . . and the future of his clan. How could the king—whom his father had served with unlimited loyalty and devotion—believe he would throw everything away simply to acquire a jewel?

"We'll hold this wretched thing until we have our proof, then return it to the king." He lifted the purple silk at one end of the display box and dropped the bag into a shallow hole that had once held a banner pole. "I can only pray that Grant's sister gives me the information I seek."

"Still no luck?"

Aiden shook his head.

"There must be something you can do to encourage her."

A sharp memory of kissing her in her chamber popped into Aiden's mind. It still amazed him that she'd permitted such liberties. "My best option is to seduce the information from her lips."

"What?"

Aiden met his brother's gaze. "She's a widow. She's already known a man. I'll not be despoiling her."

"She's also a *noblewoman*. Cousin to the bloody earl of Lochurkie."

Aiden shrugged. "The earl already believes me guilty of murder and treachery. Let him add one more sin to the list. The only time she isn't cowering in fear of me is when I'm kissing her."

"You've already kissed her?"

Aiden ignored the thunderous expression on Niall's face. "This isn't a case of ransom. I do not need to return her in the same state I found her. I just need those names."

Niall was silent for a moment, his lips tight. "You are a better man than this."

Aiden frowned. "You dare to judge me? You, the man who coerced a woman into helping him enter Duthes Castle and steal a ruby necklace from a baron?"

"I never forced myself upon the lass."

Aiden grabbed the torch from its bracket and made his way back to the granite slab entrance. "I do what I must to protect my clan."

Niall put a hand on his shoulder, halting his progress. "Just be careful. We've lost everything but our honor. Do not sacrifice that in your attempt to regain what's gone. It's not worth it."

"I'll be the judge of that."

Having gone without supper on the MacCurran's instructions, Isabail's belly growled repeatedly over the course of the evening. Hungry and at a loss for something to do, she decided to seek an early sleep. She and Muirne had just settled themselves on the lumpy straw mattress and shut their eyes when Beathag entered the room with a torch.

"You're to come with me," the MacCurran woman said.

As Muirne rolled off the pallet and stood, Beathag shook her head. "Not you; just the lady."

Isabail pushed to her feet. "And where are we going?"

"The chief has given you quarters more suited to your station," Beathag said, studying the floor with odd intensity.

"Then surely my maid should accompany me."

"Nay. Now, come along."

Muirne opened her mouth to argue, but Isabail waved her hand. "Rest your ankle. I'm sure all will be well. Seek me out in the morning."

Still unhappy, Muirne nodded. "If you insist."

Isabail followed Beathag across the inner close, stars winking at her from the indigo sky above. The clouds had drifted away, leaving a crisp, cold night. Beathag stopped before a roundhouse hung with a wooden door instead of the standard fur pelts. A very simple door with no fancy pulls or hinges. She knocked.

"Come."

Isabail's heart stumbled. The voice that beckoned her inside belonged to MacCurran. She took a step back. "Why am I here?"

Beathag shrugged. "The chief demanded your presence." She pushed the door open. "Ask your questions of him."

Light poured out of the roundhouse, bathing Isabail's cold feet in a golden glow. Given the kiss they had recently shared, she was not at all certain she wanted to be alone with the MacCurran. He had a rather taxing effect on her willpower. But more than light reached her from the chief's room. Her stomach growled at the savory scents of venison broth and fresh bread.

He had refused her supper . . . but perhaps he'd changed his mind?

"In," Beathag prodded.

Still uncertain, Isabail caught Beathag's eyes and arched a questioning brow. The other woman's initial request had been for her to sleep elsewhere for the night. Surely she didn't mean here.

Beathag returned her stare for a moment, then looked away. "Ask your questions of the chief," she repeated. Then she gave Isabail a light push.

Despite the prompting, Isabail was seriously contemplating running back to Muirne. Even the promise of a warm meal was not enough to coax her into MacCurran's chamber. But the man himself stole her choice away. He appeared at the door, latched a big hand onto her arm, and dragged her into the room.

Then he shut the door with a decisive snap.

Isabail's mouth went dry.

His size never failed to make her heart pound. He towered over her, his broad shoulders blocking her view of everything. Everything, that is, except the tawny skin visible at the neck of his tunic and the barest suggestion of hair.

"This is an inappropriate time to seek an audience," she said weakly.

"You think a man willing to kidnap you concerns himself with what others think appropriate?" His hold on her arm gentled, his thumb brushing over her chemise-clad skin in a manner that set all of Isabail's senses atingle.

It was a dangerous feeling—because rather than pulling away, Isabail swayed on her feet, tempted to lean in to his touch. "I must return to my chamber. Whatever you wished to discuss can wait until morning."

"No."

She swallowed thickly. "I will not stay."

"Aye, you will." He tugged her sharply, and she fell against his chest. That solid, divinely warm chest that blotted out the room. "You will because I say you will."

Isabail's head swam, intoxicated by the masculine scent of his skin and the feel of his ropy muscles beneath her hands. It seemed impossible that such a frightening wall of man could spark desire within her—but the proof was in her heartbeat and her unsteady breath. True, she had admired his handsomeness when she'd first spotted him in the orchard at Lochurkie several days ago—had even asked the captain of her guard, the unfortunate Sir Robert, if he was acquainted with him. But that was before he attacked her carriage—and before she'd stood next to him. The only man she'd ever met of a similar stature had been her father. Andrew, her late husband, had been a mere four inches taller than she.

MacCurran's hand trailed slowly up her body, sending shivers rippling through her. So large . . . and yet so gentle. When he reached the nape of her neck, he lifted the thick braid that Muirne had only just plaited and unwound the gold cord that secured it. Isabail knew she should pull away—make some attempt to stop him—but the tiny thrills that shot through her scalp as he played with her hair ran all the way to her toes. No man had threaded his fingers through her hair in many a year—and God help her, it felt good.

She let him have his way.

When he had completely unbraided her hair and spread her tresses over her shoulders with a mild grunt of approval, he paused. "Are you hungry?"

"That's a foolish question," she grumbled, casting an eye at the brazier in the middle of the room. Next to it lay two bowls of broth, the brown juices thick and floating with chunks of meat. "I've not had supper."

He crossed his arms over his chest. "I'll trade food for information."

That was cruel. Isabail had no intention of revealing the names of the five men she knew had laid their pallets under Lochurkie's roof that night. Not after he'd made such a pointed observation regarding what she'd learned about the MacCurran encampment. He would never release her. The risk of her telling someone what she knew was too great. "I will not," she said. "I prefer to go without."

"Suit yourself."

Isabail thought that was the end of it, and she turned to leave. But he did not allow her to depart. Instead, he swept her off her feet, carried her across the room, and tossed her onto the mattress.

No bed frame here, either. But there was a wealth of blankets and furs, and the mattress was stuffed with feathers not straw. Despite the comforts, Isabail immediately rolled, intent on fleeing.

She didn't get far.

MacCurran followed her onto the mattress, and his arm latched around her waist.

Isabail shrieked. Heart pounding in her chest, she flailed in a desperate attempt to get free. But her efforts were for naught. His arm was a steel band. He tugged her back against his body, his hold ruthless and uncompromising. One leg over hers, and she was effectively trapped.

"Sleep," he said gruffly.

Isabail lay there, wide-eyed and uncertain. No rape, no beating. Just slow, deep breaths and a firm hold. What should she do? His large body was curled around hers, his heat seeping through her shift. She could continue to struggle, but judging from her lack of success thus far, the chances of breaking free appeared small. She could scream, but who would come running? Or, she could wait for him to fall asleep.

"I sleep with one eye open," he murmured into her hair. "I'll fetch you back if you attempt to leave."

Those words should have frightened her. They labeled her a prisoner. Instead, his lazy voice settled her frantic heartbeat.

She studied the arm hooked around her waist. Roped with well-defined sinews and covered in a sprinkle of crisp hairs, it was as much a weapon as the man's fine sword. If he accosted her in the middle of the night, could she rely on him to be as honorable as he'd promised to be? To release her at a push of her hand and roll away? Or was she a fool to place her faith in him?

It hardly seemed possible that her heart could have softened so quickly for this man.

Two days ago, she'd been convinced he'd killed her brother and a host of other people. What was it about him that convinced her he was trustworthy? Was it his story of a man in black? The fact that he had a brother and a mother? The adoring faces of his kinsmen? Really, even utter cads had family.

Isabail sighed heavily.

Nay, it was none of those things. It was this. The warmth and the steadiness. The feeling that as long as she remained in his arms, she was safe. He'd held her precisely this way the entire journey from Lochurkie, never failing her. Never taking advantage.

She closed her eyes.

She'd fallen asleep once before in his arms. She could surely do it again.

Aiden awoke.

He stared at the thatching, wondering what had stirred him from his sleep. But the hut and the rest of the ruined broch were silent—only the faint crackle of coals in the brazier broke the midnight calm. The soft scent of Isabail Grant filled his nose, and he tightened his arms, drawing her closer. As he did so, her feet came in contact with his shins, and he sucked in a sharp breath.

Ye gods.

Her feet were like icicles. She was curled up in his arms like a wee pine martin in its nest, but without a blanket, she couldn't stay warm. He was a fool. Why hadn't he thought of that? Gently easing away from her, he sat up and snatched several blankets from the end of the bed. He tucked them around her, making certain every inch of flesh was covered. Then, cradling her weight, he lay back on the mattress.

He'd fully intended to enact his plan to seduce her tonight. Bribe her with food, heat her blood with kisses, and then coax the names from her lips. But he hadn't expected her to look so goddamned beautiful with her hair unbound. Or to enjoy his fingers threading through her silvery tresses. The way she'd closed her eyes and given up a soft sigh had nearly unmanned him. Truly, she'd had him as tongue-tied as a wee lad.

And then she had refused the food.

Stubborn vixen.

He rolled to his side, hugging Isabail close and doing his best to warm her chilled extremities. She made a soft mewl of contentment and snuggled deeper into his arms. Somehow, he'd earned a small measure of her trust, and he was loath to toss away that precious gift. If he followed through with his intent to seduce her and then betrayed her trust, there would be no going back. Her hatred would be well earned.

But how else was he to get the names?

He sighed.

Tomorrow would tell.

When Isabel awoke, she found herself swathed in furs and blankets, completely alone on the mattress. The MacCurran had departed, though she had no idea when. She peered under the covers. The delicate material of her chemise was intact, and her body felt well rested, not abused. Perhaps her faith in him was not so careless after all.

Midstretch, she had a sudden thought.

Was she free to leave? She sat up and stared at the door. It was shut; did that suggest that she was imprisoned? Scrambling to her feet, she wrapped a blanket about her shoulders. There was only one way to find out.

Her feet made short work of the cold floor to the door. Hand on the iron latch, she pulled the door open. No one called halt. She peered out. Seeing nary a soul in sight, she lifted the hem of her shift and dashed across the close to the hut she'd originally been given.

Muirne greeted her with wide-eyed relief. "Oh, my lady, I feared for you the whole night."

"I am fine," Isabail assured her. "Is my gown dry?"

The maid nodded. "And I was able to retrieve one of your shifts. Offered up my recipe for honey bannocks in trade. Replace the one you've got on, and you'll be fresh from tip to toe." Muirne's face fell. "Would that I could've protected you from that cur."

"Fear not. I slept. That is all."

Her maid arched a brow. "He did not force him-self upon you?"

Isabail yanked her shift over her head, the chill of the morning air encouraging speed. "Nay."

"Did ya give willingly, then?"

"I slept," Isabail repeated. The look of skepti-cism on Muirne's face almost coaxed a smile to Isabail's lips. "Come," she said. "Let us see what the cook is preparing to break the fast."

"Nothing appetizing, I'll wager."

"He's not a master of spices," Isabail agreed, shoving her feet into her leather boots. "I miss the sumptuous fares of our dear cook at Lochurkie. No one has as deft a hand as he."

They ducked under the furs hanging over the door and stepped into a brisk winter breeze. Raised voices drew them toward the central fire, where a group of warriors had gathered. Some poor soul had been dragged before the MacCur-ran, and the faces of the men were angry.

"Did he give his name?"

One of the warriors, a handsome lad garbed in various shades of green and carrying a beautifully carved ash-wood bow, shook his head. "Not be-fore he swooned."

"Fetch Niall's healer," MacCurran said, staring down at the body. "Fool must have stumbled upon a badger sett."

Isabail caught a glimpse of the bloodied cloth-ing amid the men's legs. None of the MacCurran men were tending to the fellow; they were simply letting him bleed all over the ground. Highland brutes. She elbowed her way between them. "If he's bleeding, his wounds need immediate attention. Step aside."

The men parted, letting her through.

Isabail avoided the MacCurran's gaze as she gained the center of the group. What do you say to a man with whom you had shared a bed but no wedding vows? The flaxen-haired man on the ground was a more suitable target for her attentions—his back, arm, and hip were shredded by something with vicious teeth. Isabail crouched and rolled the poor fellow over.

A gasp escaped her lips. "Daniel!"

His eyes flickered open, his expression dazed. "Lady Isabail?"

"Dear Lord, Daniel. What befell you?"

A large hand grasped her arm and hauled her upright. "You know this man?"

Isabail faced MacCurran, a flush rising in her cheeks. A vision of lying next to him clad only in her shift wreaked havoc with her thoughts. "Aye. Daniel de Lourdes. He was my brother's most valued personal attendant."

MacCurran frowned heavily. "So he was traveling with you to Edinburgh?"

"Make way, please," said a female voice.

Isabail was jostled as the men around her moved aside. She barely noticed. Her gaze was held by the MacCurran's. His eyes were a brilliant blue—a shade not unlike a robin's egg—and she wondered why she hadn't noticed before.

"Let's have a look at you, then," the female voice added.

"Nay!" Daniel protested weakly. "Do not touch me."

Isabail broke off her connection with the Mac-Curran and glanced down. A woman with dark red hair was leaning over Daniel—red hair that Isabail immediately recognized. Reacting instinctively, she shoved the woman aside. "Get away from him, murderess!"

The woman landed on her rump on the ground, her long braid whipping into the air and her satchel spilling its contents.

Isabail kicked the pots and herbs, scattering them. "You'll not touch him with your evil witchery!"

MacCurran's hand clamped down on her arm again. "Enough."

She whirled on him. "This woman killed my brother. Fed him poison and watched him die before her eyes. If you are as innocent as you claim, how is it she is welcome in your camp?"

Nausea rolled in Isabail's belly, and her hand went to her stomach. She'd actually begun to believe MacCurran's protestations of innocence. Had actually begun to consider the existence of his man in a black cloak. But he was harboring the woman who had been tried and found guilty of John's murder. A woman found in possession of numerous poisons.

"The bailie declared her guilty," she cried hoarsely. "She was sentenced to death by pit and would be dead now if you hadn't freed her."

"I did not poison John Grant," Ana Bisset said quietly.

Isabail spun around. "Liar. You were the only one to give him food or drink that night. You gave him a tisane to rid him of head pain."

"Willow bark tea does not kill a man," Ana said.

"Unless it is laced with dwale."

The healer's face twisted. "I am sworn to heal. There was no poison in the tea."

"And yet by the next morning, he was bedridden and delirious," Isabail accused. She had trusted this woman. Allowed her into their home, accepted her balms and unguents with innocent faith. Only to be proven a poor judge of character. "What justice is there in the world when my brother—as good a man as ever there was—lies cold in a grave while you—his murderess—walks freely about?"

Ana Bisset said nothing.

Isabail turned back to MacCurran, her heart a leaden lump in her chest. "I will see to Daniel's care myself. Please arrange to have him moved to my hut and provide me with water and bandages." A shudder ran through her. "I want fresh strips of linen. Nothing touched by this witch."

MacCurran's expression was unreadable. He returned her stare for a long moment—long enough to remind her that she had no authority in his domain. Then he nodded to Beathag. "Fetch her what she needs." To his warriors, he simply waved a hand toward her roundhouse.

As Isabail made to follow the men carrying

Daniel, MacCurran stepped into her path. "Do what you must. I'll be along presently to question him."

"He needs rest, not questions."

MacCurran's expression hardened. "The man succeeded in finding his way to my camp. If you think I intend to let that matter drop, you are mistaken."

Isabail glared at him, but did not argue further. Her time was better spent healing Daniel. She had been gulled by MacCurran once, but she would not be so foolish again. As soon as Daniel was well enough to talk, she would learn how he'd made his way here . . . and then she'd do everything in her power to leave.

Chapter 7

A iden stared at Ana Bisset.

"I did not kill him," she repeated quietly.

"Is it true he had no food or drink other than the tisane you provided?"

She frowned. "So said the kitchen gillies."

"Then how was he poisoned, if not by you?" Aiden asked, his doubt weighing heavily on his words. All he knew of the redheaded healer he had learned from Niall. Perhaps his brother's infatuation had misguided him

"If I knew that, I might have been able to raise a reasonable defense," she said. She stooped to gather her scattered pots, replacing them in her leather satchel. "I was only called to tend him the next morning, after he took to his bed. What occurred between the hour I gave him the tisane and the moment I arrived at his bedside, I cannot attest to."

Aiden frowned. "Is it possible you poisoned

him in error? Mixed the wrong ingredients for his tea?"

"Nay," she said. "Willow bark tea is a simple tisane. And its odor is very unique."

His gaze pinned hers. "Then I must insist that any further healing you do within the camp, and all medicinal preparations you make, be done under the eye of Master Tam. He's not the herbalist you are, but he knows a great deal about plants nonetheless."

Ana straightened, her shoulders stiff with pride. "As you wish." Then she slung her satchel over her shoulders and pressed her way through the crowd.

Aiden watched her go, less than thrilled at how the morning had progressed. "Back to your posts," he barked at his men. He hadn't even broken the fast yet, and half the camp was already in a furious uproar. He grabbed a piece of bread from a basket near the hearth.

Lord. The bleakness on Isabail's face when she spied Ana bending over de Lourdes had cut him deep. She had looked so utterly betrayed. And he could easily understand why. It was a simple leap of thought to tie Ana Bisset and her brother's murder back to him. But damn it, he'd had nothing to do with John Grant's death.

He'd best be prepared. It would take every ounce of charm he possessed to make up the ground he'd lost. If it were even possible.

*   *   *

Daniel's wounds were worse than Isabail originally thought. She carefully cut away his lèine, pulling bits of cloth from his torn flesh. She cleaned each gash with water, removing all of the blood and dirt that she could. The wounds on his back and shoulder were the shallowest and the most difficult to dress, so she did those first. She tied the last of the bandages about his chest and sat back.

"Good thing the badgers were still half-asleep," she told him.

He smiled at her—a weak attempt at the same charming smile he had frequently bestowed upon her brother. "I'm not much of a woodsman, I fear."

"Then it must be quite the tale," MacCurran said from the doorway, "how you came to find us."

Daniel's smile fell away. He glanced at MacCurran and then back at Isabail. "I cannot take any credit for my success. It was Gorm who led me here."

"Gorm?" Isabail instinctively glanced at the door. Then wished she hadn't—MacCurran's eyes met hers. She looked away. "Where is he now? I did not see him in the close."

"He fell, my lady," Daniel said, his eyes dark. "Defending me from the badgers."

MacCurran strode to the mattress. "Who is this Gorm?"

"My brother's deerhound," Isabail explained, her heart heavy. Gorm's unwavering affection and sweet disposition had given her great solace after her brother's death. During the two months she was in deep mourning, his was often the only face she saw. "A great, loyal beast."

"So the hound led you to us?" MacCurran asked Daniel.

"Aye." The manservant grimaced. "He and I were part of Lady Isabail's caravan. I sent him off in search of a rabbit when you attacked, fearing he would fall victim to a blade. But afterward, he tracked you through the mountains, even through the snow. He had a good nose."

"Not for badgers, it would seem."

Daniel winced. "'Twas I who stirred the badgers. I lost my footing and fell into a hole. Right onto the sleeping creatures, as it turns out. I'm certain I'd not have survived had Gorm not come to my rescue."

Tears welled up in Isabail's eyes. How silly was that? Crying over a dog, but not over the wounds done to Daniel. "He was a fine hound."

MacCurran studied Daniel for a long moment, then spun on his heel and left without another word.

"Has he harmed you, Isabail?" Daniel asked worriedly.

She shook her head. "We've been treated quite fairly."

"What was his purpose in taking you?"

Isabail no longer believed MacCurran's story about the man in black. In truth, she did not know what to think. "I don't know," she said honestly.

"We must find a way to get free," Daniel said,

sitting up. "Every moment you remain here, the risk that he will harm you increases."

"Lie still." Isabail pushed him gently back on the mattress. "Let us see you healed and then we can make plans to leave." She gave him a curious look. "Where were you when they found you?"

"We'd been following a burn. Gorm and I had just left a section of marshland, where the reeds are dried crisp by the winter chill but still standing tall, when we stumbled upon the badger sett."

"There's a burn not far from here. Think you we could escape that same way?"

Daniel nodded. "If we can leave the camp undetected."

Isabail sighed. That was the difficult part. She couldn't visit the garderobe without someone in her shadow. And that someone was likely to be the MacCurran.

To make a run for it, they'd need a diversion of some sort.

"Ana is very upset," Niall said, as they wended through the trees.

Aiden peered into the shadows left and right, but spotted no sign of a disturbed badger sett. "The tale of John Grant's murder, as told by his sister, is quite damning."

"As is the tale of John Grant finding the king's necklace hidden in your chamber."

Aiden tossed his brother a dagger of a glare. "You know the truth about that."

"Do I?"

Aiden stopped short. "Do you doubt my veracity?"

"Nay," Niall said firmly. "Because I trust my gut, and my gut says you'd never participate in such a miserable crime."

It was easy enough to follow Niall's argument. "And your gut tells you Ana is innocent, as well."

"Aye."

Aiden grunted and continued through the woods. "I'm the chief. I've not the luxury of following my gut. I must protect the clan." He ducked under an arching elderberry branch. "If your Ana is the woman you believe her to be, in time she'll earn the right to perform her craft without a watchful eye."

His brother did not look particularly happy about Aiden's judgment, but he accepted it with a sharp nod. They made their way between the trees in silence for a while, their attention on the sights and sounds of the woodland. A black grouse crossed their path some thirty paces ahead, pecking at the ground, and Aiden paused rather than frighten it into flight. Always better to pass unnoticed.

Only moments after they resumed their trek, the distinctive scent of blood drifted to them downwind. Niall pointed left and Aiden nodded, allowing his brother to take the lead. They circled a hazelnut thicket and traversed a small dip in the land. On the far side, where the earth mounded higher, the snow was pink. A large, scruffy gray shape lay under a low-hanging pine bough.

To the left, thrashed snow and broken bits of twig pointed to the entrance to the badger den.

It would seem de Lourdes's story was true.

They gave the sleeping badgers a wide berth and carefully made their way to the body of the deerhound. A hero deserved a place in the ground, rather than to provide a meal for scavengers. Aiden lifted the fir branch to look at the dog. It lay on its side, its long graceful legs extended. The animal's rough coat was matted with blood in several spots, thicker about the poor creature's neck. Badgers were one of the most vicious opponents in the woodland.

"It yet lives," Niall said, pointing to the dog's chest. Slow, shallow breaths lifted and lowered in a barely perceptible pattern.

Badly injured as it was, the kind thing to do would be to bring a swift end to its labors. Aiden reluctantly drew his dirk.

Niall stayed his hand. "Nay. Bring the creature to Ana. She can prove her healing skills to you without risking the clan."

" 'Tis barely alive. It might not survive the journey back to camp."

His brother shrugged. "If it doesn't, it doesn't. But it's surely worth a try. Deerhounds are spectacular beasts, capable of downing a buck. A shame to let it die if it can be saved."

"Agreed."

Aiden scooped the dog into his arms with a mild grunt. Heavy as a bloody woman. The dog whimpered at the movement, then lay still. Deep-

chested, with a long tapered snout, it was a surprisingly beautiful creature.

"Lead on, then," he urged his brother. "Let's see
what your wee healer can do."

Isabail next tended the bites and scratches on Daniel's arms and hip. Twelve of them, two quite
deep—one on his biceps and another on his hip.
Most of his injuries had ceased to bleed, but it was
clear the deeper ones would need more than a
strip of linen. Her healing skills were rudimentary
at best. Under any other circumstances, she would
have happily stepped aside in favor of the healer.

Her lips tightened. But she'd trusted Ana Bisset
once before, and the outcome had been dire. Daniel deserved better.

"Will I lose the arm?" Daniel asked, peering at
the wound with a tragic expression.

"Not if I can help it," Isabail said.

"Yarrow would stanch the bleeding and cleanse
the wounds."

Isabail nodded. "Muirne, fetch me some dried
yarrow from the stores in the caves."

As the maid scurried off, Daniel eyed Isabail.
"There are caves nearby?"

"Beneath the ruin." She pressed a dry cloth
against his biceps in an attempt to stop the bleeding. "Quite fortuitous that you insisted on bringing Gorm to Edinburgh with us."

He gave her a sad smile. "I'm pleased that he
led me to you, of course, but I mourn his loss most
severely. John was so fond of him. But if his sacri-

fice allows me to bring MacCurran to justice, then it was worth it."

Isabail lifted her head. "You have some plan in mind?"

A bitter edge twisted Daniel's lips. "My priority is to see to your safety, of course, Isabail. But now that I am here in his camp and I have witnessed his association with the witch firsthand, I must act on my opportunity. I can prove the wretch is guilty of killing John, whether he did the deed himself, or not."

"How?"

"By locating the necklace."

Isabail lifted the cloth to peer at the wound. The flow had eased, but the wound still seeped. She pressed it back. "Queen Yolande's necklace?"

"Aye. I must search MacCurran's camp for it."

Her eyebrows soared. "The king already believes MacCurran guilty of the theft. Why would you risk your life for no cause?"

"The queen's birthday will be celebrated in a few short weeks, on the nineteenth of March. Would it not be fitting for the king to gift it to his true love then, as he was unable to do upon their wedding day?"

"I suppose," Isabail said, a little dubious.

"Come now. Surely you believe in the grand gesture?"

She shrugged. "I'm not as convinced as you that the king is in love with Yolande."

He smiled. "Why wouldn't he be? In addition

to being quite beautiful, Queen Yolande has given him the one thing he desires most, has she not?"

"We don't know that. It's only speculation that the queen is with child."

"Nonetheless," said Daniel. "Theirs is a story that deserves a happy twist."

He sighed heavily. "In truth, I have a more personal reason for my desire to see the necklace reclaimed. To me, it represents justice for John. He died at the hands of a ruthless thief who is yet unpunished for the crime." He placed a hand on Isabail's sleeve. "It tears my heart apart to know his murderer yet goes free. I have a contact in the king's court. If I bring the necklace to him, he may be able to convince the king to expend more effort to catch the wretched cur."

Muirne ducked under the lintel carrying a small earthenware pot. "I found the yarrow," she crowed with delight.

Isabail took the pot, filled the cup of her hand with dried yarrow, and added water to create a paste. Then she removed the cloth from Daniel's wound and packed the paste into the rendered flesh. Once she was satisfied with the packing, she wrapped the wound with fresh strips of linen and tied a firm knot.

"Allow the yarrow to do its work," she cautioned Daniel. "Rest. Do not use that arm excessively."

"Thank you, Lady Isabail."

She tossed him a smile, then gathered up the

remaining bandages. It was odd to hear him address her so formally. John and Daniel had been very close for several years, and before John's death, the three of them had spent significant time together. Casual, friendly, and honest time. Many of Isabail's favorite memories of John included Daniel.

"You know, of course, that MacCurran will place a guard at my door," Daniel said.

Isabail frowned. She hadn't thought about that, but it made sense. A stranger in his camp would be cause for worry. "'Tis a logical assumption," she agreed.

"To have a hope of recovering the queen's necklace, I will need your help."

"MacCurran swears he never stole the necklace."

"That's preposterous. John's men found it hidden in his chamber the night de Coleville was murdered. And the necklace disappeared from Lochurkie a fortnight later, when MacCurran was freed from the dungeons by his brother."

Isabail nodded. Daniel was right. She'd been a fool to even consider MacCurran's wild story of a man in black. Who else had reason to take the necklace?

"It's here, hidden among MacCurran's possessions," Daniel said. "I'm willing to stake my life upon it."

"How can I help?"

"Explore the camp as best you can. Locate whatever potential caches you can. Then you and I can discuss how we might search those caches." He lightly squeezed her hand. "Whatever you do, do not put yourself at risk, not under any circumstance. Do not attempt to recover the necklace without me. I would never be able to live with myself if you came to harm."

Isabail clasped her hand over his. "If I discover anything worthy, I'll bring it to your attention. I promise."

"Lady Isabail."

At the crisp address from MacCurran, Isabail jerked. Releasing Daniel's hand, she hastily sought her feet and faced the fierce warrior. Was it her imagination, or did he seem especially forbidding at this moment? "Aye?"

His cold gaze examined her from head to boots in slow, impolite detail. What he was looking for, Isabail could only guess, but the intensity of his stare brought a hot flush to her cheeks.

"We located the hound," he said finally.

Tears sprang to her eyes. Poor, brave Gorm. "May I look upon him one last time before you commit his body to the fire?"

"It lives."

Isabail's hands flew to her chest. "Truly?"

He nodded. "You may see it once its wounds are properly dressed."

Relief and amazement drove her forward before she had time to think. MacCurran had rescued Gorm, just as he had once rescued Isabail and Muirne. Right from the jaws of death. She skipped across the room, rose to the tips of her toes, and planted a grateful kiss upon his rocklike chin. "Thank you."

A steely arm wrapped around her waist and yanked her tight against his chest. "You may thank me properly later."

Then he was gone, leaving Isabail to deal with the wide-eyed reactions of Muirne and Daniel . . . and the madcap flutter of her heart.

Aiden stood over Ana's shoulder and carefully watched her clean and dress the dog's wounds. She seemed capable enough, but his knowledge of herbs was very limited. Only Master Tam could confirm the healing properties of the unguents she was using. Thankfully, the orchard keeper was nodding and smiling.

"Will the creature survive the day?" Aiden demanded of Ana.

She looked up from her efforts. "Not without a miracle. These wounds are severe, and the poor fellow is weak from blood loss."

Aiden relived the blazing shine of gratitude in Isabail's eyes. "Then perform a miracle."

The healer grimaced. "You ask the impossible."

"Niall has great faith in your abilities. He believed you could save the animal. Are you admitting that you cannot?"

Ana stood straight. "If you leave me alone with the animal—if you give me your complete and unwavering trust—I will do all in my power to save it. But in the end, it will be God who decides whether the dog lives or dies. Not I."

Aiden's gaze dropped to the animal on the table. Its breathing was shallow and labored. In his opinion, death was a certainty. But if it died, Isabail would be heartbroken. She clearly cared for the beast. He caught Tam's eye and gave him the nod that excused him from the room. As the fur panel flapped shut behind him, Aiden delivered a fierce message to the healer.

"This dog will live, or you will face my wrath. Understand?"

Ana swept an errant lock of dark red hair from her face. She did not seem particularly fearful of his anger. No downward glances, no trembling hands—just a clean and absolute confidence in her actions. "Come back in an hour. God will have given His answer by then."

"For your sake, I hope it is the right one."

Giving her one last glare, he left her to the task.

Eager to see Gorm, Isabail went in search of MacCurran the moment Daniel's wounds were tended to. Since John's death, the hound had become a favored companion. Like her, Gorm lived for those moments when they escaped the castle walls and took to the hills on a hunt. She had added to the kitchen stew pot by way of her glossy winged merlin, while Gorm had run down rabbits with his long-legged pursuit.

She found the MacCurran chief in the lists—that section of the outer close dedicated to the warriors and their craft. He had entered into a mock duel with his brother, Niall, both men wielding wooden swords but forsaking the heavy padded cotun worn as protection by the others.

Reluctant to interfere, she stood back from the fray and watched for a time.

The two men were evenly matched. Where the chief had the advantage of size and reach, his brother gained points with speed and agility. Both had clearly spent many an hour in the lists.

With the sleeves of their lèines rolled up past their elbows and the necks unlaced, Isabail was privy to an entrancing display of rippling muscles. Neither man carried any spare flesh. As the duel continued—each whack and glide of the wooden swords as swift and strong as the last— the sheen of sweat enhanced the view.

MacCurran was surely the finest example of the male form she had ever seen. He was both long of limb and solid of shape. His movements were spare and deliberate, each one supported by heavy sinews that bunched and flexed under his smooth, tawny skin. Truly, he was the epitome of power and grace.

He was also devious.

Apparently tiring of the sport, he feinted to the left, waited until Niall was committed to that direction, then hooked a foot behind his opponent's calf and tripped him. Niall attempted to recover, but MacCurran gave his chest a quick shove and the other warrior went down.

Niall hit the ground cursing his brother with a string of ribald words that brought a flush to Isabail's cheeks.

MacCurran cut him off. "Mind your tongue, bratling. There's a lady present."

Until that point, Isabail was unaware that she'd been noticed. She advanced on the group, approaching the chief. His hair clung damply to his forehead and neck, and tiny droplets hung from his jaw.

"A word, if I may?" she asked the MacCurran. Her aim was polite nonchalance, but the words came out a tad breathless. Eyeing him from a distance never had the same effect as standing next to him. Even when Daniel's warnings were fresh in her ear.

He took her elbow and led her a short distance away. "I may have misspoken earlier," he said.

"How so?"

His blue eyes met hers. "The dog yet lives, but its injuries are very grave."

"I would see him, if I may." Gorm had given her so much comfort after John's death; she owed him whatever solace she could provide.

"Nay."

"But," she protested, "he is mine."

"If he survives the night, you can see him in the morn."

"Why would you keep me from him?"

He pointed to the ruin. "You already have a patient. Since you insisted on tending him, go tend him. I will inform you of the hound's progress."

"Daniel is fine. I wish to see Gorm."

"Go." His already fierce face took on a darker cast. "Do not test my temper over this."

The fear that had consumed her when she first met MacCurran resurfaced in a flash. Her heartbeat fluttered like a startled bird in her chest, and she had a very intense urge to run. But she did not. MacCurran had sworn that he would never strike her, or any woman, even in anger. And despite her renewed conviction that he was involved with her brother's death, she still believed that to be true. She had no idea why she believed it, but she did.

"I do not wish him to die without a familiar face to comfort him," she said quietly.

The grim look on his face eased a mite. "I understand, but I cannot allow you to see him now. To ease your fears, I will check on him. Now go."

Isabail hesitated.

"Go," he repeated.

Reluctantly, she went. She returned to the inner close, but did not give up her hope of seeing Gorm. There was no reason for MacCurran to refuse her request to comfort the dog in his last hour. He was simply being cruel. Punishing her for her bitter words of condemnation.

But he underestimated her determination.

MacCurran had promised to check on Gorm. That meant he would visit the dog, hopefully in short order. Isabail grabbed one multihued blanket from her bed and wrapped it about her waist, hiding the pale blue skirts of her gown. Then she took a second blanket and wrapped it about her head and shoulders. Anyone close to her would know immediately that it was she, but it was not intended to be a perfect disguise. Just enough of a veil to encourage the MacCurran's glance to slide past her.

Now toasty warm, she joined the other women in front of the central fire pit.

And waited for the MacCurran to enter the close.

As Aiden entered Ana's hut, she looked up. The look on her face told him everything he needed to know. "The hound died," he determined grimly.

"Nay," she protested, pointing to the piled blankets in the corner. "But neither does he show signs of recovery. I've tended the wounds and healed his hurts, but he lies still and unmoving."

Aiden crossed the room and stared down upon the animal. Blood still crusted the dog's blue-gray coat in several spots, but he could no longer see any open gashes. Linen bandages covered sections of its belly and legs. "Its breaths are deeper."

"Aye."

"Surely it just needs to eat."

Ana shook her head. "I've attempted to feed him, but he will not take food."

"Water?"

"Nothing." She handed Aiden a small wooden bowl and a spoon. "Perhaps you'll have better luck."

Aiden stared at the bowl of broth. He had far more pressing things to see to, like training the men, checking on the patrols, and solving disputes between members of his clan. But he did not want to return to Isabail with the news that her hound had passed. Nor could he send her here to Ana, the woman who had been tried and convicted of poisoning her brother. She would be furious to discover he'd sought the healer's help at all.

He crouched beside the dog.

Its head lay at the far side, close to the wall, making spooning anything into its maw near impossible. Aiden placed the bowl on the floor and scooped up the dog, once again amazed by its size. "How did you get the beast from your table to the floor?"

"Niall," she said, smiling.

Aiden repositioned the dog, then sat on the ground next to its large head. He reached for the bowl, then halted. The dog had lifted its head and laid it on Aiden's thigh. All without opening an eye.

"Och," said Ana softly. "That's a good sign."

Aiden put his hand on the dog's snout, surprised to find the wiry fur was soft and smooth. "There's a lad," he said encouragingly. "You'll eat now, or I'll take you to task."

He spooned a little broth into the animal's mouth.

It swallowed, then licked its lips in a silent request for more.

Ana looked on, amazed. "I tried the very same thing only a few moments ago, to no avail."

"He's a wise dog. Knows better than to refuse his chief."

She snorted. "Were you, perchance, the one who carried him here from the forest?"

"Aye."

Ana nodded. "He remembers your scent. He knows it was you who saved him."

For some reason that pleased Aiden. He spent the next while happily plying the beast with soup and talking to his brother's chosen woman. When he had emptied the bowl and set it aside, he was rewarded by a damp lick on his hands and a contented rumble in the dog's throat.

As he carefully shifted the dog and rose to his feet, he asked, "When will he be hunting rabbits again?"

The healer laughed. "One step at a time. Let's get him on his feet first."

"But he will recover?" he asked seriously.

She nodded. "Although, it would be best if you returned a few more times to encourage him to eat."

He frowned.

"Do you wish him to heal swiftly?" Ana prompted.

"Of course."

"Then spare him a few moments of your time."

Strangely, Aiden was not insulted by the request. A stable boy or young Jamie would have been better choices, but the task had been oddly rewarding.

He nodded.

"You did well to heal him," he acknowledged. "I will return."

*   *   *

The instant MacCurran stood up and showed signs of leaving, Isabail scurried away from the door to Ana Bisset's hut. She wasn't quite sure what to think about what she'd just seen, but one thing was certain—she did not want to be caught spying.

Darting behind the other roundhouses, she kept to the shadows and circled the central fire to the door of MacCurran's hut. Once inside, she tossed the blankets onto the mattress and ran a quick hand over her hair to flatten any hairs gone astray. Just in time, as it happened.

MacCurran entered the roundhouse a moment later.

Isabail watched him as he closed the door.

All of the anger and bitterness she had felt upon finding Ana Bisset in his camp was gone, replaced by two emotions she wasn't entirely comfortable with: gratitude for the healer's efforts to save her injured dog and amazement over MacCurran's gentle feeding of that same beast. He'd actually coaxed Gorm to eat with softly spoken words.

The sting of impending tears forced her to turn away.

Damn him.

He'd done it again. Confused her. Shaken her beliefs.

"You need not fear," MacCurran said. "The dog will live."

Isabail blinked hard, banishing her silly tears. Then she turned to face him. "May I see him?"

"In the morning," he said. "He's resting now."

Even the urge to protest had vanished. She now knew why he was keeping her from Gorm—he feared she'd be upset to discover Ana Bisset in charge of his care. And truth be told, if she hadn't seen the dog safe and secure in the healer's hut herself, she likely would have been just as distressed as he imagined.

So, how could she resent his decision?

She nodded. "I look forward to it."

"Are you feeling well?" he asked, frowning.

"Aye." As well as could be expected, given the tumultuous bend of her thoughts.

He crossed the room to stand before her. "I thought you'd be pleased to hear the dog was well."

"I am," she said. To avoid his piercing gaze, she looked at her feet. "But I was anticipating the worst and this good news has . . . disconcerted me."

His hand cupped her chin, forcing her to meet his gaze.

The rub of his callused palm on her skin stole her breath away. She suddenly craved a repeat of the intimate kiss they'd shared the night before. The press, the passion, the need. Oh aye, the need. She knew the facts pointed to him having a hand in her brother's murder, but at this moment, those facts felt vague and unfounded. The man who cradled injured dogs was real.

Excitement was a sweet taste in her mouth, and she stared into his eyes with an anticipation that was palpable. He returned her stare for a long moment, his expression still and unreadable.

Isabail was lost in the fantasy of his lips on hers, a warmth settling into her cheeks that had nothing to do with the glowing coals in the brazier at their feet.

Then, with the suddenness of a falcon strike, he hauled her up against his body. The rough press of his body against hers did nothing to calm the madcap beat of her heart. Every place her body was soft, his was hard. She barely resisted the urge to flatten her palms against the chiseled planes of his chest, to feel the evidence of his strength. But she held back. She did not want him to think, even for a moment, that she was resistant.

He tilted her head and very slowly, very deliberately, lowered his lips toward hers. Just before they touched, he said, "I'm feeling rather disconcerted myself."

And then he kissed her.

So deeply and stirringly that Isabail felt the ripples of pleasure reach right to her toes. It was a kiss of possession, a claim of rights that was primal in nature. It should have frightened her, or at the very least annoyed her, but all she felt was a hot pulse of tingling delight.

She leaned in to the kiss.

It was all the encouragement he needed. Both hands cupped her head, his fingers threading deep into her hair, and he crushed his lips against hers. The sweep of his tongue along the seam of her lips demanded her surrender. Isabail wanted to resist—knew deep down that she should—but her desire for him was shockingly potent.

He made her feel alive . . . and beautiful. The passion he stirred in her body was like an unrestrained melody, full of thrilling notes and soaring chords that vibrated through her entire being. Why MacCurran possessed the power to stir her so deeply, she couldn't fathom. He was as different from Andrew as two men could be. And he was her enemy. A cad, a cur, and a scurrilous knave . . . who fed soup to dogs.

Isabail sighed and opened her mouth.

Her hands found their way to his arms, gripping his powerful biceps with clenched fingers. She loved the contradiction—a man capable of ferocious strength but willing, on rare occasions, to cede the moment to gentleness. Like *this* moment.

He sucked her bottom lip into his mouth and bit. Not hard enough to break the skin, but firmly enough to send a host of tiny sparks coursing through her body. Isabail's knees went weak and she sagged against his chest.

MacCurran broke off the kiss. He held her close for a long moment, his forehead touching hers, his eyes closed. Twin flags of color graced his cheeks, and his breaths were ragged. The pulse in his neck beat fast and strong. Isabail enjoyed seeing the visible evidence of his desire.

Slowly, he regained control and opened his eyes. "Have your maid fetch your belongings," he said. "From now on, you'll sleep here."

Then he left.

Isabail was tempted to call after him, to complain that she had no belongings to move, but she decided she'd tugged on the lion's mane enough for one day.

Chapter 8

Isabail stood in the center of MacCurran's round-house and slowly pivoted.

Daniel had asked her to search the camp. She could think of no places in the old ruin where one would hide anything of value—except here. Everywhere else, the walls were crumbling or the comings and goings of people made tucking something away impossible. In truth, though, his quarters were no grander than hers. Everything was starkly simple—a pallet on the floor, a brazier, and a leather sack stuffed with his belongings. A clan prepared to run at any moment.

Still, to be certain, she carefully searched the walls for any loose stones and searched the floor for any spot that looked recently disturbed. There was no sign of the queen's necklace—or anything else of value.

She returned to Daniel with the news. He was lying on the pallet covered with a blanket, while Muirne patched the holes in his lèine.

"Muirne and I searched this room, too," he said. "But found nothing."

"Beathag said they had little notice of MacPherson's attack and that they took only the necessities when the women and children escaped Dunstoras into the night. Perhaps the necklace is still there?"

"Nay," Daniel said firmly. "He would not leave it behind. Not when he's sacrificed so much to acquire it."

"Then there's really only one other place to look."

He looked at her curiously. "Where?"

"The caves beneath the ruin."

His face lit up. "Yes, I recall you mentioning a cave."

"It's not a large space, but it's where most of the items they took from the fortress are stored."

"That sounds like just the place."

Isabail shared a look with Muirne. The maid was well aware that MacCurran had forbidden her to reenter the cave. "It's very dark, and the tunnels are carved into the rock. We saw no evidence of another room or a vault of any sort when we were hunting for spices."

"Nonetheless," Daniel said, sitting up, "I am certain that's where MacCurran has hidden the necklace. How do you access the tunnels?"

"Behind a granite slab in an old storeroom at the far end of the close." Isabail frowned. "It will be very difficult to enter the tunnels without being seen. There's always someone in the close."

"You must find a way," Daniel urged.

"I'm a prisoner myself," she pointed out. "I do not have free rein."

"At least you can leave this room." Daniel smiled. "You are a woman of great ability, Lady Isabail. I've always been amazed by your management of castle affairs. I'm sure you'll find a way back into the tunnels." He pointed to his shoulder. "As soon as I'm rested, I'll start preparing for our departure. My plan is to steal several horses and ride for the swamp. We can lose any pursuers easily in there."

"MacCurran's men are skilled woodsmen."

"Fear not," he said. "I have a few tricks up my sleeve. We'll make our escape without difficulty. I just need the necklace."

"Then Muirne and I will continue to look for it."

"Be as diligent as you can," Daniel advised. "I have no confidence that MacCurran will keep me alive. I am a burden and a risk."

Isabail's eyebrows rose. "Surely you don't believe he will slay you after allowing me to tend your wounds."

"You forget, my lady," he said grimly, "that he was willing to murder loyal members of his own clan to get the necklace. A number of them fell to the same poisoned stew that killed the king's courier."

Muirne looked up from her darning. "If that were true, why would the clan still follow him? I've seen nothing but respect and loyalty displayed for him. No fear."

Daniel shrugged. "No doubt they believe whatever tale of blame he tells. That just makes them fools."

Isabail glanced away. Count her among the fools. Until Daniel had shown her the error of her thoughts, she too had swallowed the tale of the man in black. Aiden had spoken with such conviction and bitterness that she still had moments of doubt.

"A shame that we were unable to reach Edinburgh and the king," Daniel said. "If he awarded this land to you, justice would truly be served."

"Sir Robert felt that my claim was unlikely to win the day, because the king seeks more than justice—he has alliances to win and peace to maintain." Which was why she'd been traveling to Edinburgh—in hopes of swaying the king with a personal plea.

"The king is a man with many favors to return," Daniel agreed.

"If we escaped now, if we left without searching for the necklace," Isabail said, "we might yet reach the king before he awards the land."

Daniel met her gaze. "Possession would certainly allow you to rout the MacCurrans and search for the necklace at your leisure."

"Aye," responded Isabail eagerly.

"But there's no guarantee the king will give the land to you, and justice for John is dependent upon gaining the necklace. Nay. This is our best hope." His face grew ruddy with anger. "Any other plan runs the risk that MacCurran goes free. We must stay the course. We must find the necklace."

Isabail sighed. She understood his desperate need for justice. Daniel was the only person who had loved John more than she. He had sobbed into her arms, quite unlike himself, for hours when John gave up his last breath.

Isabail's father had beaten John black-and-blue over the years, threatened him with castration, and sent him off to be toughened in regions beset by war, all in hopes of ridding John of his "unnatural interest" in other men. There were laws against such behavior, after all. But Isabail had accepted her brother's sexual preference, seen it as just one of the many facets that composed the fine man that her brother had been.

His love for Daniel had not made him a poor earl, as their father had feared. John had been strong, decisive, and politically astute. He had strengthened the earldom by becoming justiciar of Glen Avon and enriched it by hiring and training skilled weavers to craft their wool into fine, sought-after cloth. Daniel, too, was a learned man, fluent in Latin, French, English, and Gaelic. They had spent many an hour in heated debate over the political affairs of Scotland, England, and Europe.

If Daniel was convinced that gaining the necklace was necessary to see justice done by John, then so be it.

"If the necklace is here, I will find it," Isabail vowed. "I swear it."

Darkness settled over the glen, and a low mist rose off the snow. The moon was bright enough to see by, so Aiden gave the order to douse most of the torches. Firelight was visible for long distances, even between the trees. MacPherson rarely sent out evening patrols, but why take the risk?

"Did you succeed in getting the names from Lady Macintosh?" Niall asked as he returned to the ruin after standing the evening watch.

Aiden tossed his brother a cool stare. "After she discovered your healer in the camp? I think not."

"But you returned to your quarters at midday," Niall reminded him. "The men were taking bets on how long it would take for you to coax the information from her lips."

"The men have more important concerns."

"Aye, that they do," said Niall. "And they're ready."

"I hope you're right."

Niall glanced at him. "It will be easier to break into Dunstoras than it was to enter Lochurkie."

"Don't underestimate MacPherson."

The two men left the perimeter wall and made their way into the inner close, where a boar was roasting on a spit and the cook was handing out bread rounds. "He's a sorry excuse for a garrison commander. Only a laggard fails to attend the lists."

"He may be lazy, but he's also smart," Aiden said. "I've met him several times, and I assure you his wits are as sharp as fine Spanish steel."

Niall used his dirk to slice off a piece of boar. "You're not suggesting we leave our lads to hang for poaching, are you?"

"Nay." It was galling enough that his people were imprisoned inside the very keep that once protected them. Standing by and watching them swing would be impossible. "I am merely warning you not to be cocksure. The guards at Lochurkie were not expecting you to break in. MacPherson will be prepared."

"No one knows Dunstoras better than we do."

"Agreed." Aiden didn't bother to repeat his warning; he simply stared at his brother as he ate his meat.

Niall acknowledged the message. "We'll take proper care."

"I'll be taking the lead."

Niall frowned. "Are you sure that's wise?"

"Are you doubting the value of my sword arm?"

"Nay," Niall said. "Fearing the loss of it. If I am captured, you can continue the fight. If you are captured, the fight is over."

Aiden shook his head. "The clan will go on as long as a single MacCurran breathes. Our lads are under MacPherson's knife because I failed them. I'll not sit back while you attempt to free them."

His brother shrugged. "If you insist."

"I do."

"When shall we leave?"

"Gather the men. I'll join you in a moment. Isabail has asked to see the hound."

One of Niall's brows raised. "Does it yet live?"

"Aye." Aiden hesitated, then added, "Ana did a fine job with the beast."

One side of Niall's mouth lifted. "Do you trust her now to treat the rest of the clan without Master Tam hovering nearby?"

"Give it time," Aiden said. "If all is well in a day or two, I'll give her free rein."

"I'll hold you to that."

Snatching his brother's round of bread from his hands, Aiden strode across the close to Ana's quarters. Nodding to the healer, he crossed the room and gently gathered up the dog. "I've found someone to care for the hound tonight. I trust you've no objection?"

"Nay." She rolled up the dog's bedding and tucked it under Aiden's arm. Then she gave the dog a kiss on the head. "Sleep well, Gorm."

Aiden crossed the camp, ignoring the broad grins he received from some of the men. Udard opened the door to his hut for him, and he stepped inside.

Isabail was seated on her pallet while Muirne braided her white-blond hair. She turned as the door clicked closed behind him. "Gorm!"

She scrambled to her feet and raced across the room. The dog opened its eyes to her crooning but did not stir. Aiden handed her the bedding. "Lay it beside the fire," he instructed. When the bedding was unrolled, he lowered the dog to the blankets.

"You told me I could not see him until morning," Isabail said, crouching beside the dog to pet it.

Aiden shrugged. "He's doing much better. He has eaten and gotten to his feet, though he is still too weak to walk. And I will not be able to look in on him during the night."

"Why not?"

"I've something important that needs my attention." Digging through the leather bag leaning against the wall, he found a dark gray lèine and a black brat. Sneaking into Dunstoras would require extra diligence on such a bright night. He strode to the door and then paused. "If for any reason Beathag comes to you and tells you to flee into the tunnels, do not hesitate. Gather everything you see, save for the brazier, and run."

"Do you anticipate an attack?"

He shrugged. "It's possible."

"If someone attacks your encampment, would that not suggest my rescue is imminent?"

Aiden favored Isabail with a flat stare. The thought of returning to a camp that did not include Isabail was disagreeable. "Do you not recall what I told you of MacPherson's army? Mercenaries are hard men capable of heinous acts. Stay with the other women and children; you will be safer."

"Oh."

"Take care." He tugged open the door.

"Wait! Where do you go?"

He turned back to her. "It matters not. I'll be back by morning. If you wish, Muirne can pass the night here as well."

Isabail rose to her feet. "Is it dangerous, this important task you must see to?"

He met her gaze. "Not overly," he lied.

"So a prayer to Saint Andrew would go amiss?"

A faint smile touched his lips. "That would depend on what you pray for, lass, but a prayer to Saint Andrew rarely goes to waste."

And then he left her.

"What are you doing?" asked Muirne, a frown upon her brow.

Isabail wrapped the dark brat she'd pulled from MacCurran's sack around her shoulders. It was much less bulky than the blanket, yet it still hid a great deal of her pale blue gown. "Seizing the moment."

If the MacCurran was leaving for the night, it surely meant a sizable portion of his warriors were leaving, too. The close should be nearly empty. There would be no better time to search the tunnels than right now.

"But what about Gorm?"

Isabail scurried to the door, opened it, and peered into the night. "You can tend to him."

"What if he doesn't heed me?"

"Speak firmly to him," Isabail advised. "He's not as strong as he was when he knocked you over at Lochurkie. He's unlikely to even rise from his bed."

With that, Isabail slipped out of the door and darted for the deepest shadows. As she hoped, the courtyard was almost entirely empty—the men were gathered at the outer gate and the women of the clan were seeing them off. With one eye on the gillies who were cleaning away the last of the supper, she crept along the wall toward the far end of the close.

One of the older bakers shuffled toward her, and she halted, hugging the wall with a pounding heart. If he looked up, he would surely see the pale blue cloth of her dress against the moonlit stones. But thankfully he did not. He picked up a platter of bread rounds, tipped it into a canvas sack, and then walked off with the sack.

Isabail continued along the wall to the ancient storeroom. The entrance to the tunnels was hidden by a tall slab of granite. Until Beathag had shown her there was a gap between the huge granite stone and the wall, she'd not seen the entrance. Now that she knew it was there, slipping into the tunnel was a simple affair.

The tunnel was narrow and poorly lit but not difficult to navigate. Isabail's only fear was meeting someone else in its damp confines. She paused every few paces to listen for the footfalls of a gillie. At every stop, she examined the walls for signs of another room or vault, but saw nothing. The walls were remarkably smooth, worn down by strong, skilled hands and the passage of time.

When the tunnel opened into the torch-lit cave, Isabail breathed a sigh of relief. She had no fear of the dark, nor of small spaces, but found the tunnel rather airless and smoky.

Isabail spun slowly around, studying the walls. If there was a second room or an alcove of any sort, it was not immediately obvious. Of course, the cave was piled with sacks and barrels and furniture, so much of the walls were not visible. She squeezed between two barrels. A small space behind a pile of flour sacks seemed conspicuously empty. Climbing upon the sacks, she peered into the gloomy space . . . and frowned.

A winch?

Why would there be a winch here? With a rope that disappeared into the rock behind it? It made no sense. What purpose could it possibly have? At Lochurkie, the only winches she had seen were used to raise heavy stones into place on the walls. What did this one lift?

There was only one way to find out.

Carefully searching for foot- and handholds, she climbed down the sacks to the winch. The base of the winch was a carved stone etched with several Pictish symbols. It seemed unlikely the wooden shank and the rope were as old as the stone; they appeared to be freshly carved and corded.

She grabbed the handle of the winch and applied all the force she could muster. It turned with surprising ease. Not so easy that it didn't tax her arms, but not so challenging as to render her efforts useless, either. As she turned the handle, a low rasp of stone on stone echoed through the tunnel. After a half dozen turns of the crank, the winch locked and she could turn it no more.

She crawled out of the space and looked around, but saw no door, nor any sign that a stone had been moved. So what had the winch done?

A cold clamp of fear seized her throat. A vision

of the granite slab at the entrance to the tunnel rose in her mind. Dear Lord. Had she just sealed herself in?

Lifting her skirts, she ran.

Aiden and his men approached Dunstoras from the west. It was the side most heavily protected by the mountains. Massive shards of shale had broken away from the side of the mountain, making navigation treacherous for anyone not familiar with the terrain. As a result, MacPherson wasted few guards on the west side of the keep.

At the crest of a narrow ridge, Aiden paused and allowed himself a brief moment. The castle stood before him in all its glory—a graceful tower reaching toward the night sky, a crenellated curtain wall, and a sturdy gatehouse with an iron portcullis. A year ago, he'd stood inside those walls and watched his father's body lowered into the crypt beneath the kirk. Now he stood outside the walls, an outlaw.

God surely knew how to test a man.

The moon was high as the Black Warriors wended their way between the rocks, allowing them to avoid random slides of shale. To a man, they wore dark brats and equally dark lèines. In days of old, they would also have carried a symbolic black targe, but tonight such a weighty implement would only slow them down. Silently and swiftly they made their way to the base of the castle wall. The two visible guards on the ramparts were felled at the same time—one by Cormac with his large ash bow and the other by Niall with a crossbow.

Duncan and Ivarr, the largest men among them, swung iron grappling hooks atop the ramparts, then retreated to the rocks. A few moments later, a second pair of guards appeared to investigate the noise. They were silenced by Cormac and Niall before they could raise the alarm.

Aiden sheathed his sword and ran for one of the two ropes dangling from the ramparts. Niall was the first to reach the other.

Aware that Niall considered him to be a little soft due to his role as chief, Aiden put substantial effort into the climb. He reached the top of the forty-foot wall ahead of his brother and grinned at him in the dark.

"A sennight ago, I took an arrow in the chest," Niall whispered with a shrug.

"Impossible."

"Ask Ana."

Aiden took stock while he waited for the others to gain the wall. A dozen soldiers huddled around a fire pit in the close, warming themselves against the winter chill. Another six, armed with bows, stood at various spots along the wall, looking out at the forest.

To succeed, Aiden's men needed to reach the donjon without attracting attention. Not an easy feat, given that the only way into the tower was through the big wooden door in the close. But they had to move—it was only a matter of time before someone spotted them in the shadows.

When all ten men were crouched on the ramparts, he waved them forward.

"Take three men and fetch our lads," Aiden told Niall. "I'll create a diversion on the south wall."

Niall and his three men went right, keeping to the shadows. Aiden went left, his gaze firmly locked on the young archer immediately in front of him. The lad's peripheral vision caught his movement when he was a dozen paces away, and the short but powerful bow he carried swung in Aiden's direction.

Aiden gave up stealth in favor of speed. The foolish fellow neglected to call the alarm as he scrambled to nock and loose an arrow. Aiden's sword ended his effort swiftly and with little more than a gurgle. He caught the archer's falling body and dropped it over the wall.

A moment later, he entered the door to the gatehouse. To create a successful diversion, he had to pose a credible threat to the castle. As long as the portcullis was lowered, the additional men he had waiting outside the gate were little more annoying than a swarm of angry bees.

He took the stairs to the middle level two at a time. The two soldiers on gate duty drew their swords as he reached the bottom of the stairs. Having been in the winch house numerous times, Aiden knew the layout well. He leapt from the stairs to the huge rope roll that fed the portcullis and kicked the weapon from the hand of soldier number one. Then he pivoted to parry a thrust from soldier number two.

That's when Aiden's luck ran out.

The first soldier had the sense to raise the alarm before retrieving his weapon, and the man he was dueling turned out to be a highly skilled swordsman. Aiden blocked a skillful slash. He had but moments to dispatch his opponent before the guards bunking in the first-floor garrison came thundering up the steps.

Isabail stared at the open entrance to the tunnel and breathed a huge sigh of relief. Her exit was unimpeded. The ancient winch had not sealed the door. Her heartbeat slowed and her panic receded. Should she give up the search and return to her bed, or go back into the tunnel?

It was very tempting to call an end to her adventure. But this was a rare opportunity—who knew when she would enjoy this much freedom again? And the winch had moved something.

Something important, her gut told her.

She took a deep breath. Back into the tunnel, then.

Returning to the cave, she began a thorough examination of the walls. She traced every crack in the stone and pushed every protruding bump in hopes of finding a hidden passage. Nothing. She stepped back into the tunnel and studied the mouth of the cave. A series of glyphs were carved in the archway, but none seemed to stand out more than any other.

Turning slowly, she eyed the flat wall that announced the end of the tunnel some twenty paces farther along. Although the torch light barely reached that far, she could see that it, too, was covered with symbols. Strange. None of the other walls of the tunnel were marked in a similar fashion.

She walked toward the wall, studying the symbols. Unlike other Pictish stones she'd seen, all of the markings on this slab of granite were depictions of animals: a boar, a bull, a wolf, a goose, a fish, and a snake. Nary an enigmatic circle or bent arrow to be seen.

Curious.

John had been fascinated by the symbols left behind by the Painted Ones and had amassed a collection of smaller stones, which he had kept in the stables. He enjoyed knowing that the land he owned had once been walked upon by an ancient people.

Isabail traced the etched shape of a goose with her finger. Some barbaric warrior of old had painstakingly chiseled this symbol into the rock.

Why?

She peered through the half-light at the rock wall. The shadows in the corners were deep, and she could not make out where one wall ended and the next began. Sliding her hands along the rock, she felt for the corner . . . and found the faintest of grooves—a groove that ran all the way to the floor and was echoed on the other side.

A thrill ran down Isabail's spine.

It was a door.

Flattening both hands on the slab, she pushed with all her might, but the rock did not budge. Perhaps it required more strength than she possessed to open it.

She stood back, hands on her hips. Or perhaps the animals were trying to tell her something. Putting her weight behind her, she pushed the salmon and then the snake. Nothing. Not willing to give up, she shoved the goose and the bull. Still nothing.

"Open, you bloody wretched thing," she snapped. With two hands on the boar, she vented her frustration. And it swiveled open. Not enough to let her pass, but enough to coax a euphoric shout from her throat. "Aye!"

Isabail put all her weight behind another push on the boar. The giant slab opened farther, with an accompanying groan of stone, and Isabail stepped inside. The corridor on the other side of the slab was pitch-black, so she ran back and retrieved a torch from the cave.

Much better.

She could now see the floor in front of her, including a decorated pathway of stones leading around a curve in the corridor. Isabail stepped forward.

The harsh rasp of rubbing stones immediately told her something was amiss, and she pivoted . . . just in time to see the great stone slab swivel back into place and another stone drop from the ceiling to seal it shut.

*   *   *

Aiden swung his sword with power and precision. He had only one chance to fell this soldier. He could not afford to miss. His blade collided with his opponent's with bone-rattling force, sending a shower of sparks into the air. The soldier stumbled under the brute power of the attack and took a step back.

It was exactly the opening Aiden had hoped for.

Vaulting from his position on the rope roll, he gave the soldier's exposed knee a ruthless kick. The man screamed and collapsed. His weapon dropped from his hands as he grabbed his leg. Without pausing, Aiden whipped around and stabbed the other guard in the sword arm.

Both men now disarmed, Aiden pounced on the winch. The furious beat of boots on the steps accompanied every crank of the winch handle. He barely got four turns in before the garrison soldiers reached the top of the stairs. He threw the lock to hold the portcullis in its partially opened state and then leapt for the dark stairs to the third level.

He counted the stairs as he climbed, and when he reached the eighteenth stair, he dove to the left. Crashing through a wooden shutter, he fell out a small window and landed on the slate roof of the stable one story below. The impact temporarily robbed him of breath, but he managed to roll off the roof to the hay piled next to the animal stalls.

The metallic clash of swords told him the rest of

the Black Warriors had entered the close through the partially opened portcullis and engaged the soldiers. He pushed to his feet and raced to join them.

Cormac had already taken out several of the archers on the walls, but Aiden played it safe and veered left and right with erratic movements as he closed the gap between himself and his men. The moment they saw him, the Black Warriors began a strategic retreat—they ran for the three-foot opening beneath the iron spikes of the portcullis.

A shout went up from the captain of the garrison. "Drop the portcullis! Quickly."

Aiden knew it would take only a well-aimed slice of a sharp blade to sever the rope and drop the portcullis to the ground. He ran. He was still ten paces away when he saw an ax swing toward his head from the doorway of the gatehouse.

He parried the ax with his sword but felt the weight of the mighty two-handed blade vibrate up his arm, numbing his fingers. The sword slipped from his grip, flying off into the dark, and his boot slipped in the mud.

Mourning the loss of a good weapon, he recovered his balance and resumed his run for the gate. He could only pray his delay was not costly—if he rolled under the portcullis at the wrong moment and it fell upon him . . . well, Niall would be forced to wear the mantle of chief.

Aiden sent a prayer skyward and dove for the mud under the gate.

*   *   *

Isabail bit her lip, trying not to panic. She was trapped in a secret room in the dark of the night, with no one aware of her location. Even if Muirne came in search of her, the maid would never realize she was buried behind a huge rock.

Isabail's hand massaged her throat.

Breathe, Isabail. Do not assume the worst. Perhaps there is another way out.

Holding the torch aloft, she turned away from the door and faced the tunnel. Several feet along, it changed direction, making it impossible to see what lay ahead. Praying that none of the other tiles in the footpath were about to bring the ceiling down upon her head, she walked forward. Thankfully, the only sounds she heard were the shallow draws of her breath and the soft pad of her boots on the stone floor.

She rounded the corner and entered a small chamber. A sepulcher, it would seem, complete with a large stone burial chest. Atop the chest, a loose bolt of purple silk served as a bed for several silver items.

Isabail stepped closer.

One of the items lying on the silk was a sword. Half as long as the chest and clearly well maintained, the sword gleamed in the torchlight. But it wasn't the sword that held her attention. The centerpiece of the display was a simple silver band set with the most glorious sapphire Isabail had ever seen. Perfectly cut to catch the light, it glowed with a noticeable fire under the torch.

It was clearly a crown.

One worn by a Pictish king, perhaps?

Isabail wrinkled her nose and studied the markings on the burial chest. Quite likely, whoever had worn the crown lay within this stone box. Unfortunately, there were no symbols or words on the stone chest that Isabail could read.

She stepped back.

An unexpected treasure, but no help to her. It was neither the necklace she sought, nor the answer to her escape. There were no other exits, no other tunnels leading into the mountain.

Her only hope for a rescue lay with the MacCurran. Had he not just marched off to do some sort of battle, that hope would have more weight. Back by morning, he'd said. But how much longer after that would it take him to realize she was missing?

She might well starve to death before anyone came.

Isabail licked her lips. For some reason, most probably because water was beyond reach, she had a sudden thirst. Lifting the torch high again, she explored the entirety of the small room. There was no miraculous second exit. The only way out was the way she had come in.

Swallowing a cold lump of fear, she made her way back to the huge granite slab that held her prisoner. Surely there must be some way to open the door from this side. She tried stepping on the tile that had sealed her in, tried several other tiles, and even tiles in combination. The door and the smaller rock on the ledge above her that held it shut remained exactly where they stood.

Isabail slid slowly to the floor and sat with her back to the tunnel wall. She remained surprisingly calm as she ran through her options and once again came up dry.

Her calm held, despite her desperate situation.

Until the torch began to flicker.

Chapter 9

Aiden hit the ground and rolled. He heard the heavy rumble of the iron portcullis dropping in its frame and prayed he'd rolled far enough. When it hit the ground an instant later and he still lived to note it, he grinned.

But he had no time to rest on his laurels. More archers had flocked to the walls, and although Cormac was doing his best to keep them at bay, if Aiden didn't move quickly, one of them would find him, even in the dark.

He scrambled to his feet and darted for the bushes. He rolled behind a tree trunk just as an arrow drove into the heel of his boot.

"Bloody hell," he muttered, snapping the shaft of the arrow at the base of the arrowhead.

"Are you wounded?" asked Cormac.

"Nay," said Aiden. "But my finest pair of boots are ruined."

Cormac laughed. "Well, that ought to have been

enough fuss to get Niall *into* the dungeon, but how in bloody hell are we going to get them out?"

"We're going to start a fire."

From his spot behind a dead elm tree, Cormac tossed him a scandalized stare. "You're going to set Dunstoras ablaze?"

It was a shame, to be sure. "Any damage to the keep can be repaired in time. Kin can never be replaced."

Cormac's shoulders sagged. "Aye, you've the right of it. Tell me what you need me to do." He spied an archer between two parapets and lobbed an arrow neatly between the stones. The man fell.

"Nothing more than you're already doing," Aiden said. "Shoot a well-placed arrow."

"Over the wall and into the haystack, perchance?"

"Aye," said Aiden. "I emptied the farrier's oil lamp onto the hay, so one arrow or two ought to do the trick."

"Well played," acknowledged Cormac with a nod of his head. "But we need a flame to lob over the castle wall, and all the wood in sight is as wet as a sow's teat."

Aiden dug into the pouch at his belt and pulled out his flint and a little tangle of sheep's wool. "Keep the vultures on the wall off my back, and I'll make you a fire."

"Done."

Working quickly and behind the protection of a broad-trunked maple tree, Aiden struck his flint with the blade of his dirk repeatedly, causing spark after spark to fly into the loose knot of wool in his hands. When the wool began to smoke, he lightly blew on it. The glowing threads burst into flames. Placing the burning bundle in a divot between two roots of the tree, he carefully added the straw he'd stuffed in his lèine to the flames, fueling them to greater strength. He yanked several strips of cloth from the hem of his lèine, wrapped them around the arrowhead from one of Cormac's arrows, then set the linen alight.

"Don't miss," Aiden warned Cormac. "I've enough for three arrows. Four at most."

Cormac snorted. "Miss? I don't know the meaning of that word." He nocked the burning arrow, then let it fly.

It sailed high into the air before beginning its descent, a radical drop not unlike the dive of a falcon onto its prey.

The moment the flame appeared in the night sky, the soldiers on the wall begin to shout a warning to those gathered in the close. Fire could have terrible repercussions in a keep—many of the inner buildings and supporting braces were crafted from wood—and there was a desperate edge to the soldiers' voices.

They needn't have worried.

The arrow landed, but no fire ensued.

"You missed." Aiden said, handing Cormac a second arrow.

"Not possible," he responded. "Perhaps the hay is wet."

"Nay, it's not," Aiden disputed. "You missed."

The bowman nocked the second arrow and freed it to the midnight sky. There was another chorus of shouts as the arrow began its descent, this time ending in laughter.

"I told you your aim was off," Aiden said, handing Cormac a third arrow. His small fire was fading without new fuel. He wrapped a fourth arrow, trying not to consider the possibility of failure.

Cormac nocked the third arrow.

Aiden watched him, his heart thudding heavily in his chest. There was no better marksman among the MacCurrans than Cormac. If he could not land the arrow true, then no one could.

Cormac closed his eyes, then loosed the arrow.

"Are you mad?" Aiden snarled. "You didn't even aim."

The bowman opened his eyes and watched the arrow's trajectory. It went up, high over the castle wall, then down hard and fast toward the earth. As it landed, Aiden heard a host of panicked shouts from the soldiers. There was a brief bloom of orange light behind the wall, and he dared to hope. But a few moments later, it died.

Echoes of congratulations rang out among the soldiers as they praised one another for their efforts in putting out the blaze.

"Where exactly did you spill the lantern oil?" Cormac asked quietly, holding out his hand for the fourth—and last—arrow.

"The lantern was hanging at the edge of the roof.

I tugged it free as I rolled off into the hay and tipped the oil into the hay before I leapt to the ground."

"Around the middle of the pile then," Cormac said, nocking the arrow.

"Aye," Aiden said, holding his frustration in tight check. Interfering with Cormac's concentration would not be wise. He had to have faith that the bowman could complete the task. The little fire in the tree root flickered and died. Aiden sucked in a deep breath and held it.

Cormac closed his eyes again, but this time Aiden said nothing. The arrow shot into the sky, but Aiden's gaze did not follow it. He locked his gaze on Cormac's face and listened to the shouts of the soldiers instead.

The swell of shouts grew louder, and he knew the arrow was on its way down. He heard panic rising in their voices, then a soft *whoosh*, followed by loud screams for water.

Cormac opened his eyes and smiled.

Aiden followed his gaze. Bright yellow flames leapt above the castle walls in the direction of the stables, and the attention of all—even the archers— was captured by the drama taking place inside the close.

Someone screamed for the animals in the stables to be freed, and he knew the fire was threatening to spread to the wooden horse stalls. He grimaced. MacPherson's men were an undisciplined lot if they couldn't douse a fire with reasonable haste. To his relief, the captain of the garrison ordered his men into lines shortly thereafter, and within minutes, there was an organized disbursement of water from the well, and the fire was wrestled under control.

Niall sank to the ground next to him.

Aiden noted blood on his brother's lèine and frowned. "Trouble?"

"Nothing a few MacCurrans couldn't handle," said his brother with a grin. "Fear not. It's not my blood. I freed every lad I could find. Twelve men in all."

The rescued men joined the other warriors, amid great smiles and hearty pats on the back. When the hunting party approached Aiden, the looks turned sheepish.

"Our apologies, laird," Hamish said to Aiden. "We should have been more diligent. MacPherson's men had never come so far down the glen before, and we were caught unawares. It won't happen again."

"See that it doesn't," Aiden acknowledged. "I cannot afford to burn any more of my castle."

Under a volley of arrows aimed at the keep walls, they slipped back into the depths of the forest and headed back to the old hill fort.

The torch sputtered and died.

The room was pitched into darkness.

Isabail's heart leapt into her throat. She'd never been in such a complete absence of light or sound. The stone wall at her back, which only seconds before had seemed solid and comforting, now felt cold and pressing. Each breath she drew provided less and less satisfaction, and she worried that she might suffocate.

Although she knew it was pointless, a scream rose in her throat, and she pounded her fist against the great stone portal.

"Help!" she cried. "Help! Please help me!"

It was near dawn when Aiden and the others returned triumphant to the encampment. The rescue of the captured men sparked an impromptu celebration that lasted until well past sunup. Only after he had consumed a well-deserved horn of ale and broken the fast did he withdraw to his chamber in search of Isabail.

When he entered the room, he found it empty. The brazier was cold, and there was no evidence that Isabail had passed the night.

The vixen had no doubt disobeyed him and laid her bed in her old hut. Had Aiden not been so weary, he would have sought her out and dragged her back to where she belonged. But her punishment could wait until after he was rested. Aiden dropped onto the pallet and, in a few short moments, found sleep.

"Laird MacCurran?"

He opened one eye and found Muirne staring down at him, her hands wringing the apron tied about her waist.

"How long have I been sleeping?" he asked, sitting up on the mattress and sweeping his heavy brown locks away from his face.

" 'Tis noontide."

Perhaps not the sleep his body craved, but it would do. "What is it you seek, Muirne?"

"I fear for Lady Isabail," she said.

The last cobwebs of his sleep-addled brain were swept aside. "Lady Isabail? Why?"

"She has disappeared," Muirne said, tears falling. "She's not been seen since late last night."

Aiden shot to his feet. "Last night? Why did you not say anything?"

The tears came in earnest now. "She swore me to secrecy. Made me promise not to tell anyone what she was about."

A cold stillness settled over Aiden. "And what was she about, Muirne?"

"You have to promise me you won't punish her," Muirne begged, dropping to her knees and holding her head. "I would never tell you what I'm about to, save she's been gone for far too long. I'm certain something terrible has befallen her."

Her fear was so strong that Aiden's heart did a tumble in his chest. "Where did she go, Muirne?"

"Into the tunnels," she whispered. "But I searched for her, and there was no sign. It's as if she just vanished."

The tunnels? Aiden's breath caught in his chest. Dear God. Was it possible she'd discovered the tomb and become trapped inside? He tore out of the room and raced across the close. Diving into the tunnel, he jogged down the narrow corridor to the cave, leapt over the flour sacks, and turned the winch. When it was locked into place, he ran for the end of the tunnel and pushed at the great granite slab.

But it would open only partway. Something was blocking its movement.

"Isabail," Aiden called. "Move aside. I cannot open the door if you remain there."

No sound came from the pitch-black interior of the tomb.

"Isabail?"

He leaned in as far as the slab would allow and listened carefully. Was that she sound of her breathing? He couldn't be certain. "Isabail!" he called loudly.

Still no answer.

Striding back to the tunnel, he snatched one of the torches from a wall bracket, then returned to the tomb. He shoved the torch through the narrow gap in the door, lighting the passage beyond. And spied a hand. *Her* hand. The long, elegant fingers that were uniquely Isabail's. She was on the floor directly behind the door. If he forced the door open, he would crush her.

"Isabail, you must move," he urged. When that didn't work, he allowed the tightness in his gut to bleed into his voice. His words came out cold and clipped. "Get up, Isabail. Now."

Even that had no effect.

Her hand lay there, still as death.

Placing the torch in the nearest wall bracket, Aiden steadied his thoughts. To free her from the tomb, he had to move her, willing and able though she might not be. He lay facedown on the stone floor, wedged as far as he could through the opening, and took her hand.

It was cold.

Aiden's heartbeat slowed. Once before, when he was a wee lad, a man had gotten trapped in the tomb. Not one of his kin—they knew better—a traveling minstrel who'd heard the legends of an ancient Pictish treasure and decided to try his luck. They found his body three days later and buried him in the mountains.

Pushing that thought aside, Aiden tugged gently on Isabail's hand, pulling her to one side. His position was awkward and the gains he made were slow, but eventually he could see her blond hair through the gap. With the majority of her body clear of the stone slab, he was able to open it all the way.

He snatched her to his chest.

"Isabail," he commanded. "Wake up."

Her head lolled against his arm. Was she . . . ? No, he refused to believe she was dead. He bent an ear to her mouth, hoping for evidence of the sounds he'd heard when he first found her. Surely she was still breathing.

The faintest of breaths stirred the hairs at his temple. He surged to his feet, with Isabail's chilled body clamped to the warmth of his chest, and sprinted for the tunnel entrance.

"Beathag!" he yelled as he entered the busy close. "Fetch me Ana Bisset. Quickly!"

He advanced to the large cooking fire, hoping

to warm Isabail's ice-cold body. The heat from the stoked coals drew beads of sweat to his forehead, but he remained there until Beathag returned with the healer.

"Blankets!" Ana demanded, pointing to the ground before the fire. Women offering blankets appeared swiftly, and when a suitable bed had been laid, she waved to Aiden. "Lay her here."

He did so, parting with her reluctantly.

Isabail's face was as white as her hair. Not a mote of color graced her lips or her cheeks—her skin was like marble.

Ana did not ask what happened. She simply closed her eyes and placed her hands on Isabail's cheek and chest. After a long moment, punctuated only by the heavy thuds of Aiden's heart, she sat back.

"Well?" he demanded.

Ana lifted her gaze to Aiden and gave him a look he didn't care for. "She is alive," the healer said, "but something is wrong."

"*Something is wrong*? What am I to make of that? Fix it, then. Heal her."

The redhead rose to her feet. She cast a glance at Niall, who had shouldered his way through the crowd around the fire. "I'm not certain she can be healed. I saw a similar case once—a child who fell into the pond and was found sometime later."

"I will not accept that," Aiden said. "Heal her."

She nodded. "I will, of course, do my best."

Her response was too tentative for Aiden's liking.

To him it already carried the suggestion of failure. And the notion of Isabail never again opening her eyes, of never again facing him with stiff shoulders and a brave stare, pinched his chest so painfully he could barely breathe. "If you can heal her bloody dog, you can heal her, too. No excuses. You will heal her. Now tell me what you need."

Niall stepped forward, his gaze firm and his stance clearly protective of Ana. "Not everyone can be saved. That is God's will, not the healer's."

"Step aside and let Ana do what she must," Aiden ordered his brother.

"If anyone needs to step aside, it's you," Niall responded, remaining at Ana's side.

"Cease, both of you," said the healer. To Aiden, she added. "Clear the inner close, and I'll do everything I can to save her."

It was an easy enough request to fulfill. Aiden barked an order to all those hovering in the close, and a few moments later, the courtyard was empty . . . save for Niall, Ana, Aiden, and Isabail.

"You must leave too," Ana told Aiden.

"Nay."

Niall grabbed his sleeve. "Come, brother. Let us leave her to her work."

Yanking his arm free, Aiden cut his brother a cold stare. He'd left Isabail alone, locked in the tomb for hours. He was not about to leave her now. "I said nay."

Niall and Ana exchanged glances.

"Go ahead," Niall encouraged.

Ana shook her head.

"All will be well," Niall said. "You've nothing to fear."

She glanced at Aiden and snorted. "He is full of anger and hate. I have everything to fear."

"Enough blather," Aiden said, his gaze falling to Isabail's pallid face. "If she dies while you debate who stays near the fire, I swear I will run you both through. Heal. Her."

"This is on you," Ana said darkly to Niall.

She dropped to her knees and rolled up her sleeves. "I need a bucket of cold water and uninterrupted silence."

Niall fetched the water and placed the bucket next to her. He gave Ana's shoulder a quick squeeze before crossing to stand at Aiden's side.

It would have been a comfort to have him there if his brother's hand hadn't been firmly positioned on the hilt of his sword. Apparently, his brother was prepared to take a stand between him and the healer.

The redhead rubbed her hands together, then placed one of them on either side of Isabail's head. Bowing her head, she appeared to be praying.

Aiden had no issue with an appeal to God for help. For centuries, his family had honored both the pagan gods of his ancestors and the Christian God preached by Saint Columba. But as Ana remained silent and still for painfully long moments, making no effort to bleed Isabail or create a healing poultice, he grew impatient.

"Hold," Niall whispered. "Look at her arms."

Aiden's gaze slipped to Isabail's arms, but the

sleeves of her gown hid them from view. Then he noticed Ana's arms.

"Sweet Danu."

A ruddy pattern of swirls and dots was growing like a mystical vine down both of Ana's arms. Aiden had never seen anything like it, and as the vines crept over the backs of her hands, reaching her fingers, he took a step forward. They would soon be touching Isabail's flesh.

Niall's hand flattened against his chest, staying further movement. "Have faith."

It took all of Aiden's willpower to resist the urge to throw off Niall's hand. His heart pounded in his chest with a fear like he'd never known before. But he trusted Niall. And he desperately needed Isabail to awaken.

Drawing in a shuddering breath, he subsided and allowed Ana to work her magic. And it *was* clearly magic. But if this was what it took to bring Isabail back from the brink of death, so be it.

Ana removed one hand from Isabail's face and sank it into the bucket of water. A few minutes later, she switched hands. A wince flickered across her face, and she began to shiver uncontrollably.

Niall tensed.

Aiden could see that his brother wanted to go to Ana, to hold her, but he did not. He waited, as impatient as Aiden, for the healing to take its course.

Finally, after a long, unbearable length of time, Ana dropped both hands to her sides. She appeared utterly drained. Dark circles had formed under her eyes, and Aiden swore she'd gotten thinner in the hour or so she'd taken to complete the healing.

Niall rushed forward and dropped a blanket over Ana's shoulders. Displaying more tenderness than Aiden had ever seen, Niall scooped the redheaded healer into his lap and sat with her before the fire, her body cradled against his chest.

"Is it done?" Aiden asked hoarsely.

Isabail still had no color, and he feared the worst.

"Aye," murmured Ana from the depths of Niall's arms. "I've done all that I can do."

"Will she awaken?" he asked brusquely.

"I believe so. Let her rest."

The promise of a happy resolution seemed weak, but Aiden chose to believe in it. He gathered Isabail and her blankets into his arms and strode toward his chamber. Just before he left the close, he called back to his brother, "The door to the tomb is open. Seal it as soon as you're able."

Isabail awoke with a scream on her lips.

"Hush," said a familiar deep voice that vibrated against her cheek. MacCurran. "You are safe."

Midafternoon sunlight poured into the chamber through an open-shuttered window, creating a thick stream of golden air, which highlighted every mote of dust in the air. The dark void was gone, and the steady beat of MacCurran's heart had replaced the unbearable silence.

Safe.

Cocooned in his embrace, supported by the well-stuffed contours of his down-filled mattress,

Isabail could easily believe her hours in the tomb had simply been a dreadful nightmare. Except her throat was sore from screaming and her fingers throbbed from tearing at the granite slab.

"You found me," she whispered.

"Aye."

"How?"

"What possessed you to venture into the tunnels alone?" he asked.

Isabail's cheeks flushed with guilt. How could she tell him she'd been seeking evidence that he was a liar and a murderer? True, she'd done it more for Daniel than to answer any of her lingering doubts, but it was still betrayal. "I was curious about the winch. I spied it while looking for spices and wondered what it was for."

"Curiosity drove you from your bed in the middle of the night?"

Here at least, she could be honest. "I knew you would be angry if I ventured into the tunnels again, so I did it when I knew you were gone."

"Foolish lass."

Indeed. The last thing she remembered from her ordeal was the tight feeling of airlessness in her chest and a dizzy lightness in her head that made it difficult to think. She had been certain she was drawing her last breath.

"Who is buried in the tomb?"

"That's not important."

"A king or a prince of some sort, judging by the crown," she guessed, unwilling to let the subject die. She'd spent a lot of time wondering whom she would be buried with. "A Pictish king, if the symbols on the door are to be believed."

He tipped her head to look in her eyes. "What do you know of Pictish kings?"

"Lochurkie was once owned by the Picts. There are standing stones etched with their symbols all over the land." She bit her lip. "John was curious about them and told me stories of the Painted Ones. Savages, he said, who once roamed the land, hunting and slaying the Gaels at will."

He grunted. "Your brother knew naught of what he spoke."

Isabail pushed at his chest, separating them. "He knew they were just tales. No one truly knows anything of the Picts. They are long gone."

MacCurran released her and rolled from the pallet. "Barbarians do not build stone fortresses like this one," he said, pointing to the walls. "Skilled craftsmen do."

She looked around. "Surely the walls of this fort were built by Scots."

"Nay," he said. "The walls, like the rest of this broch, have stood here for hundreds of years, slowly crumbling away. The MacCurrans have occupied this glen for three hundred years, and it was here when we arrived."

She frowned. "The walls are sturdy still. Why did you not claim it as your own, then? Why build a new keep?"

"Because for a very long time, a druid lived here," he said, "and swore it was a hallowed ground deserving of respect."

"He knew of the tomb," she guessed.

MacCurran nodded. "In his own way, he guarded it."

"Yet you now trample that hallowed ground without care," she pointed out. "Why allow the palace to crumble and overgrow with weeds when you do not follow the druid's beliefs?"

"Did I say we did not honor the druid's beliefs?"

"You occupy the fort."

"We begged sanctuary, and it was granted."

Isabail sat up. Her boots had been removed and placed neatly beside the mattress. She slid her feet into them and pushed to her feet. "Begged sanctuary? From whom? I thought the druid was dead."

"Did I say that?"

She could not be certain if he was serious or making a jest. "The druid yet lives?"

"Enough. I must ask you never to speak of what you found in the tunnels," he said. "Let us get some food. You've not eaten for nearly a day."

Judging by the closed expression on his face, she would not be getting any further information. And he was right about the food—the ache in her belly was a persistent sign that she was hungry. Still, one question yet nagged her. As she tied the laces of her boots, she asked, "Can you not tell me the name of the tomb's inhabitant? We very nearly shared the same final resting place."

He turned to her, his eyes dark and serious. "If I told you, you would never again be permitted to leave the glen."

It was such a preposterous statement that Isabail started to laugh, but MacCurran's frank and completely humorless delivery froze the chuckle in her throat. Dear Lord. What kind of secret could this clan be hiding that prompted such coldhearted threats?

"You found her inside the tomb?" Niall repeated, eyes wide.

"Aye."

"She saw the crown and the sword?"

Aiden sighed. Had he not already explained this? "Aye."

"By the gods. You were right to fear her return to Lochurkie. She'll reveal the location of the tomb."

The risk was very real. Only one thing worked in their favor. "She does not realize the importance of what she found."

"That might be worse," Niall said with a groan. "She might casually change the future of Scotland as she tells an amusing tale to her admiring beaus."

The image of Isabail surrounding by admiring beaus proved surprisingly annoying. "I'll make certain she tells no one of what she's seen."

"How? Once she's returned to Lochurkie, she'll be beyond your control."

"Leave Isabail to me," Aiden said firmly.

Chapter 10

Daniel was dozing when Isabail entered the bedchamber to check on his injuries. Most of the wounds were healing well—scabs had formed and the new flesh was pink and healthy. Even the deep slice on his biceps showed the early signs of knitting well. But one cut, a gnawing on his left wrist, was angry red and oozing yellow pus.

Isabail cut away the putrid bandage and carefully cleansed the wound with a fresh linen cloth. She was studying the wound with a frown when Daniel opened his eyes.

He lifted his arm and peered at the bite. "It needs an aggressive treating," he pronounced calmly. "Soak strips of linen in vinegar or wine and wrap them around my wrist."

"Are you certain?"

"As certain as I am that if we do not do this, I will lose my hand," he said with a faint smile.

When she returned with a bowl of vinegar, he was sitting up, his back against the stone wall.

"My apologies, Isabail."

"For what?" she asked as she dipped the bandages in the bowl.

"I neglected to ask how you were. Muirne and I spent much of the night worried for your safety."

"I am fine. A wee embarrassed perhaps, but otherwise unharmed." She washed the wound with the wet linen.

"Would that I could have left my bed to go in search of you. You would not have spent long hours in despair." He met her gaze. "Muirne informed me that you went into the tunnels alone."

Isabail shrugged. "There is nothing more dangerous in the tunnels than a spider or two."

He cocked his head. "But you got lost?"

"Nay, not lost," she disputed. "Trapped."

"Dear Lord. I truly did fail you," he said. "Did a section of the tunnel collapse?"

"Nothing so dire," she assured him.

Arching a brow, he waited for her to continue.

Isabail hesitated. Revealing her discovery of the crown did not feel right, even to Daniel, whom she trusted explicitly. "I stumbled upon a small room off the tunnel. Unfortunately, having found my way inside, I could not locate a way to exit."

"You could not simply retrace your steps?"

She grimaced, reliving the terror she'd felt. "The door locked behind me."

He took her hand and squeezed. "I should never have sent you looking for the necklace. Finding it is my cross to bear, not yours."

Isabail agreed, but she did not have the heart to

say so. Finding the necklace was important to Daniel—but not to her. She no longer believed MacCurran had the necklace. She smiled ruefully. "If only I had found the necklace, it would have made the ordeal worthwhile."

"You saw no other evidence of a hidden cache? No locked chest? No shrouded repository?"

"I looked everywhere," she said truthfully. "Searched every corner and crevasse. The necklace is not in the tunnels."

"Forget the necklace. I'm just relieved that you were found." He shook his head. "I would never have forgiven myself had anything befallen you. Promise me that you won't take such risks again."

"We cannot give up the search," she said. As long as Daniel believed she was looking for the necklace, he would relax and let himself heal. "But now that I know how I triggered the door to lock, I will avoid decorative floor tiles if I ever see one again."

His jaw dropped. "A floor tile caused the door to lock?"

She nodded. "The Picts were surprisingly skilled. The entrance to the room was a huge granite slab that pivots. Quite a feat."

"I would enjoy seeing such a marvel," Daniel said, as he watched her rebandage his arm. "Perhaps when I am on my feet again, you can show me."

A lump settled in Isabail's belly. She had not meant to say as much as she had. Showing Daniel the hidden room in the tunnels was impossible. "Perhaps," she said, knotting the bandage snugly.

"But frankly, I'm more eager to explore the rest of this ruin. There must be other places to hide a necklace."

"Surely," he agreed. "But you've already risked your life. I cannot ask you to do so again. Give me a day to two to heal, and I'll take up the search."

"You have a guard at your door," she reminded him. "And even if they cease to guard you, they will watch you closely. There are fewer eyes upon me."

His gaze met hers. "Do not take offense, Isabail, but it's obvious you harbor doubts as to whether MacCurran stole the necklace."

He did not add *and poisoned John*, but Isabail heard the echo of those words anyway. Her face flushed. "It's true. I have every reason to believe the man is a blackguard, but if you could have seen his face as he told the tale of the man in black, you might have doubts too."

"You have a tender heart, Isabail. I think sometimes you see what you prefer to see."

She sat back. "Are you not angry with me?"

Daniel adjusted his position against the wall, wincing as he moved one hip. "I will not lie. I am disappointed that you do not seem as eager as I am to claim justice for John," he admitted.

Guilt was a sharp stab in her chest.

"But," he added, "I have known you too long to believe you disloyal. I know you will demand justice if the proof of his crimes is irrefutable. That's another reason to find the necklace."

"And if we never find it?"

He offered her a faint smile. "Do you ask if I can then accept that MacCurran is innocent?"

She nodded.

He looked away. "Failing to discover the necklace is not the same as proving he did not steal it. Nay, I will not easily be shaken from my belief that MacCurran killed John."

A fair and honest response. And exactly what she had expected of Daniel. "I will continue to search for the necklace"—she caught his worried frown—"with great care. You must focus on healing. Is there anything I can bring you to help speed your recovery?"

"Some willow bark tea would not go amiss," he admitted. "Just be sure to make it yourself. I do not trust any made by a MacCurran."

"Or Ana Bisset."

He smiled. "Indeed."

An irrefutable sign that his clan had been in hiding too long was the volume of complaints that were brought before Aiden when he held court. Small issues, all. Accusations of hoarding, cheating, and idleness. Petty bickering that at its root lay lack of purpose. Hiding in the hills, there were no lands to tend, no pigs to feed, no tools to repair. And whose fault was that? His. The only cure for what ailed his kin was regaining Dunstoras.

Aiden ruled on the last of the grievances and ended the court session with a demand for tolerance.

Then he left the broch in search of a task to soothe his turbulent thoughts.

The horses were kept in the outer enclosure. The old stable master had been one of the casualties of their escape from Dunstoras, so the animals were now loosely assigned to younger lads for care. To the amazement of all, Jamie had taken a leadership role since returning to the camp with Niall. When Aiden approached, he was teaching several other lads how to coax a stubborn horse into offering up its hoof to be cleaned.

Aiden picked up a curry brush and wove through the other horses and across the snow to where his stallion was staked. A bay with two white stockings and a white blaze, the destrier had been a gift from his father upon his majority. Well trained and strong of heart, the horse had quickly proven to be Aiden's most valuable tool in battle. Aiden ran a hand over the stallion's velvet-soft muzzle. The horse responded by pushing against his hand and giving an approving snort.

Using long, smooth strokes, he began to brush the beast.

"You've no need to do that, laird," Jamie said, jogging to his side.

Aiden paused. The boy had matured a great deal in recent weeks, for which Niall deserved a great deal of credit. Aiden had left the boy in his brother's care, hoping the two would fare well together, and it seemed it was the right decision.

"I value the service you provide to the horses," he said to Jamie, "but a soldier must bond with his horse if he's to demand great things of it in battle."

He resumed his brushstrokes. "For all he does for me, I owe this horse more than a brush or two."

Jamie nodded. "My father is of a like mind."

His father, Aiden's cousin Wulf, had disappeared the night the necklace was stolen. The same night Jamie's mother and younger brother had been poisoned. It was probably long past time the lad accepted that his father was gone, but Aiden didn't have the heart to tell him so. The boy had lost too much already.

Locating Wulf's dapple gray destrier among the small herd of horses, he asked, "Who rides your father's horse to keep him in good form?"

"No one," confessed Jamie. "He's a tad difficult to handle."

"He responds well to you, I suspect."

The boy nodded. "He knows my voice."

"Think you can mount him?"

Jamie's eyes widened. "Aye."

"See to his exercise, then. Not alone, mind. Take him out when the other Black Warriors take to the saddle."

A grin broke across the boy's face. "Aye, laird." He started toward the horse, then stopped. "Thank you, laird."

Aiden nodded. If that's all it took to lighten the lad's burden, he should have done it weeks ago.

"Chief?"

A glance over his shoulder confirmed that Cormac was standing behind him, a frown creasing his brow. "Aye?"

"The rescue of Hamish and the others was a worthy undertaking," the bowman said, the tone of his voice serious.

"But . . . ?"

"But it was a costly venture. We lost more than thirty arrows."

Aiden bent to brush his horse's gaskin. Without a smithy, they were unable to forge new arrowheads. Although they reclaimed every spent arrow while hunting, that hadn't been an option during the raid on Dunstoras. "How many are left?"

"Fifty-seven."

Not a dreadful number, if hunting was all they were needed for. "You fear that we've not enough should MacPherson's men come a-calling." Which was a likely occurrence after the raid—MacPherson's wounded pride would demand that his men comb the woods in search of them.

"Aye."

"A fair concern. I'll have the men assemble a hearth." The reason they hadn't created one already wasn't the challenge in building a smithy—it was the smoke. Smelting required a very hot fire maintained for a considerable amount of time—the sort of fire that was difficult to hide. A small cooking fire or a warming brazier gave off little smoke by comparison.

Cormac nodded and departed, his mission accomplished.

Neither man mentioned the length of time it would take to acquire new arrowheads. It was pointless.

Aiden brushed his horse until its coat was shiny and smooth. The soothing nature of the task was no longer working. Time was hounding him. They had already lived in this temporary camp for far longer than he'd originally envisioned. When he had gathered the clan here, his hope had been that it would be only a matter of weeks before he could ascertain his innocence and reclaim his family's land. But almost three months had passed, and he was no closer to identifying the man in black.

Now their supplies were running short. Food and the other necessities were becoming scarce. It wouldn't be long before the prophecy Isabail had made on her arrival would come true. His people would go hungry and his warriors would not have the strength of arms to protect them.

He tossed the curry brush into a bucket with a loud clatter.

The horse snorted and shifted uneasily.

Aiden gave him a reassuring pat on the neck, then turned away. He had only one clue to the identity of the man in black, and that was Isabail. If he did not soon prove his innocence, his clan would starve.

He marched into the inner close and across the snow to his hut. When he stepped inside, it took a few moments for his eyes to adjust to the dimness. Isabail was seated on his pallet, her head bent over a piece of cloth. She continued to wield her needle and thread even though the stiffness in her shoulders told him she was aware of his presence.

"Tell me the names of the men visiting Lochurkie that night," he demanded.

"Nay."

Closing the gap between them in three easy strides, he grabbed her shoulders and hauled her to her feet. "Enough, Isabail. You've played this foolish game too long. Give me the names."

She lifted her gaze. "And what will you do if I give you the names? Seek out each man and force him to confess on pain of death?"

Possibly. He hadn't actually formulated a plan.

"If I tell you who they were," she said, "four innocent men might come to harm at your hands. I cannot live with that outcome."

"You are protecting a murderous villain, a slayer of children. How can you live with *that*?"

She returned his glare. "I'm not convinced any one of those men is a murderer."

Which meant, of course, that she still harbored some belief that *he* was the murderer. "If I were the murderer, why would I trouble myself with searching for the man in black?"

"Who knows? Perhaps he has some other bauble that you covet."

He thrust her away. "Look around, Isabail. Where is the evidence that I covet pretty baubles? Tell me what a necklace like the queen's would gain me."

"Food for your clan, perhaps. I don't know."

"I had everything I needed to support my kin before the necklace was stolen. There was no gain for me, only loss." He raked a hand through his hair. "And what thief who is willing to sacrifice the lives of his own kin then stays to protect and feed and clothe those very same people?"

A frown settled on her brow.

"Should I not have taken my spoils and made for the Continent? Surely I could have lived a fair life in France with the coin such a necklace would have gained me."

"Perhaps you never anticipated being caught," she said slowly. "Perhaps you still want the life you had before the theft."

He studied her. Blond hair flowing loosely over her shoulders, her dress wrinkled and stained. Not the same woman he'd pulled from the carriage a few short days ago. "In your opinion, is a murderer a man of strength or a coward?"

"A coward," she said easily.

"Cowards do not stay and fight for what they desire, especially when faced with overwhelming odds," he offered quietly. Then he turned on his heel and left the hut.

Gorm whined from his blanket by the fire.

Isabail stopped staring at the spot where Mac-Curran had stood and favored the dog with a wry smile. "Aye, he's a difficult man. You've got that right. Saving you from a horrible death one minute, shaking the life from you the next."

She scooped some water from the bucket by the door and brought it to the deerhound.

"I've no meat for you, lad. Until you're well enough to try your hand at bringing home a fat hare, you'll have to eat what the rest of us eat—bread, cheese, and turnips."

He drank the water, then downed a stale crust of bread in a few hearty crunches.

"There's a lad," she said encouragingly. "Since you appear to be faring well, I'll bring you a bone after the evening meal."

As she stood, she heard several loud shouts outside and then the pound of numerous boots in the snow. Isabail raced to the door. The inner close was a jumble of men snatching weapons and running for the walls. The women doused the cooking fires, gathered the children and their belongings, and scurried for the tunnels. With surprising speed and economy of movement, each person headed for their designated spot.

"What's going on?" Isabail asked a boy who was darting for cover.

"Soldiers," he tossed as he tore past. "Headed this way."

Soldiers? MacPherson's men? Isabail chewed her lip. She was supposed to follow the other women into the tunnels, but the promise of rescue was a sweet ache in her chest. What she wouldn't give to sleep in her own bed, to visit the graves of her mother and brother, and to wear clean clothes. If only there were some way to reach Tormod MacPherson without revealing the existence of the hill fort. She wanted to be rescued, but not at the expense of the people in the camp.

MacCurran's fierce form appeared out of the

crowd of warriors in the close. "Get in the hut and stay there until I tell you it's safe to come out."

Isabail hesitated.

His hand cupped her chin with surprising gentleness. "Please."

She retreated into the dim hut. *Wretch.* How dare he be kind to her when she was anticipating harshly worded threats. Sliding to the floor just inside the door, she leaned against the wall and listened. There were few sounds with which to re-create the events occurring outside—after the first shouts, no one spoke.

Silence reigned.

Isabail closed her eyes and listened intently. Were MacPherson's men advancing up the slope to their position? Was mayhem about to ensue? Over the past few days, she'd come to know a great number of the MacCurrans who called this old ruin home. Whether the MacCurran had stolen Queen Yolande's necklace or not, these people did not deserve to die.

She crossed her chest, bowed her head, and prayed.

MacPherson's men crept from the trees to the protection of a scattering of boulders.

Aiden watched their progress from his position farther up the slope. The rugged path leading up to the hill fort was not an obvious one, especially with the extra rocks they'd moved into place. It would take a very determined man to find them, but he feared today might be that day. MacPherson must be livid that Aiden had freed his men right under his nose. He would not accept that loss with grace.

Twelve soldiers inched toward the ruined broch below.

Once they were within striking distance, the leader of the men gave a hand signal, and together they charged toward the ruin with an aggressive roar. Only to find the broch empty. Clearly disappointed and muttering with undisguised frustration, the men searched the ruin. They turned over rocks, kicked apart portions of the walls, and examined every piece of loose rubble for clues. When that got them nowhere, they expanded the search, slowly but inexorably advancing up the slope.

Aiden's men tensed. He had seven archers deployed among the rocks, two of which were exceptional and the others decent. More than enough to turn away this group. Their ability to defend the hilltop fort was, however, limited by supplies. Fifty-seven arrows would not last long. In an extended battle, they would be at a severe disadvantage.

Two MacPherson spearmen climbed over some rocks and gained another few feet of path.

Giving the order to shoot them would bring an end to their hiding, and Aiden's thoughts went to the women and children currently under his protection. He couldn't risk their lives. As satisfying as it would be to engage MacPherson's men, he had to maintain their secrecy for as long as possible.

"I found a boot print!" cried one of the two spearmen, tossing aside a small chunk of shale.

Instantly, twelve pairs of eyes tipped upward, peering into the rocks with renewed eagerness.

"Are you certain?" the sergeant asked with a skeptical frown. In spite of his doubt, he left the wall he was exploring and headed for the path.

"Aye, 'tis definitely the mark of a bootheel frozen in the mud."

Aiden drew a long, deep breath. His hand tightened around the leather-wrapped hilt of his sword, but he still did not give the signal to shoot.

A half dozen soldiers joined the spearmen and began to clear the rocks. The farther they advanced up the slope, the easier the path became. They were about to discover the hill fort, to run amok and possibly slay his kin. Aiden was out of options. He glanced down the line of archers, his face grim. With a silent wave of his hand, he ordered his men to shoot.

The sergeant and the two spearmen were downed in the first volley of arrows. Two other soldiers farther down the slope also dropped. The remaining soldiers raised their targes and drove up the hill with an aggressive roar.

They swiftly reached level ground, and the battle switched to a duel of sword and spear.

Aiden dove out from behind a boulder and took on a broad-shouldered swordsman in chain mail. The fellow was talented, and their swords collided again and again with neither gaining the advantage. They circled each other, testing strength and speed, pushing footing and grip to the limit. In the end, it was the soldier's armor that did him in. He tired quicker than Aiden, and after nimbly parrying a swift thrust, he made his first error—he left his leg exposed. Fighting for the lives of his clan, Aiden didn't hesitate—he drove his sword into the man's thigh and brought him swiftly to the ground.

Unfortunately for the men of MacPherson's patrol, they were outmaneuvered and outnumbered. Trapped between the two walls that surrounded the fort, they fought fiercely and with the seasoned skill of arms for hire, but circumstances played against them.

None of MacPherson's men ceded defeat easily. Only three of them survived the melee—including Aiden's opponent. The MacCurran injuries, by comparison, were minor. A few sliced chests and legs, but no deaths.

Aiden lowered his sword.

The camp was safe—for the moment. But that moment would be short-lived. MacPherson would send another patrol in search of the first, and when he did . . .

Wiping his blade on his sleeve, he ordered Niall, "Gather the arrows. Have the men round everyone up. We've a need to find a new camp."

"Surely we can simply bury the bodies?"

"MacPherson will not yield so easily. He'll comb this area until he finds the bodies . . . and then he'll wreak vengeance upon us."

Aiden left Niall to direct the men and strode

across the inner close to the roundhouse. He almost missed Isabail when he entered. She was seated on the floor with her back against the wall.

When she spied him, she released a sigh. "You're safe."

"Gather your things. We must move."

Isabail gained her feet and did her best to brush the dirt from her skirts. "Move? Move where?"

A very good question. Aiden had given thought to that question many times over the past few months as he planned for the future. Nowhere in the glen would he benefit from stone walls, good storage, and a highly defensible position. But with almost sixty souls under his care, secrecy was better than defensibility. "There's a thickly wooded area farther west. We'll head there."

"Why? Why not remain here?"

Aiden laid the blanket on the floor and began piling items in the middle of it: his clothes, his spare pair of boots and some personal items. "Tormod MacPherson believes his mission is to destroy the MacCurran clan. He'll soon learn that we are camped here, and when he does, he'll attack in full force. I cannot defend my clan against the strength of his army with little or no supplies."

Isabail was silent for a long moment. "You fear that he'll come looking for his missing men."

Aiden didn't bother to answer. He tied the corners of the blanket and swung it over his shoulder. Holding out a hand, he said, "Come."

She did not take his hand. "What if there were no men to be found?"

"It wouldn't matter; he will continue to hunt until he finds us."

"Unless he believed the men were elsewhere when they died."

He stared at her, slowly lowering his hand. "Are you suggesting we move the bodies?"

Isabail blushed. "I've no idea what I'm suggesting. Just thinking aloud. Is it possible to move the bodies?"

"Aye," he said. A thoughtful frown settled on his brow. "It's possible. Moving his men from one spot to another won't be enough to deceive MacPherson, however. To be successful, we'll need a wee bit of cunning."

He dropped the blanket bundle onto the mattress. Then he grabbed Isabail by the shoulders and gave her a quick, hard kiss. "Stay here. I'll be back anon."

Chapter 11

"What age are you, Morag?" Magnus asked as they sat down to sup on the hare he'd snared that afternoon. He was very curious about the woman who'd nursed him back to health, and up to this point, she'd been very vague about her history.

But he was done with mystery and incertitude.

She lifted her gaze from her meal. As their gazes collided, he could see the swirl of thoughts in her green eyes. Perhaps she read the resolve in his own, because for once she did not attempt to fob him off with some whimsical retort. "I am four and twenty."

"And where are your kin?"

She tore the meat off a leg bone with her fine white teeth and chewed. "I am shunned. I have no kin."

Her answer wasn't entirely surprising. After all, few women of a marriageable age lived alone in a bothy in the woods. Still, it made him wonder. "Why?"

"What did I do that warranted a shunning?"

He nodded.

"I lay with three men, two of whom were brothers."

She said it calmly, without heat or embarrassment. There was no attempt to excuse her behavior or apologize for it. She simply stated it as fact. As beautiful as she was, he had no trouble imagining men fighting to have her. Even brothers.

He arched a brow. "At the same time?"

A faint smile rose to her lips. "Nay. One at a time. But the second brother was not pleased to find he'd shared my body with his younger kin."

"So he involved the friar?"

"Aye."

It was more information than she'd given him in three months of sharing an abode. Magnus was loath to cease asking her questions while she was in so generous a mood. "Did you live at the castle?"

A shadow fell over her face. "I did."

Aware that he was stirring unpleasant memories but unable to help himself, he said, "Then you would know whether I made my home there."

Her lips tightened. "What I knew then and what I know now are two different things."

"That is not an answer," he growled, pushing his bowl away. "Just tell me the truth, woman. I'm man enough to handle it, no matter how unpalatable it might be."

"You are not ready," she said. "Your leg is still weak and you suffer great headaches."

He stood up. "You call up the same excuses no matter how much time passes. I do not even know my true name," he said. "Do not deny me answers."

"The truth will only harm you."

"Better that swift fate than to slowly waste away in ignorance here," he bit out. "Did I live at the castle or no?"

She sighed heavily. "Aye, you did."

Rage seared through him like fire in his veins. "All this time I've been but a stone's throw from the truth." He pivoted and began to pack a bag.

"But you are no longer welcome at the castle. You are outlawed now."

He paused. Outlawed? "For what crime?"

"Murder, theft, and treason against the king." She, too, pushed away her bowl. "You were run through by the king's men. I saw it with my own eyes."

"And yet you took me in and healed me," he said, frowning. "Why?"

She shrugged. "We are all more than the sum of our crimes. I am not simply a harlot, and I do not believe you are simply a murderer and a thief."

"Given the charges against me, you took a considerable risk," he pointed out. "Would you do that for everyone?"

Morag shook her head. "I have much cause to be wary of men."

"Then why help me?"

"You were kind to me," she said. "On the day I was cast out, you braved the disapproval of the friar and stopped to carry my satchel."

Magnus leaned back against the wall of the hut. That story rang true; it felt like something he would do. The accusations of murder and treason did not sit as easily. "You know my real name? Why did you not tell me when I awoke?"

"In the early days after I rescued you, several patrols from the castle passed us by. Based on what I witnessed, it seemed unwise to call you by your true name." She played with the tip of her long black braid. "And you were too confused by the injury to your head to grasp two names and keep them straight."

"I am not confused any longer."

She met his gaze. Her smile was rueful. "Indeed not."

"So tell me." He pulled away from the wall, waiting.

"Your name is Wulf."

Disappointment cinched his chest tight. Damn. How was that possible? The name meant nothing to him. It did not bring to mind a single memory of his past or clue to his identity. Nor did it give cause to the nagging sense that he ought to be elsewhere.

"Wulf," he repeated. The name was even strange on his tongue. It did not seem to suit him like Magnus did. He was a large man, so Magnus fit his physical form. He'd chosen that name for himself after three weeks had passed without memory. Now it seemed familiar. Wulf did not.

"Do I have kin?"

Morag shook her head. "That I cannot answer. Many at the castle perished or were driven from the land. Others were imprisoned. I visit the castle only on faire days, so I've no sense of who lived and who died."

Magnus couldn't be certain she told the truth. She avoided his gaze, which suggested at least some part of her tale was a lie.

"Are you and I kin?"

She choked out a laugh. "You and I? Nay. I am naught but a weaver. You lived in the castle proper. Save for the day I departed, we never exchanged words."

That did not fit with Magnus's beliefs about himself. Well, not entirely, anyway. He knew from the calluses on his right hand that he was familiar with a blade, so the notion of not being a common laborer felt real enough. But holding himself above those who were of lesser status? He couldn't imagine possessing such a surfeit of pride.

"I need to strengthen this leg," he said, lightly pounding his lame leg with his fist. "I cannot remain here forever. I must seek out those who know me."

Morag tightened the woolen shawl about her shoulders. "Take to the hills, then. Climbing will strengthen the leg. Just be wary of soldiers. They seem to be venturing into the woods with more frequency of late."

Magnus crossed the hut to stand before her. He lifted her chin with his hand and peered into her pretty green eyes. "I'll forever be grateful for the aid you've given me. Be assured of that. If I can ever repay you, I will."

She flushed and stepped back, forcing him to release her. "Just chop me a good supply of wood before you go, and I'll be rewarded enough."

He let her walk away.

The woman was too proud by half. Her supplies were limited—purchased from the castle in exchange for the fine cloth she wove on her loom—and yet she had shared them unsparingly as he healed. Once he was able to hunt, he had supplemented her food with the odd hare, but he had a hearty appetite, so her pot on the fire was forever in need of new ingredients.

He would pay her back.

He just wasn't sure how or when.

Just as he wasn't sure when he would leave. It bothered him immensely to imagine her alone here, fending for herself. She was young and beautiful. She ought to be some man's wife, not chopping her own wood and risking her very life traveling to the castle to trade her wares. He'd accompanied her the last few times. He'd seen the harassment she had endured at the hands of the soldiers at the gate and clenched his fists.

"We'll never be even," he said softly. "I'll forever be in your debt."

"I don't want your debt," she retorted.

"You have it anyway."

His words annoyed her—he could see it in her sharply angled eyebrows. She did not want anything from him except for him to stay. But what she wanted was impossible. Not because of who he was, but because of who he had once been. Until he knew his past, he could not settle with a woman. For all he knew, he was already wed.

He studied her elegant profile. He only prayed that he wasn't. Otherwise, the thoughts he had about Morag would surely see him in hell.

The MacCurran returned to the hill fort as the light was fading. Isabail spied him at the entrance of the inner close, looking like some barbarian warrior of old—his hair a tangled mess and his lèine spattered with bloodstains.

He was as far from a gentleman lord as she could imagine, and yet her heart did a funny dance in her chest as he marched through the gate. Perhaps it was the purposeful look that took control of his face when he caught sight of her, or perhaps it was the rippling muscles of his thighs and calves as he strode toward her. Whatever it was, her body reacted instinctively, flooding her with heat and eager anticipation.

He grabbed her hand and led her away from the central fire and toward the hut he had claimed as his own.

"Where are we going?" she asked breathlessly.

"I owe you a proper thanks," he answered, pulling her into the hut. He shut the door, then released her briefly to change his lèine and splash his face with water. Then he advanced toward her with a wolfish grin, slowly backing her against the wall. "Your idea to move the bodies was inspired. We built a fire pit half a league from here and left several of our broken tools there, along with some furniture and the bodies. MacPherson will believe his men found us camped there and were ambushed."

Isabail heard everything MacCurran said, but she had difficulty concentrating. His hands were wandering places they had no right to be. A proper noblewoman would take him to task. But as his fingers swept down her back and over her rump, she relaxed against the wall and let him have his way. It felt so good to have a strong man offer her such exquisite moments of pleasure.

Her softened stance encouraged him to go further. The words stopped, and his lips found more adventurous tasks to perform. Like nibbling the skin along her collarbone and tracing a red-hot path to her earlobe. The heat of his kisses sent a tremble of need through every nerve in her body.

She should despise this man for all he'd done, even though he denied it. Yet she found she could not. All she could remember as his lips made merry on her flesh was the gentle hold he'd kept on her for two days in the saddle, the care he'd shown her and Muirne when they were snowbound, and the fierce desire that leapt into his eyes each time he looked at her.

Logic said that he had done all that Daniel insisted he had done, but her heart disagreed.

When he scooped her up and carried her to the mattress, Isabail did not protest. She thrust her darker thoughts to the back of her mind and faced the man lowering himself next to her with a steady stare. She was a wee bit nervous, but there was no doubt in her heart that she wanted him to kiss her.

He lowered his mouth to hers, and she met his kiss eagerly. Opening to his press, her lips parted with a soft sigh of contentment. None of his kisses were gentle. They had the potent force of a man whose ardor was barely held in check—and that filled Isabail with a weak-kneed pleasure. He wanted her, badly, but he restrained himself as best he could. For her.

"You are a rare beauty," he murmured against her throat. "As lovely as a snow-white lily."

Isabail melted a little beneath him, surprised by the compliment. He did not seem the sort to offer a woman unnecessary praise. And she knew that the desire he felt for her conflicted with his anger over what had been dealt to his honor and his kin. Much as her desire conflicted with her need to see justice done for her brother. What a pair they were.

His hand tugged at her skirts, lifting them and baring a thigh. As his broad hand found her warm flesh, he groaned, a deep, primal response that made Isabail's heart beat faster. To be wanted so clearly, so freely, was new to her. Andrew had always been admiring but reserved. In the bedroom, there had been few words and ever fewer spontaneous groans of delight. MacCurran was a much more earthy man, and for some reason that pleased her.

As did the rough caress of his callused hand over her bare thigh. It was a delightful friction that made her breath catch in her throat.

Tentatively, a little unsure of how to behave, Isabail lifted a hand to MacCurran's face and allowed herself to explore the raw masculine beauty of his face. The hard line of his jaw, with its late-day stubble of beard, the high arch of his cheek-bone and the curve of his ear. He seemed to approve of her wandering, leaning in to her hand and kissing her with deeper intent.

Isabail's fingers slid into the damp waves of his hair, lost in a wondrous explosion of sensations—the rasp of his lips on hers, the duel of their tongues, and the thrill of his daring touch on her inner thigh. Sparks of exquisite awareness built in her belly, making her restless with anticipation. She wanted more.

She lifted her hips against his and felt the telltale evidence of his desire. A throaty mewl escaped her lips as she struggled to convey her growing sense of need.

He raked her skirt higher and laid a gentle hand over her mons. Isabail's knees fell open, giving him wider access, and she closed her eyes. As his thumb began to tease her most intimate flesh, she gave herself up to the full gambit of pleasurable sensations. MacCurran knew precisely how to touch her to cultivate the stormiest responses. A finger entered her, and then two. His strokes were a perfect rhythm, and the tension inside her built to a near unbearable level. Just when she thought she would burst, he eased down her body and replaced his hand with his lips.

Isabail was scandalized. But only for the briefest of moments.

When he suckled her gently and played the instrument of her desire with his tongue, she forgot about her ideas of what was proper and let the MacCurran take control. He took her places she'd never been, and only moments after his mouth touched her, she was rocked with the sweet shudders of release.

"Oh, my Lord."

MacCurran kissed his way back up her body to her lips. "I promised you a proper thank-you."

Still relishing the gentle trembles that rippled through her body, Isabail did not open her eyes. To be honest, she wasn't sure she could look him in the eyes. Andrew had never done that. Never kissed her *there*. "That was a unique expression of gratitude."

He chuckled and pulled her against his chest. Placing her cheek next to his strong and steady heartbeat, she snuggled deeper into his embrace. Her hand slipped beneath the soft linen of his tunic and flattened against the chiseled plane of his chest. Warm and solid.

"Are you not eager for some respite yourself, MacCurran?"

He covered her hand with his, holding it in place. "You have my leave to call me Aiden," he said, his voice a deep rumble in her ear.

She smiled. She'd heard others call him by his given name, but most of his kin simply addressed him as the MacCurran. The clan chief. In her mind, MacCurran was a splendid name for him—strong, fierce, and bold. "You are the chief. I'm comfortable to address you thus unless you would be offended."

"Not offended," he said. "But you are entitled to a more intimate address. I call you Isabail."

"I am your prisoner," she said dryly. "You may call me whatever you wish."

"I would dispute who is the prisoner," he responded quietly. "I have but to look into your eyes and I am captured."

Isabail's heartbeat, which had been settling into a normal pace, sped up again. He delivered the pretty words with such a perfect note of seriousness, she was tempted to believe them. Certainly, a hope she had not yet dared to give voice to sprouted to life. *If* he truly cared for her, and *if* they could find some way to prove his innocence . . . perhaps . . . just perhaps, a future was possible. But she was reluctant to dwell on the notion; it was such a tender bud.

"Then, as my prisoner, you are commanded to complete the task you have started. Leave us both sated and replete, and I will honor you with a prize."

Another chuckle rumbled through his chest. "And what prize will that be? You've not much to offer."

"Och, you would be surprised." She tilted her head and put her lips to the warm skin of his throat. "Will you do as I command?"

With a swift movement, he rolled and pinned her to the mattress. Dark and purposeful, he swooped down to claim her lips. They were still plump and full from his previous kisses, and she opened to him as she had before. Only this time she responded with more than just her body—she offered a piece of her heart. Ah, who knew what the future might bring?

Aiden woke to a cold, wet press against his arm. His eyes flew open, and his hand instinctively reached for the sword that lay beside the pallet. But he halted midgrab. It was the hound. Standing next to the bed, looking down at him with its soulful brown eyes.

As Aiden stared back, the beast tilted its head, as if curious.

"Away with you," he whispered to the dog. Isabail's head lay on his chest, her limbs sweetly entwined with his, and he had no desire to see her disturbed.

The dog did not leave. Instead, the great animal lay down and continued to stare at him. As if it expected something. Never having owned a hound, Aiden had no notion as to what that something might be.

"Go," he said, pointing to the door.

The bloody beast just continued to stare.

A very focused stare. Rather unnerving. Aiden tried to ignore it and return to sleep, but a feeling of being watched continued to haunt him. Sure enough, when he opened one eye to check, he found the creature still staring.

"What is it you want?" he asked gruffly.

"Breakfast," Isabail murmured sleepily.

"Not you," he said, grinning into her silken hair. "*It*. What does it want?"

She lifted her head and spied the dog. "Gorm!"

To his great vexation, she pushed away from him and sat up, her face lit with happiness. "He's on his feet. How splendid." Grabbing up her shift, she pulled it over her head and stood.

Aiden was not convinced anything about this event was splendid. The beast had ruined a very promising morning. He pillowed his head on his arms. "Why is it staring at me?"

"John always took Gorm for a walk in the morn. No doubt he's looking to you to continue that tradition."

Aiden frowned. "Why me? Why not you?"

Isabail shook her head. "I've no idea. He must like you."

A dubious honor, to say the least.

"Will you take him?"

Aiden looked at Isabail. She was braiding her glorious blond tresses, denying them to his fingers. "Nay. If I must get up, then I've other business to see to about the camp. I've no time to gad about with a dog."

He rolled from his pallet and tossed the hound a pointed glare. To his mind, the morning should have started with a leisurely kiss and perhaps a bout of lovemaking. Not like this.

"I'll take him, then," Isabail said, tugging her blue gown over her shift.

"Do you not have any other gowns?" he asked. "You've worn that same one every day since—" He stopped there, searching for a neutral term to describe his capture of her and coming up dry.

A flush rose up her throat and into her cheeks. "Since you attacked my party and kidnapped me? Nay, I do not have any other gowns. All my things were taken."

He frowned. "But we gathered some of your belongings."

"And gave them to the other women in the camp," she said sharply. "Nothing was returned to me."

He watched her lace her boots, anger in every harsh tug on the leather cords. He'd never made it clear to his men that the clothing was to be given to Isabail, and he could see how they'd misinterpreted his request. The women in the camp had not seen new clothes for several months. Many of their gowns were threadbare from numerous washings.

"You'll have plenty of lovely gowns when you return to Lochurkie," he said to reassure her.

Unfortunately, that seemed to fuel her ire rather than dissipate it.

"Are you reminding me that all I have to do is provide you the names of my guests and I can walk out of this camp without a backward glance?" she asked, her voice the snarl of a wildcat.

"Aye," he said. "Have I not said that from the beginning?"

Her blue eyes were like chips of ice in the pale beauty of her face. "Oh yes, you made that quite clear . . . in the beginning."

"Then what is the source of your anger?"

She took several deep breaths before responding, calming herself. "In the beginning, we had not lain with each other," she said.

He blinked. "But you are not a maid. Surely you did not have an expectation that our dalliance would lead to anything."

"An expectation?" she asked coolly. "Nay, I am not a woman given to expectations. Few, if any, of my expectations have borne fruit. A hope that there might be more meaning attached to our dalliance than a simple roll in the hay? Aye, *that* I had."

"In the eyes of the king, I am a thief, a murderer, and a traitor," he said. "An outlawed laird. I have nothing to offer a woman of your ilk."

"Except the odd night of pleasure."

"Aye," he agreed. "Save for that."

She nodded sharply. "We are clear now." Turning on her heel, she headed for the door. "Come, Gorm."

The dog, it seemed, had other ideas. It remained precisely where it was, seated at Aiden's feet, staring at him with unwavering eyes. Aware that Isabail sought to leave the room with an angry flounce, he nudged the dog with his foot. But the beast wouldn't budge.

Isabail reached the door, and upon realizing the dog was not at her side, turned. "Gorm, come!"

The dog's gaze did not flicker.

Isabail stomped across the room with very unladylike expression and grabbed the hound's scruff. Then she pulled him toward the door. The beast was large enough to resist her tug, but it did not.

It finally broke off its uncanny stare and trotted alongside Isabail to the door.

When they were gone and silence descended on the room, Aiden dropped back onto the mattress and raked his fingers through his hair.

Well, that had definitely not gone according to plan.

Isabail walked the deerhound around the perimeter of the hill fort twice. The brisk chill of the morning helped to cool her thoughts. It annoyed her that she had indeed developed expectations for how her future might roll out, especially as those expectations were apparently closely aligned to the suggestion Lady Elisaid had made when she first arrived.

She had avoided MacCurran's mother quite successfully over the past week, but she had not managed to avoid the promise in her words.

What had she been thinking? Daring to dream of a more permanent arrangement with the MacCurran was a foolish mistake. Her original plan had been to seek an audience with the king and convince him to give her Dunstoras in recompense for her brother's death. As part of that plan, she'd intended to offer herself in marriage to a man of the king's choosing, so that he might use the land to forge an alliance, as well. It had been such a straightforward and reasonable plan.

Until she'd given her heart to a rogue.

Damn him. Why could he not have remained a villain in her thoughts? A brutal fiend, like her father? Her life would have been so much simpler. Instead she'd come to see him as honorable and valiant—the consummate defender of his kith and kin.

Isabail nodded to the two men guarding the entrance to the inner close and strode toward the hut used by Daniel. She swept aside the fur door panel. Gorm growled low in his throat and balked at entering. She shook her finger at him. "Fine, then. Stay outside."

Daniel was standing before the brazier, holding his hands to the heat. He turned as she entered and then crumpled with a wince. Falling to one knee, he groaned. "Damn this blasted leg."

Isabail scurried to his side and helped him to his feet. He leaned heavily on her as she guided him back to the mattress. "You are attempting too much, too fast."

Settling himself with his back to the wall, he shook his head. "I hate being an invalid. You are without a champion in this nest of vipers. I should be at your side, not lying about in bed."

"Do not overtax yourself on my account. I am fine." A wee lie, but the truth would not help Daniel. "Give yourself the proper time to heal, and you'll be up and about in a few days. Stress the wounds unduly and you may find yourself a permanent lame-leg."

He grimaced. "Not a fate I desire."

"Then take your rest." She glanced around. "Where is Muirne?"

"Fetching some food to break the fast."

Isabail made a quick check of his bandaged wounds. None were seeping. The injuries were knitting, which was good, but Daniel's face showed signs of strain—dark circles beneath his eyes and a glitter in his eyes that she normally associated with fever. But his face was pale, not rosy-cheeked.

She put a hand on his forehead. Cool, not hot. No fever.

"Have you slept well?"

"Nay," he said, adjusting his hip on the bed. "I cannot stop thinking about the necklace. I know it's here. I must find it."

"I've looked many places," she told him. "The necklace is not here. Daniel, it's possible that Mac-Curran does not have it."

"He has it," Daniel insisted.

Isabail could have argued further, but she was not of a mind to defend MacCurran at this moment. "I have a need to return to the cave, so I shall look again while I am down there. Now rest."

He let his head fall back against the wall. "Take care. Do not let him see what you are about."

"He's off playing lord of the ruin. He will not take heed of my actions, I assure you."

She stood, intending to leave, but he grabbed her skirts. "If you find it, return to me immediately. I must know that you have it."

"I will." He did not release her skirts, so she gently peeled his fingers away. "Sleep, Daniel. And eat something when Muirne returns. You don't look well."

Exiting the roundhouse, Isabail looked for Gorm. But the disloyal beast had not obeyed her command to stay. The spot before the door was empty. Exasperated by the behavior of all the males in her life this morn, she headed for the entrance to the tunnels.

"You've acquired an admirer I see," Niall said as he handed Aiden a fresh roll of thatch.

"What?" Aiden cast a quick glance around the close, expecting to see Isabail watching him from a distance. She was nowhere to be seen.

"The hound, brother," Niall said with a laugh, pointing to the base of the ladder on which Aiden stood. There, performing a repeat of the stare he'd given Aiden upon waking, was the blue-gray deerhound named Gorm.

"What does the bloody thing want?" he asked his brother. "It won't leave me be."

Niall shrugged. "Ignore it. Perhaps it will tire of watching you and wander off."

They repaired the roofs on the huts for the better part of the morning, but the dog remained ever at Aiden's heel. It did not whine or bark; it lay quietly somewhere within a hand's reach at all times.

"Curious," said Niall, as they paused to eat the noontide meal and down a horn of ale. "It seems to need nothing but to be near you."

Ana crossed the close to Niall's side and graced him with a kiss on the cheek. "You left early this morning," she said.

Niall pointed to Aiden. "Blame him. He fetched me from my bed before the cock's crow."

Aiden, in turn, pointed to the dog. "Nay, lay the blame where it properly lies. The beast stirred me from a restful slumber."

She eyed the dog. "That will teach you to save a wounded animal. It's yours now."

"Mine?" Aiden frowned. "Nay. The hound belongs to Isabail. It was her brother's."

"Tell that to the dog," she said with a wry smile. "I must return to tending MacPherson's wounded men. All of them, you'll be relieved to know, will survive their injuries."

Aiden's frown deepened. "And what am I to do with them once they are whole and hearty? We've no dungeon in which to lock them."

She shrugged. "If they are sell swords, perhaps you can turn them to your cause with a coin or two."

A fair notion. One definitely worthy of exploration. "Let me know when they are well enough to gain their feet. I'll speak to them."

Ana nodded and walked away.

Aiden watched her depart, then eyed the dog. What was he to do if the beast insisted on remaining at his side?

Chapter 12

Isabail took young Jamie with her into the tunnels. In part it was because the very thought of returning to the narrow and dark confines terrified her. But it was also because she had need of a strong helper and the lad was solidly built.

"Which of the men is your da?" she asked the boy as they entered the dimly lit passage.

"None," Jamie replied. "My da disappeared the night the laird was arrested by the earl of Lochurkie."

"Oh." If he had disappeared, was it not possible *he* was the thief Aiden sought? The man in black? Not that she would dare suggest such to Jamie.

"My da is the finest of the MacCurran's warriors," Jamie offered as they picked their way along. "No one can best him with a sword, not even the laird himself."

She smiled. A very proud son. "Your mother must miss him sorely."

"Nay. She's passed on. She was poisoned by the thief, as was my wee brother, Hugh."

Isabail halted and turned to face the lad. "Och, I'm so sorry, Jamie. I've no sense at all, stirring those memories for you."

His gaze dropped to his feet. "My da is off searching for the madman as we speak. He'll not return until he finds him."

The truth, or just a wishful thought? She put a hand on Jamie's shoulder. "Then I'm certain he'll return anon."

He nodded. "What is it we are seeking in the storeroom?"

"A small chest," she said, continuing down the tunnel until she reached the open space of the storeroom. She immediately breathed easier. "I saw it here a number of days ago."

"What's inside?" he asked curiously.

"A gift for the laird," she said, holding the torch high. "It's a small brown chest banded with brass. I think it's behind those flour sacks."

He scrambled over the sacks in question and climbed down the other side. "I think I see it."

"Good. Can you lift it out?"

She heard him grunt. " 'Tis heavier than it looks. Is it filled with gold?"

Isabail laughed. "Nay, but something nearly as precious to the laird, if I'm not mistaken."

He heaved the chest atop the flour sacks, then climbed over. When he had both feet planted firmly on the tunnel floor, he lifted the wooden box with a grunt and clasped it to his chest.

Seeing the gritted teeth and taut muscles in his arms, Isabail quickly led the way back out. When they reached daylight, Jamie called for a halt and set the box on the ground. "What's in here?" he asked, out of breath.

"It's a secret."

"Can I be there when he opens it?" the lad asked as he bent and reclaimed the box.

Isabail nodded. "Of course."

They marched across the close to where Mac-Curran and his brother were eating their midday meal. Isabail tossed a short glare at Gorm, who was lying contentedly at MacCurran's feet. *Traitor.* She waved Jamie forward with the chest, and the lad lowered the box to the ground next to the dog.

MacCurran offered her an arched brow.

His stare was intent, and Isabail blushed. "You may recall that I offered you a prize," she said, suddenly very aware that Niall was listening with avid attention. "I keep my word. Here it is."

MacCurran looked at the chest, then back up to her face. "I assumed it was a jest. You've no need to gift me anything."

"You assume many things, I've noted," she said briskly. "In truth, the item is already yours. I found it in the caves. Open it."

MacCurran gave the last of his bread to Gorm, then bent and unlatched the chest. He opened the lid and stared at the contents for a long moment.

"What is it?" asked Jamie. "May I see?"

MacCurran nodded, and the boy leapt forward to look in the chest. He frowned, clearly disappointed. "Arrowheads?"

Niall dove for the box. "Truly?" He grinned as

he lifted a steel broadhead and studied it. "Where did you find these?"

Isabail's eyes met MacCurran's. "In the cave. Had you a seneschal, you'd likely have found them yourselves some time ago."

He smiled faintly. "I seem to recall someone suggesting that very same notion a few days past."

"There you have it, then," she said. "My debt is paid."

"Nay," he said. "You still owe me the names of your guests at Lochurkie."

A cold lump dropped into Isabail's belly. How eager he was to see her gone now. It was as if the night of bliss they'd shared had never been. She wrapped her arms about her waist, feeling a little nauseous.

"Fetch me a quill, a pot of ink, and some parchment, and I will give you the names," she said quietly. Then she spun about and headed back to the hut she'd once shared with Muirne.

Niall dropped the arrowhead back into the chest with a soft clatter. "She seems a wee bit angry."

"She is not pleased with me at the moment," Aiden admitted.

"But you've got what you desired. She's going to give you the names."

Aiden frowned. So she had said. But why now? Why give him the names today when he had pressed her repeatedly for them to no avail? If anything, he had expected her to be more stubborn than ever, after their discussion of this morning. Anger, yes. Compliance? That seemed out of place.

And why did the knowledge that he would soon have the names he sought not fill him with joy? Those names were the very reason he had risked everything to capture her. "In truth," he admitted, "I had not thought much beyond gaining the names. I've no plan for how to coax the truth from these men."

"Ask them each to don a hooded cloak," Niall offered. "Perhaps you'll recognize the thief simply by the way he holds himself."

"Perhaps."

"The camp will certainly be a quiet place once Lady Macintosh has departed," Niall said. "And your mother may venture out of her rooms more often, God help us. She seems to be avoiding the lady for some reason."

Aiden was no longer listening. His thoughts had come to a crashing halt with the words *once Lady Macintosh has departed*. She had been in his camp only a sennight, and already he could not imagine the place—especially his own hut—without her.

"Who among the older men can count?" Aiden asked his brother.

"Hamish, I believe . . . and perhaps Gordon."

"Tell Hamish he's now the seneschal," Aiden said, handing his brother the chest of arrowheads. "And have these made into arrows."

Niall's eyebrows soared. "Where are you going?"

"To speak with Lady Macintosh."

"Are you certain that's a wise idea? Perhaps it would be best to wait until she's written the names of her guests."

Aiden quelled his brother's suggestion with a hard stare, then marched across the close to his hut.

Daniel was standing near the back of the hut when Isabail entered. He was dressed in a cream-colored lèine and laced leather boots. For the first time since MacCurran's men dragged his bleeding body into the close, he looked tall and self-assured—every bit the handsome Frenchman who had drawn her brother's attention.

"Where's Muirne?" she asked, glancing about.

He turned to face her. "Beathag had need of her services."

"I have need of her, as well. We need to pack up our belongings."

Daniel frowned. "Why?"

"I've promised MacCurran the information he seeks," Isabail said. "Once he has the names, he will set us free."

"Don't be a fool. We know the location of his camp. He cannot set us free without compromising the safety of his people."

Isabail paused. *She* did not know the camp's location—because she had been blindfolded. But the same could not be said for Daniel. Nor had MacCurran said he would free Daniel. She had simply assumed . . . "In truth, he said nothing of setting *you* free," she admitted.

"Because he intends to slay me," Daniel said grimly.

"Nay," she protested. "You were insensible when they dragged you into camp. You are no more certain of its exact location than I."

"Gorm led me near enough to cause MacCurran worry." He grabbed her arm, his grip painfully tight. "He cannot risk setting me free. Not if he is truly committed to protecting his kin. We must leave of our own accord. Now, while he believes you acquiescent."

"MacCurran is not the villain you believe him to be."

Daniel's expression softened. "I know you think well of him, but put yourself in his boots, Isabail. What if he set me free and I revealed what I know? What if MacPherson made sense of my ramblings and was able to derive the location of the camp?"

A chill slid down Isabail's spine. The outcome of such events would be horrific. "But to kill a man simply for what he knows . . . that's barbaric."

"A chief must be willing to do what other men cannot."

Isabail stared at Daniel. His words rang true. MacCurran was first and foremost a Highland chieftain, responsible for the men, women, and children of his clan. He would do anything to protect them, including sacrificing his own life. She knew that without a doubt. Was he capable of slaying a good man to accomplish his aims? Aye, he was. Sir Robert had been a good man, and Mac-Curran had slain him to capture her.

"But how can we escape?" she asked. "There's a guard outside the door."

He took her hand and drew her toward the back of the hut. "While you've been out and about the camp, I've been busy." He unsheathed his small eating dirk and cut the last tongue of wood holding a panel in the wall. The square of wall fell onto the grass outside, and the crisp winter breeze blew across Isabail's toes.

Not entirely certain she was doing the right thing, she followed Daniel through the hole.

As Daniel led her quickly behind one of the other huts, keeping to the shadows, Isabail glanced over her shoulder. "Where are we going?" she whispered. "The horses are staked at the opposite end of the fort."

"We cannot leave without the necklace."

She dug her feet in, coming to an abrupt halt. "Are you mad? I've searched the camp thoroughly. The necklace is not here."

He faced her. "It's here."

"If you truly desire to leave, we must go now," she urged. "Once MacCurran discovers me absent, escape will be near impossible."

"I will not leave without the necklace," he said stubbornly. "It's the reason I am here."

The dark circles around his eyes and the tight pull of his skin over his cheeks reminded Isabail that Daniel was still ill. She tempered her frustration and once again attempted to reason with him.

"Why are you so convinced MacCurran has the necklace?"

"Niall MacCurran brought it with him from Duthes."

Isabail blinked. *Duthes?* "But the necklace was stolen from Lochurkie. How did it get to Duthes?"

He tugged. "None of that matters. We are wasting time. We must enter the caves quickly, before we are discovered."

"Nay." If they did not make it to the horses soon, all of this effort would be for naught. She tried to free her hand from his grasp and failed. "Cease this madness, Daniel. The necklace is not worth our lives."

He snorted. "It's worth far more than you know." Yanking her sharply, he threw her off balance. As she stumbled, he caught her around the waist and pulled her toward the entrance to the caves. "I'm not leaving without it. Protesting will only cause further delay."

Even ill, he was considerably stronger than Isabail. He dragged her along with surprising ease. Aware that she was slowing them down at a time when speed was of the essence, she reluctantly ceded the moment to him and ended her struggles.

He smiled down at her. "A wise decision."

As they ducked into the ancient storeroom at the far end of the camp, they came face-to-face with young Jamie MacCurran. He slid the sack of dried beans he was carrying to the floor and eyed Daniel with a heavy frown. "Lady Isabail? Is all well?"

*   *   *

Pushing open the door, Aiden peered inside his chamber. There was no sign of Isabail. Even the brazier had gone cold. Where could she be?

He scanned the close, coming to an abrupt halt at the roundhouse with a guard standing outside. De Lourdes. He covered the distance between the two huts in a dozen long strides. But when he swept aside the fur drape, he found that room, too, was empty.

"Where is de Lourdes?" he asked the guard.

The man's expression turned to surprise, and he peered inside with a perplexed frown. "I don't know."

"That's a very poor answer," Aiden said softly.

The guard gulped. "I'll find him," he promised. He jogged around the hut and returned to Aiden's side. "There's a hole cut in the back wall. It seems he's escaped, laird."

Escaped.

An icy calm filtered through Aiden's veins. Spinning on his heel, he hailed the guards at the entrance to the hill fort. "Seal the entry! No one is to go in or out." To the men milling about the close, he said grimly, "Find me Daniel de Lourdes."

Every gillie immediately ceased what he was doing and searched for the missing man, checking every hut, lifting every tarp, opening every barrel. The hill fort did not boast many hiding spots, and it quickly became clear that their wounded visitor wasn't the only one missing. Isabail had disappeared, too. Aiden's chest grew painfully tight, every breath a chore. There was only one conclusion to reach—the vixen had never intended to give him the names. She had plotted an escape with de Lourdes.

"Fetch me my horse!" he roared.

One of the lads raced forward with his mount in tow. He swiftly saddled the horse and mounted. The hound, Gorm, remained at his side throughout, even when Aiden wheeled his mighty steed about and tore out of the hilltop enclosure.

Daniel immediately released Isabail and grabbed Jamie, clasping a broad hand over the boy's mouth. "One more word and you're dead, lad."

"Let him go," Isabail urged, suddenly beyond weary. This madcap attempt to escape was quickly becoming a farce. "He's just a boy. He has no part in this, Daniel."

"He stinks," Daniel said with a laugh. "Do you perchance tend the horses, lad?" Easing his hand away from Jamie's mouth, he allowed the boy to answer.

"Aye."

"Marvelous. The Lord is surely guiding our efforts. We'll need you when it comes time to depart." Daniel tossed a lopsided smile at Isabail. "Let us continue."

"Nay," she said. "I will not involve this boy in our affairs."

The smile fell away, and Daniel's eyes narrowed. "You will do as I command."

Isabail took a step back. Never in all the years she had known him had Daniel spoken to her in such a tone. Not a hint of the charming scholar remained. In his stead stood a cold, hard stranger. "I will not."

"You speak too hastily, Isabail." He held up his eating dirk. "Enter the tunnel, or the lad's blood is on your hands."

"You would not hurt an innocent boy," she protested, aghast.

"Are you willing to test my resolve?"

She shook her head, her mouth sour with dread. Turning, she led the way into the tunnel. But her feet dragged. Several of the torches that normally lit the way had burned out, and the walls felt unusually close and damp. Memories of being trapped in the darkness sucked the air from her chest.

Daniel gave Isabail a hard shove in the back that sent her to her knees. Rock bit into her knees and hands as she hit the floor. "Move," he snarled. "Quickly, or the boy will suffer for your stubbornness."

She scrambled to her feet, pressing her stinging palms to her skirt. "Let him go, Daniel. If you need a hostage, use me. You do not need Jamie."

She turned to face him.

He held Jamie's head in the crook of his elbow, one hand firmly clapped over the boy's mouth and nose. Jamie's eyes were wide, the whites clearly visible. Isabail's heart clenched for him. This was all her fault. She had believed Daniel's greatest wounds were physical when, in fact, they were of the soul. He had lied about his interest in the necklace—and he had made a fool of her.

A hot rush of anger surged through her veins.

"Let him go, Daniel," she repeated. "Please."

Daniel waved the dirk at her. "Cease your dallying. The hand I hold over his mouth and nose can either grant him air to breathe or deny him. Your actions decide his fate, Isabail."

Isabail met Jamie's terrified gaze, and she spun on her heel, continuing down the corridor. The shadows around her were deep and thick. Finding her way in semidarkness was a challenge she was ill prepared for. A few days ago, she would have found the task a simple one, but after her ordeal in the tomb, the creeping shadows gave rise to goose bumps on her arms and thoughts that made her heart pound.

When the tunnel opened into the wide storage area, she breathed easier. Again, she confronted Daniel. "We are here. Now let him go."

"Nay," snapped Daniel. "He'll bring the Mac-Currans down upon my head. He stays." He looked around. "Where's the tomb?"

Isabail swallowed. She had no intention of revealing the tomb's whereabouts to Daniel. In his current state, he wouldn't hesitate to disturb the final resting place of the unnamed Pictish king. And who knew what he would do with the crown and sword?

"The tomb holds only a dead body," she said. "This room is where the necklace will be."

"Do you think me a lackwit?" he sneered. "No ordinary tomb is protected by such an elaborate trap as the one you described. This one surely contains a treasure, making it the perfect place to hide the necklace. Show me where it is, or I will kill the lad."

Daniel de Lourdes had lived with her brother for more than five years. She knew him well. He was a gentle scholar—an herbalist of some renown—not a warrior. His expertise lay with the quill, not the sword. He was not capable of killing Jamie. "You will not kill him. I know you, Daniel. Let the boy go, and I will help you search for the necklace."

A humorless smile rose to Daniel's lips. "You do not know me at all, Isabail. You've no idea what I'm capable of. I loved John—that much is true. Indeed, I loved him more than I have ever loved anyone in my life. But I'm also the one who killed him."

Isabail's heart skipped a beat. "What?"

Daniel's face twisted. "It was an accident, of course. I did not mean for him to die. I brewed a potent poison, to which he was exposed. The moment I realized what had happened, I wished with all my heart that I could take his place. But it was too late. By the time I found him, the poison was already making him delirious."

"Nay," denied Isabail, clutching her chest. In all her wildest imaginings, she would never have believed Daniel would kill her brother. "It's not possible."

"I'm afraid it is," he said coldly. "So, you see, your belief in me is unfounded. Open the door to the tomb, or I will kill this boy as surely as I killed our dear, sweet John."

Isabail swallowed the bitter lump in her throat. *Daniel* had killed her brother. Not Ana Bisset. Not Aiden MacCurran. Daniel. The man she believed had entered the MacCurran camp to rescue her was a charlatan, a liar, and a murderer.

"Open the tomb, Isabail."

With eyes blurred by a sudden onset of tears, she saw him draw Jamie against his chest, the arm about the boy's neck tightening like a drawstring—squeezing, choking. Jamie's face reddened, and he began to flail, kicking Daniel's leg and clawing at his arm. But Daniel did not waver.

His eyes met Isabail's as he slowly but surely strangled the boy before her eyes.

"Cease," she cried. "I will show you."

"Hurry, Isabail. The boy doesn't have much time."

She dashed to the twin barrels and squeezed between them. Then she scrambled up the flour sacks. "The door opens with a winch. It will take me time to wind it. Please let him breathe."

As she reached the top of the sacks, she heard Jamie gasp for breath. Fearing that Daniel would permit him only one, she dropped to the winch below and began to turn the crank. Six turns of the crank and the winch locked into place, just as it had done before. And just as she had recalled, the clink of the lock was followed by a harsh grind of rock on rock.

Isabail climbed over the flour sacks. Jamie was breathing in short, raspy draws.

"Show me," Daniel demanded.

She led the way to the flat wall at the end of the tunnel. Daniel stared at the symbols engraved on the slab for a few moments, then waved the dirk again. "Open it."

Remembering the entirety of her ordeal in stark clarity, she placed both palms over the boar and pushed with all her might. The big granite slab pivoted, opening into the tomb chamber.

"There," she said. "You can search the tomb yourself. Nothing but the withered bones of an old corpse inside."

Daniel sheathed his dirk and snatched a torch from the wall sconce near the entrance to the tomb. "I haven't forgotten your tale, Isabail. You lost your way inside and were trapped for hours." He released Jamie, handed him the torch, and shoved him toward the opening. "Search diligently and bring back everything you find that looks valuable. Go."

Jamie stumbled forward, one hand on the wall and the other on his throat. His legs were obviously weak.

"Stop!"

Isabail halted Jamie before he could step on the tile that would close the door and seal him inside. "I'll go with him."

"Only one of you goes," Daniel said, grabbing Isabail's arm. "Tell him what he needs to know to succeed. And if you're wise, you'll not give him incorrect instructions. The longer we wait for him to return, the shorter my temper will get." He pinched her arm until she whimpered. "And believe me, you will not enjoy my company if it comes to that."

Isabail shared a look with Jamie. "Leap over the tiles in the floor near the door. The tomb is around a bend in the tunnel ten paces ahead."

Jamie nodded, then advanced into the tunnel.

"Pray he does not betray us," Daniel said, pulling her toward him. "I would hate to have to kill you."

Isabail had been this close to Daniel many times over the years, often while engaged in some sort of playful banter that included her brother. But this time a shiver of fear ran through her. The icy tone of his voice left her in no doubt: He would fulfill his promise to kill her if Jamie did not return.

It was difficult to imagine John's death at Daniel's hands. She'd only ever witnessed amusing or tender moments between the two. Had her brother known the identity of his murderer? She prayed not. It would have made his last moments unbearable. John had trusted Daniel like no other. He had forsaken a wife in favor of continuing to share his life with Daniel, even though it meant the earldom would pass to a different branch of the family upon his death—and that was no small commitment for John to make.

"How could you betray him that way?" she asked honestly.

Daniel's grip on her arm tightened. "Do you not think I have berated myself time and time again for my mistake? Believe me, I have. I even contemplated throwing myself upon his sword simply to make amends."

Torchlight flickered in the cavern of the tomb. Jamie was returning.

"But my death would not have brought John back," he said grimly. "And so I dedicated myself to a greater purpose."

"Accusing MacCurran of your crime?"

He snorted. "MacCurran deserves what has come to him. He and his kin are the cause of many a grievance."

Jamie appeared at the mouth of the narrow tunnel, his arms clasping the sword and the crown to his chest. He struggled to hold the torch aloft as he walked, but he remembered to avoid the tiles on the tunnel floor as he exited.

"What have you got there, lad?" Daniel asked, releasing Isabail. He stepped forward to grab the silver crown. He grinned as he spied the large sapphire set in the band. "Nothing but a few moldering bones, eh, Isabail? And here I thought lying was beneath you."

Then he spied a velvet bag in Jamie's hands, and he snatched it from the boy's fingers. Tugging on the drawstring, he peered inside. "A gold necklace set with a magnificent heart-shaped ruby. Do you know the value of this find, lad?"

Jamie shook his head.

"Such a necklace can change the course of history. It has the power to right a great wrong, and I intend to see that power enacted. With a little help from a friend in Edinburgh." Daniel stuffed the velvet bag in the front of his lèine. "Time to make our escape, I believe."

"MacCurran will come after us," Isabail warned, hoping that her words were true.

Daniel studied her in the torchlight. "He does seem to have developed a genuine affection for you, Isabail. But perhaps I can use that to my advantage. Slow his pursuit, just a little."

"Coward." She glared at him.

He took the sword from Jamie's hands, held it up to the torchlight, and then drew the blade from its beautiful silver sheath. "And murderer. While you're tossing insults, my dear, don't forget that one."

Then, without further warning or any hint of regret, Daniel ran her through.

All Isabail knew was blinding pain in her gut and a buzzing in her ears, and then everything went black.

Cormac was an excellent tracker. When they had searched a wide strip of land around the hilltop fort and the bowman found no evidence of a trail, Aiden called a halt.

"You're saying that they're still inside the fort?"

"There's no sign that they headed into the woods, laird."

Aiden nodded. It made him happier to know that Isabail had not left the confines of the camp. He urged his stallion into a canter and rode up the winding path to the outer wall. Any pleasure he felt vanished as soon as he saw Niall at the entrance. His brother's face was gray with worry, and there was a dark stain of blood on the front of his lèine.

"What is it?" he demanded, leaping off his mount.

"Isabail," Niall said quietly. "We found her in the tunnels."

Aiden's heart stopped cold, and for the briefest of moments, he couldn't catch his breath. It was a worrisomely large stain. "Where is she?"

"With Ana."

He headed for Niall's hut.

"Aiden," Niall said, his voice grim. "The sword and crown are gone."

His lips tightened. "Have you found de Lourdes?"

"No. We found one of the lads unconscious with a bump on his head. He was watching the horses."

A dull pain flashed behind Aiden's eyes. "Cormac said there was no evidence of a trail in the woods. Where in bloody hell did the bastard go?"

"Mayhap Isabail knows."

"He hurt her," Aiden said. "Why would she know anything?"

"She let him into the tomb, Aiden. There's no other way for him to have made off with the crown." Niall's lips twisted. "He took the necklace, too, of course."

The dull pain sharpened. Niall was right. The likelihood that Isabail had shared her knowledge of the treasure with Daniel was high. The man had been injured only a few days before. It was not likely he'd spent the hours combing the tunnels that Isabail had. And the two were exceptionally friendly. Maybe even lovers.

Aiden stiffened. Lord, that made a painful amount of sense. She'd helped Daniel steal the treasure only to be betrayed herself by a false lover.

He strode to Niall's hut and entered.

Ana met him just inside the door.

"How does she fare?" Aiden asked, the muscles in his throat so tight the words came out hoarse.

"I have healed the wound," Ana said. "But the blood loss was great. Despite all my efforts, her body is weakening."

He peered over her shoulder. Isabail lay on a straw pallet, her face deathly pale. Her blue gown was rent midway down her torso, and the soft wool was soaked with blood. *Will she die?* The question was on the tip of his tongue, but he couldn't bring himself to speak it. He feared the answer wouldn't be to his liking.

"She's awake," Ana said, stepping aside to let him pass. "I've asked her to rest, but she wishes to speak with you."

As Aiden approached the bed, Isabail opened her bright blue eyes. They were the only color in her face. Even her lips were white as snow.

"It was Daniel," she said softly.

"I know."

"He took everything."

That, too, he knew. "Where has he gone, Isabail? How did he escape?"

"The marsh. His plan was to guide the horses

down the burn to the marsh." Her eyes drifted closed, whether from weariness or a relived memory, he didn't know. Nor did he dwell on which it was. It was a vicious blow to hear her speak of their plans to escape. Still, he knew Isabail had expended precious energy to tell him what she did.

"Rest now, lass. I will find him." He turned to leave.

"He has Jamie."

Aiden spun around. "What?"

"He has the lad."

Aiden swallowed tightly. Of course. Jamie would have been able to gather the horses without alarming the guards. But, by God, why did it have to be *him*? Jamie had already been through so much.

He sank on his haunches at her side and picked up her hand—the slim hand that felt so perfect clasped in his. "I must go now, Isabail. I must hunt down de Lourdes and punish him for what he's done. But while I'm gone, you must remain strong. I'll not have you die. Understand?"

Isabail smiled faintly. "Even the healer will tell you that God is the only one who can decide who lives and who dies. I bow to His will."

"No," Aiden said firmly, staring deep into her eyes. "I'm the chief. You bow to *my* will. Be here when I return, or I'll shake the life back into you. I swear."

She nodded. "As you wish."

Unable to voice a goodbye for fear that it would be the last word he said to her, he stood abruptly and walked to the door. He grabbed Ana's arm.

"Do everything you can to save her," he said, and then he left the hut.

"Mount up," he called to the Black Warriors. "We ride for the marsh."

The marsh was a perilous tract of land that cradled a bend in the burn near the northern edge of the forest. In most places, the mud was simply a thick ooze that sucked at the horses' hooves. But in others, the mud was a deep bog that could swallow a man whole. They picked their way carefully through the marsh for hours, searching for any sign that Daniel and Jamie had passed that way. Twice they spied hoofprints in the mud . . . only to lose the trail when the water deepened.

Aiden split up his men to cover more ground. He sent Cormac to the east and Hamish to the west, while he continued to ride north. He combed the marsh through and through, mowing down sheaves of dried reeds as he went, but he failed to find the wretched cur. When Cormac and the others rejoined him, they reported similar failures.

The late-January sunset was one of the prettiest Aiden had ever seen, but he could not summon a single ounce of pleasure over the glorious splashes of orange and purple that colored the sky. Jamie was out there with a man ruthless enough to run his accomplice through and leave her for dead. All Aiden could do was pray the lad proved useful enough to be kept alive.

He returned to the hill fort with a knotted gut

and a fiery determination to track down his nephew simmering in his veins.

A candle was still burning in Niall's hut when Aiden entered the close. He prayed that meant what he thought it meant—that Isabail yet lived. Niall was standing outside the door, and as Aiden approached, he stepped into his path.

"Did you recover the treasure?"

"Nay."

Niall gave him a level stare. "Ana has expended extraordinary effort to keep this woman alive. To what end?"

Aiden settled back on his heels. Isabail had lain close to death for hours, and it pained him to know she'd fought that battle without him at her side. Right or wrong, he'd come to care for her.

He released a heavy sigh. "She made an error in judgment aligning herself with de Lourdes, but no one deserves to be run through. Least of all a woman."

"She betrayed us."

Although his brother's accusation echoed the ache in Aiden's gut, he shook his head. "Reserve judgment. We've not yet heard the tale from her lips."

"She led him to the tomb."

A difficult statement to refute. "Whatever the facts, her fate is mine to decide, not yours."

Niall studied him for a long moment, then stepped aside.

Aiden entered the roundhouse.

His eyes took a moment to adjust to the light.

Ana was crouched over the pallet, spooning broth into Isabail's mouth. Both women looked up as he crossed the wooden floor.

"Did you find them?" Isabail asked.

"Nay." He gave Ana a pointed stare, demanding that she give them some privacy.

With a reluctant frown, Ana put the bowl aside and vacated her spot next to Isabail.

Aiden hooked a three-legged stool with his boot and drew it over to the bed. He sat, but avoided meeting Isabail's eyes. He had trouble looking at her face and seeing anything other than his sweetly beguiling lover. "Daniel successfully eluded us in the marsh," he said. "We were unable to catch him or recover his trail on the other side."

"Poor Jamie. He must be so frightened."

"Indeed." Her sympathy for the boy shook his resolve, but gaining the truth was paramount. He pressed on. "Are they headed for Lochurkie, Isabail?"

She frowned. "I don't know."

"Aye, you do. You know him better than anyone. Where will he go now that he has the necklace?"

Her lips twisted. "Apparently, I did not know him as well as I thought I did."

The acknowledgment of their closeness stabbed him deeply. "He betrayed you," he said with a sharp nod. "But your knowledge of him still exceeds that of anyone else. In all your conversations, did he ever give a clue where he might go?"

She closed her eyes, and for a moment Aiden

believed that there would be no answer, but she finally said, "Not Lochurkie. There's nothing for him there but bitter memories."

"Then where?"

"I suppose he might return to the Continent," she said, doubt tugging at her words. "But he is a third son, and my understanding is that there was some sort of trouble and he is no longer welcome in Bigorre."

Aiden waited, but impatience clawed at him. He was a man of action, not a man of softly spoken words. He needed answers.

Her eyes popped open. "There is *one* place where he might go. . . ."

"Name it," he demanded.

"My dower estate, Tayteath. It lies on the eastern coast, six leagues south of Arbroath."

"Quite a distance," he said. "Why would he go so far?"

"He and my brother spent a month there every spring," she explained. "He knows the castle well, and my retainers know him. He could settle there for some time without suspicion. If not there, then I have no idea where he would go."

Aiden sat back. If they pushed hard, they could make the coast in two days. But if de Lourdes wasn't there, it would be a wasted two days. "What does he intend to do with the treasure?"

Isabail licked her very dry lips. "He told me it would enable him to right a grave injustice. He suggested he had a contact in the king's court who could help."

He handed her a cup of ale and watched her wet her parched mouth. A mouth he had kissed numerous times—and still desired to kiss again. Her frailty only enhanced her delicate beauty. "So he planned to meet with someone from Edinburgh?"

"So he said." She grimaced. "But everything he originally told me was a lie. Before he ran me through, he confessed that he was the one who killed my brother."

A pang of sympathy shot through Aiden. He well understood how Isabail must have felt receiving that news. The stab of betrayal reaches deep. "At that point he had no reason to lie," he said. "His true nature had been revealed. Tayteath is an easy day's ride from Edinburgh, and a coastal castle would make a suitable place for a clandestine meeting."

He stood. Even if de Lourdes had been spouting lies, the choices were limited. There were no other clues to follow. He turned to leave.

"Is that all you've come for?" Isabail asked. "Information? Not a word of sympathy or good wishes for a swift recovery?"

Aiden halted, but he did not turn to face her. Knowing the truth about what she'd done did not make it any easier to distance himself. He still wanted her desperately, craved to draw her into his arms, bury his face in her bosom, and forgive her. But he was the chief. It was his responsibility to mete out justice. No matter how much it cost him. "Why would I offer well wishes to de Lourdes's accomplice?"

She gasped. "You think I helped him willingly?"

He spun. "He never left his hut until today. The only person he saw, other than Muirne, was you. You have a long-established relationship with the man. Of course you helped him willingly."

"Nay," she cried. "You accuse me falsely. I aided Daniel only because he threatened to kill Jamie if I did not."

"Do you deny that you and de Lourdes are lovers?"

Isabail's eyes darkened, and her mouth twisted in a poor mimicry of a smile. "I do. Even had I suffered a tenderness for him, it would have remained unrequited. I am not what Daniel finds attractive. He and my brother were lovers."

The ache in Aiden's heart eased. She did not love de Lourdes, nor he her. "You still aided him. He could not have known about the tunnels or the location of the tomb had you not told him."

"Label me a fool, if you must, but not a traitor. He was my brother's companion for more than five years. I trusted him. Did I tell Daniel about the tunnels? Aye, I did. But only in passing, as I explained where the stores were kept and shared the tale of my misadventure. I never told him of the crown."

"So you say."

Isabail broke eye contact, and she stared at the glowing coals in the brazier. "It appears you have little respect for me."

"Actually, I have the deepest respect for you,"

he said quietly. "I believe every word you've told me this eve, because you've never given me cause not to. In spite of everything that has happened to you in the past sennight, you've remained forthright in your comments, helpful in your suggestions, and unwavering in your opinions. You've shown genuine affection for your maid, your dog, and even your brother's traitorous lover. If I did not wear the mantle of chief, I would be begging your forgiveness for doubting you, even for a moment."

She stared at him, mouth agape.

"But I am the chief," he said. "And a chief must do everything in his power to protect his clan, even if it means hurting those he cares for. As such, I must withdraw my promise to return you home. Names or no names, you know too much."

"What are you saying? That I'll forever be a prisoner here?"

He shook his head. "Not a prisoner."

"What then?"

"Wife. *My* wife." The words felt good on his tongue, even though he suspected they didn't sound quite so appealing to Isabail. There wasn't much about being wed to an outlaw laird that prompted a smile.

"Wife?"

"Aye," he said. "When I return, we'll say the proper words before a priest."

"And if I choose not to say those words?" Her expression was suspiciously calm.

"Do not be hasty," he urged. "Think on it."

"I will have a hand in choosing my husband," she said slowly. "Whether it suits you or not. Simply being a wife is not enough for me. My mother was a wife, and that did not save her from my father's fists. She ended her life at the bottom of the castle steps, a blossoming bruise upon her cheek."

Aiden's gaze dropped to his large hands. Ah, that explained so much. How brave his lass had been to face his wrath under such circumstances. "I've told you before, I'm not a man who beats women. I will never hurt you, Isabail. You have my word on that."

She smiled faintly. "I know."

"Then why caution me with a tale of your father?"

"Because I want more than a simple vow before a priest. I married once for practical gain, but I am a woman of means now. If I wed again, it will be for love."

He smiled. "We'll speak again on my return."

Then, to avoid the argument he could see building in her eyes, he turned on his heel and left.

Chapter 13

Isabail lay back on the blankets and stared up at the thatching. Had MacCurran truly just offered to wed her? Without a single mention of love or devotion? Was he mad? Offers of marriage were supposed to be delivered on bended knee and accompanied by some sweet-smelling bouquet. Not delivered in the form of a threat.

"Did he truly say I could never leave?"

"He's not thinking straight at the moment," Ana said. "He'll come to his senses in time."

Isabail turned her head to look at the other woman. A woman she had falsely accused of killing her brother and condemned to die in a pit. The very same woman who had just healed a near-fatal wound in Isabail's gut.

"How can you be so forgiving?" she asked.

Ana wielded her pestle with mastery, crushing handfuls of dried leaves in a small wooden bowl. "I've been on the wrong side of a judgment or two," she said ruefully.

"I accused you of a crime you did not commit. Why would you agree to heal me?"

Ana paused to wipe sweat from her brow with her sleeve. "There is no room for intolerance in healing. I simply do what I am called upon to do. I can no sooner turn from a wounded person than I can cease to breathe. Whether the patient lives or dies is a decision to be made by God, not by me." She smiled. "I am not worthy of such power."

Isabail blushed and looked away. During the trial, she had called Ana Bisset a godless demon. Now she was writhing in shame.

"Do not feel any blame, Lady Isabail," Ana said. "You, like many others, fell victim to the twisted mind of Friar Colban."

Isabail shook her head. "Surely you must feel some anger toward me. No one can be as understanding as you profess to be."

The other woman chuckled. "Aye, I felt anger. And aye, I cursed your name when I was wasting away in that pit. But before John's death, before I was accused of poisoning him, you were kind to me. When I tended to the talon strike on your arm the day you got your merlin, you blessed me and pressed a gold coin into my hand. First one I'd ever seen."

Isabail smiled. "Aye, well, I was rather certain I was going to lose the arm. When you told me it would heal within a fortnight, I was overjoyed."

All that seemed so long ago. It was as if it had happened to another person. Isabail felt no connection to the young widow who'd lived for nothing more than to hunt at her brother's side. So much had happened in the last year, not much of it pleasant. John's death, the trial, the arrival of Cousin Archibald to take up the reins of the earldom.

Before that she'd been happy. As happy as any woman can be who had lost her husband prematurely and been left without children.

"Did Daniel truly threaten to slay Jamie?" Ana asked, her expression frank and serious.

Isabail nodded. "Choked him to near death right before me. He would have killed him if I hadn't opened the tomb."

"He's a good lad," said Ana. "And he's already been through much."

Meeting her gaze, Isabail swallowed heavily. "I fear for him. I truly do. Daniel will not hesitate to end his life if he feels the need."

"Niall and the laird are going after him," Ana assured her. "They will see to his safety."

An image of MacCurran approaching the gate at Tayteath sprang into Isabail's mind. She pushed herself weakly into a sitting position. "Tayteath has never fallen to a siege."

"They will find a way."

Isabail groaned in frustration. "If I could accompany them, they could enter the castle freely. My soldiers will open the gates to me."

"You are not well enough to travel," Ana pointed out, setting her pestle on the table. "And I do not believe the MacCurran would want you in his party."

Isabail put a hand on the bandages wrapped

about her waist. She felt surprisingly well, considering the grievous wound she sported. Only a wee bit weary. "Please," she begged. "Ask the laird if I can accompany them. It would save many lives on both sides if the castle can be entered peacefully."

Ana looked dubious.

"Please. I will never forgive myself if I don't make the attempt."

Heaving a heavy sigh, the healer nodded and ducked under the fur panel over the door.

Isabail downed the rest of her cup of ale, then set it aside. She was feeling stronger by the minute. Whipping aside the blanket, she swung her feet to the floor. The MacCurran would never agree to take her along if she could not stand on her own feet.

Gathering her resolve with a deep, indrawn breath, she shoved against the straw mattress and thrust herself upright. All might have gone well had a wave of dizziness not washed over her at that moment. She teetered to one side, reached for the wall, and missed. Crashing to the wooden floor, she narrowly missed landing on the brazier.

"You foolish lass," growled the MacCurran as he strode across the room and scooped her into his arms. The comforting warmth of his chest competed with the throbbing pain in her hip from the fall. "You lay near death only a few moments ago. You should yet be abed."

Isabail gave in to her desire and pressed her cheek against his chest. "You cannot go without me. Tayteath is unbreachable."

"No castle is unbreachable," he said gruffly.

"If I accompany you, it will not be necessary to try."

To her regret, he lowered her to the mattress and stepped back. "You cannot come. Speed is of the essence, and you will only slow us down."

She pushed to her elbows. "What good is speed if you can't get past the castle gate?"

He crossed his arms over his chest, the muscles of his forearms rippling in the firelight. "If de Lourdes is not there, the sooner we know that, the sooner we can consider other possibilities. And it's vital that Jamie know we have come for him. That knowledge might be all that keeps him alive."

Two excellent arguments.

"But if Daniel is there," she countered, "he will lock down the gates and hold you off. He might even threaten Jamie's life as a means to repel you."

"I have no intention of simply marching up to the gate and announcing my presence." He favored her with a steely stare. "No matter what arguments you use, I will not agree to take you with us."

She studied his face. "If we were already wed, would you take me along?"

"Nay."

"Fine, then," she said with a pout. "Leave without me."

He continued to stare at her with his fierce blue gaze. Then he sank to a crouch beside the mattress and cupped her chin.

"Take care, lass."

Whether he intended it as a warning or as a

wish for her safety, she did not know. Nor did she get the opportunity to ask. In a blink he was gone, leaving Isabail staring at the fur panel flapping in the wind.

Aiden accepted a bundle of dried meat and cheese from Beathag and packed it in the pouch slung over the rump of his horse. They would not be stopping for food, only to sleep. That meant they would eat in the saddle, and any supplies had to be easily consumed.

"Did she tell you anything about the castle defenses?" asked Niall as he strapped his bow to his back.

"Save to say it was impregnable, nay."

Niall snorted. "Grand."

Aiden put his foot in the stirrup and hoisted himself into the saddle. He was taking a small party—his best twelve men. "It's a sea-bound fortress, so unless you can swim, there's only one way in."

"Through the front gate."

"Aye."

Niall swung into the saddle. "Bonnie bloody hell. Have I mentioned how much I enjoy our little excursions, brother? Truly, without you, my life would be dull."

Aiden snorted and turned his mount toward the path. " 'Twasn't I who insisted you break into Duthes Castle, enrage a mad friar, and rescue a maiden from a burning pyre. I think you find enough trouble without my help, bratling."

He urged his massive bay warhorse into a canter and led the way down the hill and out of the glen. The one advantage to leaving in the middle of the night—they were unlikely to meet up with one of MacPherson's patrols.

"Ha!" crowed Isabail as she reached the door. "I told you I was feeling stronger. You truly are a miracle worker, Ana."

The redhead rolled to her side of the mattress and pulled the blankets up around her ears. "You should be sleeping," she grumbled. "Not wearing a groove in the floor."

"We cannot stay here and allow needless deaths to occur. I would have thought a healer would be more concerned about the loss of life and limb."

"You are a madwoman," tossed Ana from beneath the covers. "We are but two lasses. We cannot cross the length of Scotia on our own. No matter how great the benefit."

"Why not?" demanded Isabail, walking slowly but successfully over to the bed. "I can wield a bow, and I've seen you fillet a fish with that knife. We are not so helpless as men would have us believe."

"I will not do it," Ana said, sitting up. "I've been alone on the road, and I assure you it wasn't pleasant. There are dangers you cannot imagine. Don't be a fool, Isabail. Give up this ridiculous notion."

Isabail plopped down on the stool. "I cannot."

The healer sighed. "Why not?"

"It is my fault that the crown was stolen. And my fault that Daniel took Jamie hostage. If I had but held my tongue instead of sharing all that I did with the traitorous cur, he would still be lying in the hut under guard, and the crown would be safe."

"Nay." Ana braided her hair and tied a leather thong around the end. "Daniel came here with the intent to steal the necklace. One way or another, he would have found a way—or died trying. You are not to blame for his scurrilous acts."

"Even his presence here was my fault," Isabail said with a shake of her head. "He followed me."

"Nonsense." Ana tugged a gown over her shift. "He followed MacCurran."

Everything Ana said rang true, but her words did not ease the dread in Isabail's belly. She knew she held the key to breaching the walls of Tay-teath, and if she did nothing to help, good men would die. Jamie might die.

Isabail surged to her feet. "If you will not come with me, then I must go alone."

Ana grabbed her arm. "Nay, Isabail. If you insist on going, let us try to convince some of the Black Warriors to come with us."

A notion Isabail had already considered and dismissed. "I'm a prisoner, remember? He has surely instructed them to keep me here, and they will never disobey their laird. Believe me, I attempted to sway their loyalty once before—to no avail. Nay. I must go alone and I must go now."

A resigned look crept over Ana's face. "I cannot let you go alone. I will come with you."

Relieved beyond measure, Isabail clasped Ana's hand. "Thank you. You will not regret this."

Ana snorted. "I already regret this."

Isabail smiled and helped the healer pack her satchel. She lifted a few earthenware jugs and studied them. "Can any of these put a guard to sleep?"

After the guards at the entrance consumed their ale and drifted off to sleep, Isabail led the horses quietly to the entrance and joined Ana. To lessen the noise as they descended the rocky slope, she had wrapped linen strips around their hooves. The strips would soon come loose, but so long as they made it to the forest without alerting the other guards, she would be happy.

Isabail was about to drag herself into the saddle when Gorm appeared at her side. The huge gray dog nuzzled her skirts and then *woof*ed softly.

"Hush," she said in a sharp whisper. She glanced around to see if the noise had attracted any attention, but nothing moved in the darkness. "Go back," she ordered the dog, pointing up the rocky slope.

Gorm just stared at her and gave a slow wag of his tail.

"Why not bring him with us?" Ana asked.

"He's still weak from his injuries."

"If he's half as stubborn as you, that won't slow him down," the healer said dryly.

"I feel fine."

"Of course you do. And even if you didn't, you would never admit it. Bring the dog."

Isabail shrugged. "I suppose he might provide a bit of extra protection. He can be quite alarming when he growls." She mounted, feeling the strain in her gut but refusing to acknowledge it. "Let's be off."

.

Magnus awoke with a start, rolling from his pallet and instinctively grabbing for the sword lying next to him on the floor. But there was no sword. Because he was no longer a warrior. He stood, silent and still, wondering what had roused him.

Morag slept on the other side of the bed, her dreams as yet undisturbed.

Then he heard it, the soft jingle of horses' bridles coming from the yard outside the bothy. Morag did not own a horse, so the sound sent a tingle of awareness down his spine.

He reached down and gently prodded Morag. "Someone is outside," he whispered.

She sat up abruptly, her eyes wide.

Magnus snatched up a dirk from the tabletop. There were no windows in the bothy, so he slipped to the door and, ever so carefully, cracked it open. His view was limited. All he could see was a riderless horse standing in the yard. Dawn was still an hour away, and the darkness was deep and heavy.

Morag pushed him out of the way and opened the door wide. "Who goes there?" she demanded.

A blond woman stepped around the flank of the horse. Slight of body and holding a hand to her side, she did not pose much of a threat. "Our sincere pardons, mistress. We did not mean to wake you. We simply hoped to partake of your water and then be on our way."

"We? Who do you travel with?" Morag asked, looking about.

A second horse walked forward from the shadowed trees. Another woman, judging by the slender shape in the saddle. Two women traveling alone in the dark. If ever there was a call for trouble, this was it. Magnus shook his head.

"Why do you hold your side?" Morag demanded in her usual forthright manner. "Are you injured?"

The blond woman dropped her hand and stood a little straighter. "Just a wee bit sore. May we fill our oilskins in your rain barrel?"

"Just tell me who you are and what you are doing in these woods at this hour of the night," Morag said crisply. Although she wore only her shift and a woolen shawl, she stood tall and spoke with firm authority.

Magnus had a crazy desire to kiss her.

The two women exchanged a flurry of whispers, some of them harsh, and then the blond woman faced Morag.

"I am Isabail Macintosh, and this is my companion, Ana Bisset. We are on our way to Tayteath on the coast. A mission of some urgency, I might add, involving the rescue of a young lad."

Whatever Morag had expected them to say, it wasn't that. For the first time since he woke to her face, he saw her speechless. Magnus left the shadows and stepped around Morag and into the moonlight. "Are you from the castle?"

Isabail retreated a step. "Nay."

Her lack of explanation spoke volumes. Not aligned with the MacPhersons, it would seem. "Who is the lad of whom you speak, and why does he need rescuing?"

His question opened the floodgates. Isabail launched into a breathless tale of theft and murder and betrayal that lacked detail but not passion. On at least two occasions, she paused to wipe tears from her eyes and then doggedly returned to her story.

"So," he said when she finally fell silent, "some scurrilous rat has stolen a necklace, kidnapped a boy, and made off to Tayteath. You, believing yourself vital to this rat's surrender, have disobeyed your laird's orders and set off on your own to bring him to justice. Is that a fair assessment?"

She nodded.

Magnus wanted to laugh, but the lass looked so serious and woebegone he dared not. "In my opinion," he said gently, "it's best to leave such matters to your menfolk. Go home and await their return."

"Nay," Isabail said. "I cannot. May we partake of your water? We must continue on our way with all due haste."

Morag waved at the barrel. "By all means. I can also supply you with some dried hare and bannocks, if you've a need."

Isabail smiled gratefully. "That's most kind."

Magnus pulled Morag aside. "You should not encourage them. This venture is sheer madness. Two women alone cannot survive the trek to the coast. Brigands and thieves abound. They will surely meet a most unwelcome fate."

"They do not need to travel alone."

He stared at her. "What are you suggesting?"

"That you go with them."

To say he was surprised did not do his shock justice. Morag had repeatedly discouraged him from leaving her and the bothy. She had met his every plan with a strongly worded warning of how he would end up in the gallows. "Do you not fear what will become of me if I leave your side?"

She shrugged. "These women are not from the castle. They hold no grudge against you; nor does it seem that they have any reason to believe that you are more than a simple woodsman. Accompanying them seems like a rather safe way to test your memories."

"What memories can I test with strangers?"

Morag crooked a finger. "Come with me."

He followed her to the back of the hut, where she kept sheaves of dried grass for the goats. Curious, he watched her dig through the grass. When she found what she was searching for, she paused and then hauled out a four-foot-long bundle wrapped in burlap. Judging by her grunt, the item was heavy.

"Take it," she said softly. "It's yours."

He relieved her of her load, recognizing the weight the instant he accepted it. "A sword."

She nodded. "The men who left you for dead were in a terrible hurry. They did not stop to loot your body. The sword was still in your hand when I found you."

Magnus unwrapped the weapon and admired the craftsmanship of the blade. The steel was very hard—most likely from Toledo—and the blade was honed to a razor-sharp edge. But it was the bronze hilt wrapped with tan leather that truly made the sword. Intricately patterned with hundreds of tiny Celtic knots, it snared the moonlight so well that it appeared to glow.

"It's a bit too pretty for a man like you," Morag said, "but I suspect that your ability to wield it makes up for it."

"How do you know it belongs to me?" he asked. "Perhaps I stole it."

She snorted. "I've seen you practicing with the wooden blade you carved. Your body flows into each position like it was made to dance with a sword. You are a warrior; of that I have no doubt."

"You are risking two ladies' lives on an unfounded belief. Are you sure that's wise?"

Her eyes met his, her expression suddenly serious. "I've never told you this, but I saw the soldiers attack you that night. Eight of them, all wearing mail and helms, while you were attired only in a tunic. God has graced you with a true talent, Magnus. You struck half of them down before you were defeated."

Magnus resisted the urge to shuffle his feet. Praise did not sit easily upon his shoulders, and inwardly he scoffed at her description. And yet, as he grasped the hilt firmly in his palm, all sense of discomfort vanished. He raised the weapon high, and his muscles rose smoothly to the challenge, lifting the blade like it was simply an extension of his arm. He might not recognize the sword, but it seemed to know him.

But accepting the sword and accepting the mission to escort Isabail and her companion to Tayteath were not the same thing.

"This adventure might test my sword arm, but it will not test my memory," he said. "I do not see how going to Tayteath will give me what I need."

Morag's face was a mask of blandness.

As he stared at her, the truth sank in—she did not want him to recover his memory. Not if it meant that he would leave her side. With this mission to rescue a young lad, she was hoping to tame the restlessness in his soul. To calm him enough to stay.

He should be angry, but he wasn't.

If he were honest, he'd admit that he could have left many times over the last month. His memories were stubbornly eluding him, but his health had improved every day. He was held here by his fondness for Morag, not by anything else. But just as she made no direct plea for him to remain at her side, he was not ready to openly acknowledge his affections for her. They shared a bed each night, but had never shared a kiss.

He needed to be certain of who he was before he could stake a claim on Morag. And he might need to sort that out without the benefit of his memories. If his knowledge of the past never returned, he would have to carve out a new identity. One of his own making.

"I will go," he said finally.

She nodded.

"But," he said, laying the sword upon the woodpile. "I would have a boon from you before I leave."

"What boon?"

He cupped her face in his hands and tugged her close enough that he could count the freckles scattered across the bridge of her nose. Her eyes widened, but she did not pull away. Drawing in a breath, inhaling the same sweet fragrance that he fell asleep to each night, he lowered his lips to hers.

Kissing her was the culmination of many dreams. He had resisted the lure of her earthy, carefree loveliness for so long that the connection of their lips was like lighting a bonfire in his chest. A surge of heat and passion overwhelmed him, burning a fiery path from his lips to his groin. His hands tightened their hold on her, and he deepened the kiss.

She tasted so much sweeter than he had imagined. The urge to scoop her up and carry her into the bothy was fierce. Making mad, passionate love to her became a need he could barely resist. But resist he did. A kiss would have to do for now.

He slowly, reluctantly, withdrew.

Morag stared back at him with flushed cheeks and a smoky look in her green eyes.

"Do not do anything foolish while I am gone," he said.

She settled back on her heels, smiling faintly. "What would constitute foolish?"

He gathered the sword and strapped the leather baldric to his chest. "Trading your cloth at the castle, taunting the soldiers when they ride past on patrol, taking a bath in the loch, climbing the tall oak in the—"

She threw up her hands. "Och. You mean I'm to have no fun at all."

"I mean that I want you to be here, safe and sound, when I return," he countered firmly. He caught her chin, pressed another quick kiss to her lips, and then let her go. "And I will return. I promise."

Their eyes met and held for a long moment.

And then he left.

In the dark hour before dawn, even under a bright winter moon, it was easy to imagine the entire world was asleep. Aiden peered into the obscurity of the forest around their fire and listened to the snores of his men. They had pushed long and hard before stopping for the night. He would wake them as soon as the horizon began to glow with a new day.

Out of the corner of his eye, he saw something move, and he turned his head to look closer. A vague shape, low to the ground, gained detail as he stared. A head, a large body, and a tail. He stood straighter.

A large white wolf.

And where there was one wolf, there were generally others. He drew his sword. Making himself as large as possible, he advanced toward the wolf. Most wolves preyed upon the weak and the helpless. In the face of strength and purpose, they usually turned tail and ran. Not this one. The fur on its neck stood on end and a vicious snarl escaped its maw.

Aiden firmed his grip on his sword.

The wretched beast had picked a poor night to take his measure. He was angry, and it would suit him just fine to be wearing a new fur cloak come dawn.

A low growl rose up in the night. And then a second. Neither originated from the wolf in front of him—they came from the other side of the camp. The wily beasts had surrounded them.

Aiden stepped back. Without taking his eyes off the big white wolf, he kicked his brother's sleeping form. "Niall, wake up."

His brother threw off his blanket and surged to his feet, his sword in hand. "What is it?" he asked, his gaze darting about, his voice rough with sleep.

"Wolves. Several of them."

Niall bent and shook Cormac's shoulder. "Wolves," he said to the bowman's startled face.

In a moment, the entire camp was awake, each man staring into the woods with their weapons aloft. The big white wolf gave a deep snarl, then edged backward.

"That's a bloody big one," Cormac said, taking aim with his bow.

"Hold off," ordered Aiden.

"No wolf disturbs my sleep and lives," Cormac said, drawing hard on the bowstring.

"I said hold." Aiden loaded the words with chilly authority. He did not enjoy repeating himself. When he gave an order, he expected it to be obeyed. Without question.

Cormac lowered his bow and his gaze. "Aye, laird."

The white wolf stood up, shook its head, then turned and loped off into the woods. Judging by the sudden lack of snarls and growls, the rest of the pack followed its lead. Aiden was about to comment on the strangeness of the encounter when he caught another movement in the shadows, this one much taller and shaped like a man.

He kept his weapon at the ready.

As the stranger neared the fire and his facial features became visible, the tension drained from Aiden's body and he sheathed his sword. "Bhaltair."

A white-haired man garbed in an ankle-length lèine and a dark wool cloak strode into the camp. He carried a tall staff and sported a belly-grazing white beard. His face was heavily wrinkled, but he looked no older than when Aiden had last seen him. Some three or four years ago.

"What brings you here?" he asked the old man.

Niall added, "We thought you were long gone to the Maker."

Bhaltair extended gnarled fingers toward the flames of the fire. "I go where I must."

Aiden sighed. The old man was fond of speaking in riddles, no doubt due to his exalted age. He claimed to be a druid, one of the ancient holy men that once roamed the north quite freely, but Aiden had never witnessed him perform any of the so-called miracles that were attributed to such men. "Quite a coincidence, meeting you here."

"Not a coincidence at all," the old man said. "Do you have any tea?"

"Nay," said Aiden, a little annoyed. "Are you suggesting you planned to meet us here?"

"Of course not," Bhaltair said. "What about ale? I haven't had ale in quite some time."

Niall offered the druid his oilskin.

"Thank ye," he said after he'd quenched his thirst. He appropriated some blankets and sat down before the fire. "I'm relieved to find you precisely where I thought you'd be. My legs are weary."

Niall exchanged a look with Aiden. They'd told no one where they'd planned to camp for the night. Indeed, they'd chosen this spot only upon reaching it.

"How did you find us?" Aiden asked.

"The same way I find all things that I have misplaced," he responded. "By reading the stars."

Aiden glanced at the night sky. It was clear, and a thousand stars competed with the brilliance of the moon, but none of them pointed anywhere. Yet the man had found Aiden's party . . . assuming he'd actually been looking for them.

"Why have you sought us out?"

Bhaltair poured more ale into his mouth. After he swallowed, he said, "There have been signs of trouble brewing. If I read them correctly, dire events are about to transpire."

Dire events had already transpired. But what harm could there be in querying the man further? "What sort of signs?"

Bhaltair threaded his fingers through the thickly curling hairs of his beard. "I spied a two-headed squirrel the day before yesterday, and this morn a wee bird dropped from a tree branch to my feet, stone cold before it hit the ground."

"It's winter," Aiden pointed out dryly. "It's not unknown for birds to succumb to the harsh clime."

"Indeed," said the old man. "A bird that dies out of sight is just that—a dead bird. But a bird that dies at my feet is an augury."

Unconvinced, Aiden asked, "And what does it foretell?"

"A death, of course."

"Whose death?"

"That I cannot say."

"Then your omen is pointless," Aiden said. Turning to the other warriors, he said, "Pack up. Since sleep has eluded us, we'll continue on our way."

The men began to collect their belongings.

"I fear I cannot bring you with us, Bhaltair," he told the old druid. "We travel light, on a mission of grave importance."

Bhaltair nodded. "To rescue the lad and recover the crown."

Aiden blinked. A bloody accurate *guess*.

The old man got to his feet, grabbing the wool underfoot as he stood. He folded the blanket and handed it to one of the men.

"Do you need a weapon?" he asked the druid. "If that pack of wolves returns, you might find yourself in need of one."

"I have nothing to fear from wolves," Bhaltair said. "I have my staff."

"Take this dirk," Aiden offered, handing him the knife at his belt. "These wolves are more ferocious than most I've seen."

The old man opened his cloak and pointed to the sickle strung at his waist. "If need be, I'll use my own blade. Keep yours."

"As you wish." Aiden replaced the knife. "If you like, you can remain in this meadow, and we'll collect you on our return trip."

"No need," said Bhaltair. "But there is one further detail of the omen that you should heed."

Plucking his saddle from the ground, Aiden carried it to his horse. "Oh?"

"The wee bird was crested."

Aiden cinched the saddle tight, struggling to find the relevance in the old man's words—and failing. "And what, if anything, am I to make of that?"

"It's an obvious reference to the crown."

Obvious was clearly in the eye of the beholder. "So the omen suggests the crown might be permanently lost?" he asked, turning to face the old man.

Bhaltair scratched his head, his brow furrowed in thought. "Perhaps."

Yet another ill-defined and uncertain response. How was he to act on such insubstantial advice? And more to the point, why was he even considering the advice of a madman? He sighed. Because said madman had befriended his father, shown him the secrets of the hill fort caves, and tasked him with preserving a legend.

"I'll keep your words in mind," he said, hoisting himself into the saddle. He nodded respectfully to the old druid, then urged his horse into a trot.

The Black Warriors followed.

Chapter 14

Isabail studied the long brown hair and the broad back of the man riding in front of her.

She'd given up her mount and now shared a horse with Ana. For good reason—their hired warrior, Magnus, was a large fellow with a very large weapon. He clearly needed a horse to himself. Not quite as tall as MacCurran, but blessed with a similar robust build, the man sat his mount with the comfortable stance of a man who'd spent many a long hour in the saddle. Which was curious. How did a peasant living alone in the woods learn to ride? Or wield a weapon—other than a pole—for that matter?

"How did you learn your craft?" she asked him, as she ducked beneath a low-hanging branch.

"Of which craft do you speak?"

"Swordsmanship." The bronze hilt of his weapon was quite impressive, certainly not the sort a common soldier would own. "Were you a soldier before you injured your leg?"

"Aye."

Isabail waited for more, but nothing was forthcoming. "At the castle?"

"Does it matter where?" he countered, slowing his horse to allow her to come alongside. "Even if my talents are limited, a weak sword arm is better than no sword arm."

"True enough," she acknowledged. "And lest I imply otherwise, we do appreciate your willingness to aid us. But it would be remiss of me not to gain some sense of how loyal you'll be in the thick of trouble." Then she added hastily, "Not that we anticipate such trouble."

"Of course not." He shrugged. "We struck a bargain. Two deniers for a fortnight of service. I'm a man of my word, so you need not fear I'll desert you. I'm yours to command."

"How long will it take us to reach Tayteath?"

"At this pace? Three days."

Isabail frowned. "That simply won't do. A lad's life is in danger."

"Alone, I could make the journey in less than two," he pointed out. "But with women in the party, there's no hope of traveling that swiftly."

"Is there no way to make better time?"

He shook his head. "I cannot demand the same of you as I would a man."

Isabail considered that. Normally, she would agree. But the image of Jamie's face as she'd last seen it in the tunnel—pale and frightened and trying to be brave—refused to be banished from her thoughts. "We are not men," she agreed, exchanging a glance with Ana, "but we are willing to keep the pace you set for as long as we are able."

Magnus studied them for a long moment. He looked as if he was biting his tongue, but no scathing comment leaked out. Instead, he sat back in his saddle and nodded. "The best gait for an extended push is the trot. The horses can maintain a good speed without tiring excessively. But the trot is hard on a rider, especially without stirrups. If you grow weary, you must let me know immediately. It would be most unfortunate if you took a tumble."

"Agreed."

He raked a gaze over the two women. "Ensure your cloaks are securely fastened and that your hold on each other and the reins is firm."

They did as he bid.

Ana's hands shook a little as she grasped Isabail about the middle. "I'm not a skilled rider," the healer whispered.

"You're strong," Isabail reassured her. "Just hold tight. We'll take turns in the saddle, and if you ever lose your grip, pinch me and I'll stop."

"Are you ready?" Magnus asked.

Isabail patted Ana's hand, then threaded the reins through both hands and nodded. "Aye."

Without another word, he urged his horse into a trot and took off through the woods. Isabail sucked in a deep breath and kneed her horse into motion. She could only pray that she had not just made one of the worst decisions of her life.

*   *   *

Aiden and his men reached Tayteath by midafternoon. He brought them to a halt at the edge of the trees and surveyed his target. The castle stood on a narrow jut of land overlooking the sea. Steep cliffs protected the keep on three sides, forcing all access through the heavily fortified front gates. To the northwest, midway between Aiden and the castle, lay a small village that consisted of a kirk and at least twenty stone blackhouses, smoke rising lazily from their chimneys.

Niall nudged his horse alongside him. "What do you think? Is de Lourdes inside?"

"The portcullis is down," Aiden pointed out. Unless the castle was expecting trouble, there was no reason to bar the villagers from the castle during daylight hours. "But I prefer to be certain. Send someone into the village. With any luck, the townspeople noted his arrival."

Niall nodded. "Shall we set up camp?"

"Aye," Aiden said, still studying the keep. "But no fire tonight."

Gaining access to the keep would be a challenge. A full frontal attack wasn't possible—he didn't have the men or the equipment required to mount a siege. If they approached the gate, the archers on the walls would cut them down like hay.

Which really only left one option.

The cliffs.

"Cormac," he called. "I have a task for you."

Halfway across a wide plain, Magnus slowed the horses to a walk to allow them to cool. One glance at the women and he knew the game was up. Isabail looked weary, but she remained steady and upright. Ana, on the other hand, despite an extended period in the saddle, looked ready to collapse. Pale faced and trembling, she was latched onto the reins with a desperate clutch of fingers.

"I was a fool to agree to this," he said, reining in his mount. He handed Ana his oilskin and watched her drink deeply of the ale within.

Isabail nodded unhappily. "'Twas unkind of me to demand this of you, Ana."

"I'll be fine," Ana said as she lowered the oilskin. But her voice quavered as she spoke, belying her words.

Magnus glanced around. "We'll head for that copse," he said, pointing to a small stand of trees to the south. "After we rest a while, we'll make our way—slowly—back to the glen from whence we came."

Isabail also glanced around. "What of the wolf?"

They'd caught sight of a large white wolf several times over the course of the day, always at a distance, always alone. Isabail's deerhound had growled upon spying the beast but seemed content to remain at their side rather than give chase. Likely a wise decision.

"There's no sign of it," he said. To reassure the women, he tapped the hilt of his sword. "But if it makes an appearance, I'll dispatch it swiftly."

They walked the horses to the trees and found a small clearing in the center in which to make camp. The remnant of a day-old fire told Magnus that it was a popular place to stop, and he did a careful search of the woods before making camp. They were alone.

Ana's legs gave out on her when he helped her from the saddle. "My legs are like jelly," she said with a laugh, as she fell against him. "I thought myself able, but I was clearly mistaken."

He scooped her up and carried her to the blankets that Isabail had laid before the fire pit.

"The pace we set would pose a challenge even for an experienced rider," he told her as he tucked the wool about her. "You've done remarkably well to make it this far. The return journey will not be nearly as difficult."

Isabail paced back and forth as he lit the fire. "How close are we to Tayteath?"

"Another half day." He caught a glimmer of renewed hope in Isabail's eyes and shook his head. "Ana is in no condition to continue. We must allow her to rest."

"I've no desire to push Ana beyond her limits," Isabail said. She turned to her companion. "I've already asked far more of you than I had a right to, but I cannot turn back. Not when I am so close. Not while Jamie remains Daniel's prisoner."

Crossing to his horse, Magnus removed food from his pack. He broke a round of bread in half and offered a piece to each of the ladies. He tossed a small piece of dried hare to the dog, as well. "Your concern for the lad is laudable, but your menfolk are already in pursuit. You must have faith in their ability to bring him home."

"I do not lack faith," Isabail said. "If it were a simple matter of who possesses the better sword arm, I would hang my favor on Aiden MacCurran's lance. He is a formidable foe. But it's not that simple. The castle is mine. I can retrieve the lad without bloodshed. Surely, the sparing of lives is a noble cause?"

"A noble cause, perhaps," he said gently. "But not a practical one."

Isabail flopped onto the blanket next to Ana, clearly unhappy with his response. She picked at her bread with halfhearted interest, her attention elsewhere.

"Hallo," called a deep voice from the trees.

Magnus whipped around, drawing his sword as he spun.

Out of the shadows stepped an old man garbed in a dark cloak, his white beard and hair shining brightly in the early-afternoon sunlight. He leaned on a long burl-wood staff as he walked.

The deerhound lifted its head as the man drew closer, but did not growl.

"Halt there," Magnus said. "Identify yourself."

The old man obediently stopped and gave them a low bow. "Bhaltair of the Red Mountains."

Magnus frowned. "You're a long way from home, old man. What brings you to the Lowlands?"

"You do."

The tip of Magnus's sword lifted. "I beg your pardon?"

The old man put a hand to his chest. "I mean that in a general sense, of course." He unhooked the burlap bag he carried over his shoulder and lowered it to the ground. Opening the drawstring, he displayed the contents. "I sell herbs and unguents to travelers in need. You look as though you might have need of my wares."

Ana peered at the earthenware jugs in the old man's sack. "What sorts of unguents do you have?" she asked.

He held up a pot. "I've this one containing goldes and Saint Johnswort." He dug deeper, and the jugs rattled. "I've also got this one with Saint Johnswort, valerian, and wintergreen."

"Let me see," she said, waving him closer.

The two of them huddled over the sack, talking in the riddles of herbalism and discussing the merits of each unguent and salve.

"They seem to have formed a bond," Isabail said quietly.

He glared at her. "I know precisely what you are thinking, madam, and I cannot endorse it. He's an old man. Hardly a reliable champion with whom to entrust Ana's care."

"I disagree. He travels the roads alone and carries a sharp sickle at his belt."

"He could be a cad, or a thief," he said. "We know nothing of him."

"The same could have been said about you," Isabail pointed out. "Sometimes we must base our choices on the options presented to us, rather than on what we truly desire." She rounded the campfire and joined the other two. "Ana? Might I have a word?"

The two women stepped away, Ana limping stiffly. To Magnus's relief, Isabail did not appear to coerce Ana into making a decision. She simply asked the healer a question and listened at length to the answer. Ana ended the conversation with a pat to her staghorn-handled dirk, and they returned to the fire.

"If it is not too much to ask, Bhaltair," Ana said to the old man, "I wonder if you might remain with me for a few days while I regain my strength? My companions have a pressing need to reach Tayteath forthwith, and I'm afraid my horsemanship is not up to the task."

Bhaltair nodded graciously. "Of course. In truth, it would be greatly to my benefit to spend a few days with such a learned herbalist."

Isabail smiled and returned to Magnus. "So, are you game to continue?"

"Aye." He helped her mount her horse. "This lad you're so determined to save must be a very worthy sort to inspire such devotion."

She waited for him to vault into the saddle. "That he is, Magnus. That he is."

By the time Niall returned with the news that Daniel de Lourdes had been identified by several of the villagers and that he had arrived at the keep with a young lad in tow, Aiden had reached a decision on how to breach the keep. Drawing a map in the snow, he shared his plan.

"Our best option is to start here." He pointed to the base of the cliffs. "At the evening low tide, we walk out to the base of the cliffs. From there, we scale the rocks until we reach the castle, and then we enter through a window."

"Climb the cliffs in the dark?" Niall asked.

"It will be difficult," acknowledged Aiden. "But the rear of the castle will be unprotected. We have a far greater chance of success with the cliffs than with a frontal attack."

Several of the men nodded, seeing the wisdom of his plan, but most remained silent. They would do whatever Aiden asked of them, but he wanted more than blind obedience. Pointing at the keep through the trees, he lowered his voice to a firm intensity. "Inside those walls lies the crown of our great ancestor, Kenneth MacAlpin. The last true king of the Picts. Do I want to retrieve it? Aye, I do. I'm sworn to protect it. But more important than any piece of treasure is kin. One of our own is held within that keep, perhaps in pain or suffering. Jamie is not only one of us; he's the son of one of our finest warriors. He's paid the greatest of sacrifices, losing his maither and his wee brother to a murdering thief. I, for one, am willing to pay the same price to see young Jamie freed. Are you with me?"

This time the response was enthusiastic. "Aye!"

Even Niall, who was a cautious fellow by nature, brought his fist to his chest with a resounding thump and joined the chorus.

"Pack lightly and pack quick. We leave for the cliffs at nightfall."

* * *

Isabail and her hired warrior arrived at Tayteath just as dusk was falling. Noting an air of quiet around the castle, she wondered what had become of the MacCurran. If not laying siege to the castle, where was he? Surely, he would have arrived well ahead of her.

She voiced her thoughts to Magnus.

"Were I him," he said, "I'd be camped in that wood." He pointed to a thick forest a half league to the west. "No sense alerting your enemy to your presence until you've gathered all the information you'll need to breach his walls."

"Do you think you could you find him?"

Magnus smiled. "Of course."

He spurred his horse into a canter and headed for the trees. Isabail did the same, even though she'd long since reached the limit of her endurance. Exhaustion tugged at her shoulders, and holding up her head had become a monumental chore. A short distance into the woods, Magnus reined in his mount and swung to the ground. "We walk from here."

"Why?"

"The horses make too much noise. They'll hear us long before they see us."

Isabail frowned. "Don't we want them to find us?"

"Find you? Aye. Find me? Nay."

"Do you have a grievance with the MacCurrans?"

"Possibly," he said, leading her through the brush and showing her where to step. At the short trill of a bird, he halted. "This is as far as I go. Head straight toward that half-fallen birch. If they've got their wits about them, as I suspect they do, they'll find you within a pace or two beyond that."

She frowned. "And where will you go?"

"I won't be far," he said. "If you run afoul of the MacCurrans, just yell. I'll find you."

Isabail lifted the hem of her dress and ripped open the seam. She removed the silver deniers sewn there and pressed them into Magnus's hand. "Thank you. I could never have made this journey without you."

He shoved the coins away. "Thank me after the lad is safe. Before that, there's nothing to be rewarded for."

He gave her a gentle push in the direction of the fallen birch, then melted into the shadows and was gone.

Niall marched across the camp to Aiden's side. "You'll never believe whom we found in the woods."

Aiden glanced about. "Who?"

He followed Niall's pointed finger and found the disheveled yet still amazingly lovely face of Isabail Macintosh. "Bloody hell."

As she stepped out of the woods accompanied by two of his men, Aiden shook his head. "How is this possible?" he asked her. "How did you get here?"

"Never mind how," she said. "I'm just glad I

arrived before you laid siege to the keep. I will go to the castle and demand entry. They are my men, so they'll raise the portcullis, and we can enter without bloodshed."

He sighed heavily. "That won't work."

"Of course it will." She shot him an exasperated look. "Why is it men always want to solve problems with their swords?"

He grabbed her elbow and led her out of the earshot of Niall and the others. He was tempted to kiss her, but thought better of it. She might get the idea that he approved of her reckless race across the countryside. "It won't work because de Lourdes has replaced all your loyal soldiers with mercenaries from France."

"What?" She blinked at him.

"Mercenaries," he repeated. "The villagers confirmed it."

"Oh."

She looked so absolutely shattered by his news that he tugged her to his chest. "I know you were attempting to aid Jamie, and your efforts are appreciated," he said softly into her hair. "Even though I should paddle your arse for coming all this way on your own."

"My bottom is quite sore enough," she said, her voice muffled against his lèine. She sagged against him. "I truly believed I could help."

"I know." He tipped her head up and planted a firm kiss on her lips. "Now, I must ask you to stay here and wait patiently for my return."

"Where do you go?"

"We enter the keep tonight."

She frowned. "How?"

"Promise me you'll make no attempt to follow." When she nodded, he explained. "Up the cliffs."

Her hands gripped the front of his lèine. "You're mad. That's a sure way to meet the Maker."

"For lads born in the Highlands, 'tis a simple feat," he assured her, even though it was no such thing. "And these Lowlanders will never expect it."

"I'll be praying for your safety."

"Will you?"

She looked at him, her eyes dark and serious. "Do what you must, but come back alive."

"I'll do my best." He kissed her again, then let her go. "Stay out of trouble, lass."

"What trouble can I get into here in the wood?"

He snorted. "You've a knack for finding it wherever you might be." He turned to leave, but she caught his sleeve.

"I love you," she said quietly, as if haste would somehow minimize the importance of her words.

His heart thumped heavily in his chest. He took her chin and peered into her face. It was a moment that begged for heartfelt words and promises of devotion, but saving Jamie would not wait. "I'm going to hold you to those words. When I come back, we'll have the discussion we ought to have had some time ago."

And then he kissed her again. Hard. "Godspeed, lass."

* * *

When the men had departed, Isabail lit a small fire. When she was certain the wood had caught, she sat on a stump with her hands toward the flames and finally let weariness curl her shoulders. She'd raced all this way—and forced Ana to race with her—for naught.

Daniel was not at all the man she'd thought him to be. His betrayal of her was not some spontaneous thing, some madness. He'd been plotting against her for months. How else could he have replaced her soldiers? It was even possible, though it made her heart ache to contemplate it, that his love for John had been a sham, that John's death hadn't been the accident he insisted it had been.

She tossed another branch on the fire and watched a plume of sparks leap into the night air. What a fool she was. Now Aiden was risking his life scaling the cliffs to her castle and she was unable to do anything but wait and pray.

"I take it your plan to spare lives was not well received?"

Isabail looked up. Magnus stood just inside the circle of light cast by the fire, the black outline of trees at his back.

"It was a naive plan," she responded dismally. Like all of her plans.

He advanced. "It was born of a genuine desire to help the lad. Who could find a fault with that?"

"Niall MacCurran for one," she said bitterly. "I didn't have the heart to tell him I dragged Ana along on my foolhardy quest and then left her in the woods with an old peddler." She released a humorless laugh. "He'd have been completely distracted as he set off to scale a cliff to the castle, and I'd have another person's blood on my hands."

"Ah," he said, lowering himself to the log beside her. "Indulging in a wee bout of 'pity me,' are we?"

She glared at him. All of it was true. Couldn't Magnus see that?

"You've never struck me as a lass given to weeping," he said. "We are safe, Ana is safe, the MacCurran lads are about to surprise the castle guards, and your wee lad is about to be rescued. What's there to weep about?"

"All of this could have been avoided!" she cried, leaping to her feet. "If only I'd told MacCurran from the start that Daniel was after the necklace."

He stared at her. "Why didn't you?"

"In the beginning, I believed MacCurran might be guilty. Later . . . I don't know. I suppose telling MacCurran felt like I would be betraying Daniel." She shook her head. "In the end, he betrayed me."

"Well, 'tis all water under the bridge now. Daniel will not escape his just dues."

Isabail frowned. Escape. That tugged at a memory—an old memory from when she was a child. She and John had played in the empty dungeons of Tayteath, a simple game of hide-and-chase. He'd leapt out of a hidden door and sent her screaming down the corridor.

"Wait," she said, grabbing Magnus's sleeve. "There's a door in the dungeons that leads to outside. If John told Daniel, Daniel can indeed escape."

Her hired warrior surged to his feet.

"Show me where the door leads."

Scaling the cliffs was a slow, arduous task. Footholds were scarce and narrow and sometimes crumbly. There were few outcroppings big enough to hold a man, so rest was infrequent. By the time Aiden was halfway up, his thighs were aching and his fingers were raw. But quitting wasn't an option, so he pushed on.

He glanced down only once, when he was a fair distance above the beach. The tide had started to come back in, and the sand had vanished. Waves beat slow and steady against the rocks, and his head swam with a dizziness that made him cling to the rock face.

Since down was not a direction he wanted to experience, he focused on up. One toehold and push at a time.

The men who followed him were equally silent and focused. Aiden heard the occasional scrape of a sword or a knife against rocks, but nothing more.

When the gray stones of the castle came into view, Aiden found renewed strength. Their goal was in reach. He felt for a grip among the rocks over his head, found purchase for his right boot, and heaved his body another three feet up the cliff.

A wide ledge was his next target—the ground on which the castle was built. Eager to plant his feet on solid ground again, he gripped the ledge with both hands and hauled himself over the lip. He lay there for a moment, catching his breath and offering a short prayer to the gods; then he leaned over and offered his hand to Niall.

One by one the MacCurran men reached the top. Aiden could tell by the euphoric expressions on their faces that several of them had not believed they would make it.

They paused on the ledge for a short while, allowing their shaking legs to recover.

When Aiden was confident they were ready to move on, he waved Cormac forward.

The bowman swung the crossbow from his shoulder. "Any one of you could do this," he muttered. "Don't need a skilled man to shoot a bloody bolt thirty feet into the air."

Aiden patted the man's shoulder. "I need you to bury it in the stone next to the window"—he pointed above them—"deep enough to hold the weight of a man. At this angle, that requires a man with skill."

Cormac shrugged, aimed, and fired. The bolt, with rope attached, drove into the stone with a loud *thunk*. Aiden and the others flattened themselves against the castle wall and waited for someone to peer out the window. But none came.

Aiden yanked on the rope, testing its solidity. It held firm. Then he wrapped his hands and feet around the rope and began to climb. By comparison to the cliffs, scaling the castle wall and entering through the window was easy. The room he slipped into was dark and small—an antechamber intended to house guards on watch. But it was empty.

As the other men dropped into the room, Aiden quietly pulled on the door and peered into the larger room beyond. A bedchamber. Fortunately, the curtains on the bed were open and he was able to quickly ascertain this room was also empty.

Widening the door, he stepped inside.

The room was well appointed. Velvet draperies on the bed, an elaborate brocade coverlet, a ladies' table replete with combs and mirrors. Just for an instant, Aiden's thoughts went to Isabail. It was easy to imagine her here, attired in her finery, with a maid brushing her hair. Living in a ruined broch with no furniture did not suit her beauty. But this elegant castle did.

He shook the mental cobwebs away, unsheathed his sword, and peeked past the outer door to the corridor. There were four guards stationed in the corridor, and as soon as his men joined him at the door, he swung it open and leapt to the attack. With the element of surprise in his favor, he made short work of this first opponent, then moved to the next.

The clang of metal on metal soon drew other soldiers, and the battle thickened. Had they been fighting regular household guards, the fight would have ended swiftly. But these were seasoned warriors, not easily unnerved. They fought aggressively and with skill.

It took Aiden longer to dispatch his second and third opponents than he had hoped. By the time he was free to search the other rooms for Daniel and Jamie, they were empty. The door at the end of the corridor opened into a large chamber that clearly belonged to the lord of the keep.

The bed sheets were rumpled, and Aiden noted the presence of a pallet on the floor at the foot of the bed. A manacle lay on the mattress. Anger surged through him. After all the lad had been through, he hardly deserved to be chained like a dog.

"Search the chests," he ordered. "Find the crown."

Then he dove for the stairwell. They couldn't have gone far. If he was fleet of foot, he could end this now. Leaping several stairs at a time, he reached the great hall in a heartbeat. But Daniel and the boy were nowhere to be seen, Only a frightened group of gillies huddled by the fireplace.

"Where?" he demanded.

They pointed to the stairs leading to the dungeon, and he raced for the bottom.

Chapter 15

Moss had overgrown the secret exit door to the castle, and Isabail almost missed it.

"Here," she said, pointing to the dark brown wooden door. Rot had blackened the door in several spots, and it blended into the rock with great effectiveness.

"No one has come through," Magnus said. "I can enter, but I prefer you wait in the woods for me, not here on the cliffs."

Isabail had no argument about that. She was uncomfortable on the ledge, especially in the dark, with the wind tugging at her skirts. She inched her way back toward the trees, with Magnus following immediately behind her. When they reached the end of the sloping path, he lifted her up the remaining two feet to the plateau. As she paused to regain her balance, the door burst open and three soldiers stepped out onto the ledge, swords aloft.

"Run," Magnus urged her, as he drew his

weapon and joined her on the plateau. Added height and a sturdy footing were clear advantages.

Isabail ran into the trees, but did not go far. Outrunning an armed soldier wasn't a future she could foresee, and leaving Magnus behind seemed not only unfair, but unwise. She hid behind the broad trunk of a Scots pine and with one hand to her madly thumping heart, watched her hired warrior battle for his—and quite possibly her—life.

Fortunately, he quickly improved his odds. He kicked his first opponent in the head and sent him catapulting over the ledge. Less fortunately, the other two learned from their compatriot's mistake and advanced with a flurry of sword strokes that eliminated the opportunity for a kick.

Isabail sent a little prayer skyward.

She needn't have bothered—as it turned out, Magnus was a skilled swordsman. Although she had no knowledge of swordplay and could not have named a single move he made, it was apparent that her warrior was smooth, fast, and effective. He made fighting two opponents simultaneously seem easy. Twice he broke through the flurry of steel to strike a blow that resulted in blood. His opponents were weakening, and Isabail began to believe that he would triumph. But then two more soldiers rushed onto the ledge, and Magnus was forced to give up ground. One of the new soldiers leapt up to the plateau and began to engage Magnus at an equal level. Four against one did not seem like a remotely fair battle. Especially when the other three soldiers leapt up as well.

She had to do something. But what? Short of screaming for aid, she couldn't imagine what that something might be. She glanced around. Fling a stick or a rock?

Spying several fallen tree branches beneath a nearby elm, she weighed her options. Too light and it would be no more distracting than a gnat, too heavy and she wouldn't be able to toss it more than a foot. Picking up a stick, she hefted it. This one seemed about right.

Staying low, Isabail moved to the very edge of the trees, close enough to reach the nearest soldier. Then, stepping out from behind the tree, she took aim and pitched the stick with all her might.

It hit Magnus squarely on the back of the head.

Isabail gave a sharp shriek of regret and shrank back behind the tree.

To her immense relief, Magnus powered on without pause. He took down one of his opponents. A sharp jab to the leg, and the fellow was down. Magnus battled on, but took a slice on the arm in the ensuing melee. Blood darkened his lèine and dripped down to his fingers.

Fear was a sour taste in Isabail's mouth. She had a dreadful feeling she knew how this was going to end. She hugged the tree trunk with white-knuckled intent. Her gaze was locked so tightly on Magnus's brave attempt to triumph that she almost missed the flash of movement over by the cliff. A flaxen-haired man tossed a lean, dark-haired lad upon the plateau, then leapt up behind him and began dragging the lad to the trees.

Daniel!

Isabail was loath to leave Magnus, but she had to see where Daniel was taking Jamie. She sent another quick prayer skyward for Magnus, then darted through the trees in the direction she'd seen the fugitive pair disappear. Running as fast as her skirts would allow, she rounded a clutch of fir saplings and came face-to-face with the man who had attempted to kill her.

The dungeons of Tayteath were dark and dank. Water dripped from the ceilings and black mold crept up the walls, signs that the rooms were very infrequently used. Aiden paused at the bottom of the stairs and listened.

De Lourdes was down here somewhere.

His hand tightened on his sword. Although he would dearly love to kill the bastard for what he'd done to Isabail, his intent was to take him alive . . . and to save young Jamie. Preferably with the same sword strike. He had no notion how skilled a duelist Daniel de Lourdes might be, and frankly, it mattered not. He'd spent eight years of his life with the MacDonalds on the Isle of Skye, a wild and beautiful land matched only by the ferocity of its warriors. He had fought all manner of opponents while fostered there. He could handle one weasel.

The rough scrape of leather boots on stone gave him a direction to travel, and Aiden jogged down the corridor toward the very back of the dungeon.

What did de Lourdes hope to accomplish down here? Was he hiding, hoping to escape the castle after Aiden's men had come and gone? It seemed the sort of craven act a man who stabbed women and used lads as shields would do.

Peering into the dimness of the dungeon, Aiden spotted a wooden door standing open. The scent of burning pitch hung in the air, but there were no torches in view.

He approached the door cautiously. It opened into a narrow corridor, the confines of which were even darker than the dungeon. But here the smell of torch was thicker. This was the direction his rat had fled.

Ducking his head beneath the lintel, he stepped into the corridor. Blinded by darkness, he was forced to travel slowly, but he made his way with as much haste as he could manage. The corridor turned several corners, the last of which gave him sight—another door, this one swinging open with the breeze, the light of a full moon pouring in through the portal. Aiden ran to the exit and out onto a ledge on the cliffs.

The clash of metal on metal broke through the howl of the coastal wind—the familiar sound of swords engaging in combat. He dashed toward the noise, not entirely certain what would meet his eyes.

What he found was a solitary man surrounded by three soldiers, doing battle like he'd been born into it. And as the moon shone upon that grim warrior's face, Aiden was swamped with a gut-deep feeling that was equal parts pride, shock, and euphoria. The man wielding his sword on the plateau above him was none other than his long-missing and presumed-dead cousin, Wulf.

Aiden vaulted up the two-foot step to the plateau and attacked the soldiers from behind.

Isabail stared at Daniel in the bright moonlight, frozen in place.

Daniel paled. "Isabail? How is it possible? I ran you through."

Her eyes went to Jamie, who looked frightened, but otherwise unharmed. Relieved, she returned her attention to Daniel. A cold trickle of sweat ran down her back. Standing this close to him, seeing the sword in his hand, she almost lost her nerve. Every detail of the sword sliding into her—all the pain and all the blood—was vivid in her mind. The desire to turn and run was so intense, her knees trembled.

But she stood her ground. For Jamie.

And as the seconds passed, the pallor of Daniel's face and the tremble in his hand sank in. *By God*. He wondered if she were truly here. . . . He wondered if he was seeing a *ghost*. Given how he'd left her, lying in a widening pool of blood, she could completely understand his state of mind.

Drawing on an inner strength she had not known she possessed until recently, Isabail took a firm step forward. "You deserve to be punished for what you did to me."

Daniel retreated, waving his sword in front of him. "Stay away."

"You deserve to be punished for what you did to John," she said, taking another step forward.

"Stay away, I say."

"You deserve to be punished for all your sins, Daniel de Lourdes."

He closed his eyes. "You aren't really here. You are dead. You can't punish anyone."

Isabail signaled to Jamie. *Run*, she mouthed.

The lad did not need further prompting. He yanked his arm free of Daniel's grasp and took off through the trees.

Daniel's eyes snapped open. He stared at Isabail, examining her face in thorough detail. "Why would a specter free a living boy?" he said, firming his grip on the sword and circling around her. "There is no reason, unless you are not a ghost at all."

He frowned. "But I most certainly pierced you with my blade. How could you be standing?"

Isabail could think of nothing to add that might not lead him to conclude that she was real flesh and blood. The last thing she wanted was to have him run her through a second time. Ana was half a day away. Surviving another stabbing was unlikely. So, she simply repeated her original statement.

"You deserve to be punished for what you did to me."

He stared at her hard. Then he glanced up at the full moon. "Nay, you're just the moon addling my wits," he said, lowering his sword. "Nothing but a brief fit of lunacy." A sad smile touched his lips. "Guilt, perhaps, over what befell my beloved John."

His shoulders straightened and the wild look left his eyes. "But I have a new lover now and a higher purpose that must be met. Such pangs of guilt are not to be tolerated. *Adieu*, sweet specter."

He bowed to Isabail, then spun on his heel.

With no one else about, Isabail knew only one way to prevent his escape.

"Nay!" she cried. "I am no specter, Daniel. 'Tis I, Isabail. The wound you gave me in the tunnel was nothing more than a scratch. I yet live to tell the world of your crimes."

He halted.

"Your new lover will swiftly abandon you when you are tossed in the dungeon for the murder of my brother and an assault on my person. My cousin Archibald will stand beside me at your trial, and together we will see your soul rot in hell."

Daniel spun to face her, a sneer on his handsome face.

"You forget, my dear Isabail, that a dead woman tells no tales."

Working together, their combat styles strangely similar, Magnus and his mysterious new friend defeated the three guards handily. When the third and final man fell, Magnus was treated to a hearty thump on the back and a broad grin.

"By God, you're a sight for sore eyes."

Wiping his blade on the churned-up snow, Magnus considered his companion. Given that he'd been the one in sore need of aid, such a comment would have been better suited to his own lips, surely? His cohort was a tall man. Beardless and sporting the well-groomed hair that Magnus associated with nobles. If Isabail had not claimed Tayteath as hers, he would have guessed this man to be the lord.

So, if not the Lord of Tayteath . . . ?

"Who are you?" he asked.

The other man's grin fell away. "You do not know me?"

Magnus stiffened. *Ah. The fellow recognizes me.* That explained the camaraderie. "Nay, I do not," he responded honestly.

"Wulf," the other man said, "I am your cousin, Aiden MacCurran. Our fathers were brothers."

Kin. This man was *kin*. A heady blend of excitement and frustration spun inside his head. But if the man was kin, why didn't Magnus recognize him? Why did everything seem strange and unknown?

"Da!"

A slim, tousle-haired missile hit him in the gut and squeezed him tight with gangly arms.

"I knew you were alive. I *knew* it," said the lad attached to his waist as his face pressed into the folds of Magnus's lèine. "Oh, God, Da. I'm so glad to see you."

He stared at the boy, rooted to the spot in shock.

It was too much to absorb, being a cousin and a da. How could he be a father and have no memory of it? Surely such a thing was impossible. Ought not the sound of the boy's voice and the touch of his hand to stir something? Yet they did not. No fond memories, no sense of familiarity. Still, he did not have the heart to push the lad away, so he stood stiffly and allowed the boy to cling to him.

He shared a desperate look with the man who called himself Aiden, and thankfully, the man stepped into the breach.

"Jamie, lad. It's good to see you safe. How did you escape de Lourdes?"

The boy pointed to the trees. "Isabail confronted him. He thinks her a ghost."

"Isabail?" Both men spoke at once, their voices an echo of dismay.

"The wretch will kill her." Magnus attempted a step, but with Jamie stuck to him as securely as a lamprey eel, it was hardly a smooth stride. "I must go."

Aiden pointed to Magnus's bleeding arm. "You're wounded. Stay with Jamie. I'll take care of de Lourdes."

"She's my responsibility," he protested.

But even as the words left his mouth, he changed his mind. The lad had tightened his grip to a painful intensity, clearly fearful that having found his father, he was about to lose him again.

Lifting his gaze to Aiden, he nodded.

The other man disappeared into the trees, leaving him alone with Jamie. Magnus gazed down at the boy's light brown locks and placed an awkward hand upon the lad's head. The hair beneath his fingers was fine and soft. A child's hair. *His* child's hair. The tension in his gut eased.

Perhaps there was a wee spot of familiarity after all.

"Help me bind my wound," he told the boy. "And tell me everything that's happened since I saw you last."

Isabail saw a shadow move among the trees behind Daniel, and a calm fell over her. She knew that shadow well—the broad shoulders and impressive height had become incredibly dear to her these past few weeks. Aiden.

"You tried to kill me once and failed," she taunted Daniel, hoping to keep his attention focused on her. "I'm not convinced you'll do any better with repeated effort."

He walked toward her, slow and light-footed like a Highland wildcat stalking a rabbit. The sword in his hand remained low to the ground, but Isabail wasn't fooled. His grip on the hilt was unwavering.

He intended to gut her.

Praying that Aiden would reach them before Daniel slid the blade between her ribs, Isabail slowly retreated. The cliff was behind her, some twenty paces away. Plenty of space for Aiden to make his move.

"It seems that when your mouth opens, only

lies come out," she said. "Since justice for John was clearly not what you sought, why take the necklace? Why risk all this for a pretty bauble?"

He said nothing, just continued toward her, one relentless step after another.

"Tell me why my brother died, Daniel."

That sank through his icy facade. He paused. "I told you. It was an accident. But in the end, he died for a good cause—the triumph of right over wrong. Justice has been a long time coming, but it *will* see the light of day."

His response was too vague and unsatisfying. Isabail needed more. When she had believed John the victim of a thief and a traitor, his death had been understandable. Not easy to accept, but understandable. Now that Daniel had confessed to the crime, there was only confusion and a horrible sense of waste. "How do you accidentally poison someone, Daniel?"

But the answers she sought were not to be had. His brief moment of introspection passed like a cloud over the moon. Lips clamped tight, his purposeful stride resumed. With his eyes locked on her chest as if he was imagining just where he would place the tip of his blade, he came at her.

Aiden jogged into the trees, his fist tight around the hilt of his sword. He'd nearly lost Isabail once to de Lourdes's blade; he wouldn't allow it to happen again. The wretch would die before harming her. He scanned the trees for some sign of Isabail. The bright winter moon filtered down through the barren branches, creating a patchwork of dark and light. He caught a glimpse of pale blue gown, and his heart leapt. She was alive. De Lourdes was harder to see, but Aiden eventually spotted his outline in the dimness. The miserable cur was relentlessly pressing her toward the cliffs.

Slipping silently through the trees, Aiden drew closer.

As he listened to the strange conversation between the two, he frowned.

Until the moment the necklace was mentioned, Aiden had assumed de Lourdes was a thief of opportunity—that he'd stolen the necklace and the crown because he could. Not because that had been his aim all long. Which spoke volumes about how disturbed Aiden had been by Isabail's near death—he had not thought to question the cur's goal.

But de Lourdes hadn't entered the MacCurran camp to rescue Isabail—he'd come for the necklace. The same necklace that lay at the root of all Aiden's recent troubles, the same necklace that eventually led back to the man in black.

By God.

De Lourdes knew the identity of the man in black. He had to. If Aiden but questioned him, he would have all the answers he sought. Dunstoras would be saved, and his clan could return to their home. All he had to do was wring the truth from de Lourdes's lips.

Right after he rescued Isabail.

With his gaze locked on de Lourdes, he stepped around a patch of winter-dried bilberry—and very nearly trod upon a sleeping black grouse. The startled bird took flight, veering west in a madly beating flurry of wings. Aiden recovered quickly and raced for Isabail. But he was a moment too late.

De Lourdes reached her first. He wrapped an arm around her throat and swiveled. His sword flashed in the moonlight, now accurately pointed at Aiden. "Step any closer and I'll kill her."

Aiden continued forward, closing the gap to ten paces. To have a hope of disarming the cur, he had to be within striking distance.

De Lourdes shuffled back, dragging Isabail with him. "Stay back, I say."

The sword was pointed at Aiden and not Isabail, so Aiden ignored him. Eight paces. "Harm her and you'll die a very painful death."

De Lourdes retreated farther, a scowl upon his face.

Aiden followed. The edge of the cliff was only a few feet behind them. Was de Lourdes aware? "Let her go and you can live."

Isabail was clawing at her captor's arm, but her efforts did not register on de Lourdes's face. The man's attention was completely focused on Aiden. He waved his sword. "Do you think me a fool? The only way you'd allow me to live would be if I betrayed the one I live for."

De Lourdes took another step back.

Aiden's heart thumped heavily in his chest. "Let her go and we'll talk, nothing more."

"There's naught to be said," the other man said,

taking a firm step back. His voice was dark and crisp, the sound of utter conviction. The edge of the cliff lay immediately behind him, and his purpose suddenly became clear.

He intended to jump—and to take Isabail with him.

Aiden's blood pumped slowly through his veins, and a cool clarity dropped over him. He knew exactly what he had to do—stop de Lourdes before he could leap. There was no time to think twice or doubt the plan of action that sprang to mind. He simply dropped his sword and darted forward, eyes on his target.

Daniel didn't hesitate. He saw Aiden move and immediately leapt backward.

Isabail screamed.

As the two of them began to fall, Aiden's priority shifted—one hand had been grabbing for each of them, but now he dove for Isabail with both. He grasped for her wrist, but caught only the tips of her fingers as her slim hand slipped through his desperate fingers. The other hand had more luck— he latched onto the fluttering folds of her gown, gaining a fistful of material.

Aiden landed on his belly in the snow, partly hanging over the cliff. An instant later, as the full weight of Isabail's body dropped, the strength of his grip was tested. He vaguely saw de Lourdes pitch headfirst toward the water, but his gaze was locked on Isabail. She hung from his right hand, her death prevented by only a handful of finely woven wool.

Thankfully, she did not squirm.

Wide blue eyes met his, terror evident in the pallor of her face.

Aiden's balance was not secure—he was too far over the edge—and Isabail's weight, though not excessive, was enough to rock him. Heart pounding, he planted his left hand in the snow to keep him steady.

"I've got you, lass," he said reassuringly.

Digging his boots into the frozen ground as best he could, he tried to wriggle back. The sound of material ripping froze his movements. The delicate seam stitches at Isabail's waist were giving way.

She said nothing, but the stark look in her eyes begged him to do something.

There was only one option.

Aiden lifted his left hand and reached for Isabail. If they fell, at least they would fall together. "Grab my hand, lass."

Isabail reached for him, trembling badly. A foot of space separated their fingers.

Aiden extended his arm farther, but his body tipped and he had to pull back. "Stretch," he urged. "Safety is only a few inches away."

She did as he bade. Reaching. Grasping. Their fingers touched, but the melted snow on his hand proved too slippery and she fell back. The seam ripped further, and she let out a short shriek.

Aiden swallowed, his mouth dry as dust. The seam was half-gone now; a huge hole had opened up, one that Isabail could easily fall through. If she tilted too far to one side, or the rest of the seam gave way, he would lose her. "Try again," he told her.

She did. This time their fingers locked briefly before she slipped from his grasp. As she fell back, the seam ripped wide, leaving only a bare few inches of attached material . . . and the threads continued to give. Aiden knew he had only seconds to save Isabail.

"Again," he urged firmly, opening his hand and offering her the broadest grip possible. "Quickly now; there's a lass."

Desperation drove the next attempt. With a slight catch of her breath, she launched herself at his hand. The dress ripped again, completely parting. His right hand now held nothing but a swath of fabric. Luckily, Isabail had latched firmly to his left.

He dropped the fabric and grabbed Isabail with both hands. Slowly, but with increasingly sure movements, he withdrew from the edge of the cliff. When his balance was firm, he yanked her up over the edge. Giving in to a primal need, he clasped her tightly to his chest and pressed his lips into the soft hair on her head.

They lay there in the snow, breathing heavily and doing little else but listening to their heartbeats for several minutes.

"What of Jamie?" Isabail asked hoarsely. "Did you see him?"

"Aye. He's with his da."

Her hand, still clutching his, tightened. "His *da*?"

"All that will sort itself out," Aiden said. "Did de Lourdes hurt you? Are you well?"

"I'm fine."

He released her, rolled to his feet, then offered her a hand. When she was standing and he could see for himself that all was well, he pulled her again to his chest. "I love you, Isabail Macintosh."

"I know," she said with a faint smile.

"I've nothing to offer you, not a home nor a good name," he said. "Just myself. But I was earnest about a wedding."

"You are a meager prize, to be sure," she said, pressing a cold kiss against his lips. "But fear not. I have something to offer you."

"Oh?"

"I'll give you the names of the guests at Lochurkie that night"—she wagged a finger at him—"on one condition."

He frowned. "And what is that?"

"You must promise not to kill any of them."

Staring at her beautiful face in the moonlight, Aiden knew he could never deny her anything. But he still protested. "One of them cost me everything. Harmed my kin in unspeakable ways, dishonored my name before the king, and put a barrier called the law between you and I," he said. "Yet you expect me to spare him?"

"I simply ask that you let justice take its due

course. Prove without doubt that this man is guilty. We both know that innocent people can be accused of crimes they did not commit."

He kissed the top of her head.

"I will do everything in my power to honor your request. More than that I cannot promise."

She nuzzled the skin at his neck, her nose cool against his throat. "That will do."

Chapter 16

The corridor was ablaze with lit tapers, every nook and hollow illuminated, every colorful pennant and silken tapestry artfully displayed. Isabail resisted the urge to smooth imaginary wrinkles from her burgundy gown. She had walked these very halls of Edinburgh Castle once before—the year she'd been presented as Andrew Macintosh's bride—but the circumstances today were much more challenging. Today, she had one chance to make everything right. Her words must be firm and persuasive, passionate and incontrovertible.

She must convince the king to pardon Aiden and return Dunstoras to the MacCurrans.

Not an easy task.

She paused before the iron-studded doors to the king's receiving room. The guards on either side, aware that she was expected, stared straight ahead, expressionless.

"You'll do fine, my lady," whispered Cormac encouragingly. He stood several paces behind her, attired in an uncharacteristic velvet tunic. Green, of course. The bowman's presence was comforting, but Isabail would have given anything to lean against Aiden's strength at this moment, to lose her fears in the solid warmth of his embrace. An impossible wish, of course. He still had a price on his head.

Palms damp with sweat, Isabail adjusted the parchment in her hands.

With the help of her cousin Archibald, she had documented Daniel's confession to killing John Grant. The words had seemed so perfect when she'd read them a few minutes ago, but now her belly quivered with uncertainty.

Footsteps echoed on the granite tiles behind the doors, and a moment later, the heavy oak panels swung inward. With a stately bow, the king's hostarius ushered her inside, the wave of his hand guiding her across the room to a rather simple wooden throne, upon which sat King Alexander. He wasn't alone. At his right side stood Earl Buchan, the justiciar of Scotia, and next to him, the king's bastard half brother, William Dunkeld. To the king's left stood James Stewart, the high steward. None of them were smiling.

An intimidating group, to say the least.

Isabail crossed the room. She focused her gaze on the bearded face of King Alexander, telling herself the look in his brown eyes was kindly and welcoming. Her brother had been one of his favorite nobles; she had nothing to fear. Except failure.

As she neared, the king rose to his feet and stepped off the dais.

"Lady Isabail," he greeted, grasping her hand in two of his and giving her a gentle squeeze. While not particularly tall, he had the quiet strength and easy confidence that only a man of royal birth possessed. "My condolences on the passing of your brother. He will be sorely missed."

Isabail curtsied. "Thank you, Your Grace."

"Lochurkie has informed me that you have a petition."

Isabail nodded. "I do. But before I make any claim, my honor dictates you be informed of all that transpired in the past sennight." She held out the parchment. "I was witness to a confession that may inform your decision against Laird MacCurran."

The king took the letter, unfolded it, and began to read. When he was finished, he handed the parchment to the justiciar and turned back to her with a faint frown. "Based on this confession, I would willingly pardon the healer . . ."

"Ana Bisset," offered the justiciar.

"Ana Bisset," the king continued. "It would seem she was unfairly accused of murdering your brother."

"Indeed, Your Grace." Buoyed by that victory, Isabail waved Cormac forward. "There is something more. When we searched the keep where de Lourdes was hiding, we found this."

The high steward accepted the velvet bag from Cormac and peered inside. "The ruby necklace, Your Grace. The one commissioned for Queen Yolande."

A smile spread over King Alexander's face. "How excellent."

"De Lourdes was likely responsible for the necklace's original theft," Isabail said.

"There's no proof of that," said the king. "Your brother found the necklace in MacCurran's rooms. And there's still the matter of de Coleville's death. De Lourdes took credit for slaying your brother, but not my courier. And even if he had, de Lourdes failed to name his liege lord, so my judgment against Laird MacCurran must stand. His lands remain forfeit."

Isabail's shoulders drooped. She had failed. Aiden was still a wanted man.

"What of your petition, Lady Isabail?" the king asked.

She drew in a slow, deep breath. All was not lost. The fate of Dunstoras still hung in the balance. A rousing petition might yet change the future—a petition that would be a great deal easier to make if Earl Buchan were not standing a mere twelve paces away. The Comyns were her rivals for Dunstoras, insisting the land rightfully belonged to them due to some ancient description of their border.

Keeping her gaze locked on the royal seal hanging about the king's neck, she said, "I wish to formally claim Dunstoras."

"Your Grace—" began Earl Buchan.

"Not for Earl Lochurkie," Isabail added quickly, "but for myself, in recompense for the death of my brother. John served you faithfully, Your Grace, and for that, he was felled in his prime. Murdered in his bed. The person responsible remains at large, and I beg for some measure of justice, sire. Grant me Dunstoras."

"Our claim to the land dates back three hundred years," Buchan said.

Isabail pictured Aiden's face and the weary faces of his clan. She straightened, facing her detractor squarely. "Lochurkie borders Dunstoras directly to the northeast. Were the lands granted to me, I would have easy support from the earl and could provide warriors to him in times of strife. The Comyns are separated from Dunstoras by the Red Mountains. I believe fulfilling my petition is best for Dunstoras and best for Scotland."

"Strong words, Lady Isabail," the king said.

"My love for my late brother lends me strength, Your Grace."

Buchan's lips twisted sourly. "Majesty, this request has less to do with love than greed. Justice would favor the Comyn claim."

"Lord Buchan," Isabail said firmly. "Surely, the need for peace is paramount. What message do we send to the people of Scotland if we fail to end a bitter clan dispute when the opportunity is within our grasp?"

The king nodded. "What message indeed?"

"How can granting MacCurran's lands to his enemy bring about peace?" demanded Buchan.

"Much easier than you suspect," Isabail said quietly. "I will repair the castle and rebuild the village. I will welcome any MacCurran cottar who pledges his oath to me. And I will bring prosperity to a glen that has seen too much of strife." Lobbying so hard in favor of taking Aiden's home made her stomach queasy. But the thought of losing Dunstoras, of seeing it fall into anyone's hands but her own, made her feel worse.

Isabail turned to the king. "I beseech you, Your Grace. My brother is forever lost to me. Claiming Dunstoras will never make up for his passing, but seeing real justice done will ease my sorrows. Give Dunstoras to the one most committed to its redemption."

The king met her gaze, solemn. As the length of their shared glance stretched beyond mere politeness, the corners of his mouth lifted ever so slightly and he gave her the barest of nods.

"Done."

Isabail sank into the steaming hot tub with a groan of absolute delight. It had been longer than she cared to remember since she'd indulged in such a wonderfully frivolous moment. She leaned back against the wooden bathing tub and closed her eyes. The rose petals Muirne had tossed into the water added a sweet fragrance to the steam that filled her nose and curled the hairs at her nape.

The last fortnight had passed in a blur of travel, political intrigue, and audiences with the king. An exaggeration, that last bit. She'd had only one audience with the king. But, to be fair, it had been a most satisfactory one.

"Shall I wash your back, my lady?"

Isabail opened her eyes. Muirne stood next to the tub, a thick cotton towel in one hand and a bar of lavender soap in the other. The maid wore a broad smile that bordered on a grin.

"I take it Fearghus has finally arrived," Isabail guessed.

"With all of my furniture," Muirne acknowledged happily. "Including the bed, which he has already assembled in our room."

Isabail clapped her hands over her ears. "Enough. No details, please."

"He's a difficult man to please, my Fearghus," Muirne continued, draping the towel over a nearby chair and pulling a stool closer to the tub. "But he says he likes it here."

Isabail leaned forward, giving the maid access to her back. "Dunstoras is a lovely castle."

"I've only one complaint," the maid said, lathering the soap across Isabail's back.

"What would that be?"

"Lady Elisaid."

"Oh, dear," said Isabail, frowning. "What has she done now?"

"She's torn down the tapestries we hung in the great hall yesterday. She wants those dusty old ones with the MacCurran crest put back."

A sigh escaped Isabail's lips. "Fine. Wash them and put them back."

"But, my lady," Muirne protested, "if the king were ever to visit—"

"The king is not going to visit," Isabail said. "Not anytime soon, at any rate. And if we get word that he's about to descend upon us, we'll take them down."

Isabail leaned her forehead on her knees and let the tension flow out of her neck. The maid was doing an exquisite job of soaping her back. Strong, sure strokes that made her limp with languid pleasure. "Och, that's lovely, Muirne. A little lower . . . Ah, perfect."

The maid's thumbs pressed firmly in the flesh between her shoulder blades, and Isabail gave up a little moan. She had not realized how stiff her back had become of late. "You could make your fortune with those hands, goodwife."

"I'm afraid these hands are already spoken for," a gruff voice whispered in her ear.

Isabail smiled. They weren't Muirne's hands at all. She should have guessed by the roughness of the calluses. "Are they now?"

"Only my wife benefits," Aiden said. His hands reached up and unpinned her hair, letting the silky blond tresses fall over her shoulders. The ends fell into the water.

"Now you've done it," she said. "You'll have to wash my hair."

Two large male feet stepped into the bath, and water sloshed over the edge as he sat behind her. He pulled her back against his chest, one arm wrapping around her waist. A familiar sight, that arm—bronzed sinews scattered with a dusting of dark hairs. Strong, powerful, and comforting.

"I can think of worse punishments," he whispered into the hair at her temple.

Isabail relaxed against him. "You're going to smell like roses for the rest of the day," she warned him. "Be prepared to suffer ribald remarks from Niall and Wulf."

"Niall, perhaps," he agreed. "But Wulf has left the castle."

She trailed wet fingers up his arm. "He's still uncomfortable."

"Aye," Aiden acknowledged. "But it's rough on the lad."

"Does Wulf not spend time with him?"

"He does," Aiden said. "But he still doesn't remember the lad. Or Elen, or wee Hugh. They converse like strangers."

"Give them time. They'll find their way."

His hands slid up her soapy body to cup her breasts. "The passage of time is greatly overvalued as a solution to life's ills."

She covered his big hands with hers. "Daniel *was* the man in black."

He snorted. "I'm not so confident as you."

"Did we not find the black wolf cloak at Tayteath? In the very same chamber as we found the necklace and the crown?"

"Aye," he acknowledged. "But what of de Lourdes's talk of a new lover? Of his higher calling to serve justice?"

Isabail sighed. "The man jumped to his death. He was not of right mind. And we've chased down every other clue. Ana's traveling merchant bought the necklace from a man matching Daniel's description near Lochurkie last November."

"And what of the man I spied the night of the poisonings?"

"We've spoken to all five of my guests at Lochurkie that night, and none are a match to the man you saw in the corridor leading to the kitchens."

"Someone else must have been there. Someone we've forgotten."

Isabail slid her soapy hands up his arms, admiring the ropy sinews that cradled her with such tenderness. "I am as vexed as you that we've no proof to offer the king of your innocence. But, in time, the truth will come to light. Have faith."

He gently squeezed her breasts, sending a wave of sweet longing through her body. Her head rolled back, giving him access to the sensitive cords of her neck—and he obliged by lowering his hot mouth to her damp skin. "For the moment, I'm willing to put aside the hunt," he murmured. "MacPherson is gone, my people are back in their homes, and my boot steps once again echo through the passageways of Dunstoras. Thanks to the new lady of the keep."

Isabail pressed her rump against the rigid length of her husband and gave a little wiggle. "I am, of course, pleased that the king awarded me this lovely keep," she said, closing her eyes and imagining him sinking deep inside her. "But I welcome the day when we can publicly announce our wedding and you can take your rightful place as laird."

He nibbled his way up the side of her neck.

"So long as we are together and the name you whisper in the throes of passion is mine, I am content." He slipped a hand under her knees, and with one powerful push, stood up in the tub. Water splashed and dripped. Stepping over the edge and leaving a wet trail of footprints on the floor, Aiden carried her to the huge platform bed. "For now."

As he lowered her to the sheets and then slid his wet body along hers, Isabail smiled.

He was not truly content—he was merely biding his time. Aiden MacCurran was a Highland chief, full of pride, courage, and raw determination. He would not rest until he cleared his name and redeemed the honor of his clan. Which was fine with her.

But tonight, they would forget all that . . . for a moment or two.

"Well, my dearest husband," she said throatily. "All this talk of passion and contentment has piqued my curiosity. Perhaps you want to show me what truly happens when a laird takes a lady."

Glen Storas
The Red Mountains, Scotland
March 1286

Morag ceased weaving, a wooden shuttle held loosely in her left hand. Seated on a low stool, she sat back and studied the cloth taking shape on her vertical loom. A repeating pattern of green, blue, black, and red threads, aligned in straight vertical and horizontal lines, it was every bit as unique and lovely as the fine twill weaves her father had been renowned for.

She gave a soft grunt of satisfaction and resumed her task, wending the wool swiftly through the warp, lifting or lowering the four heddle sticks as needed. She wove four threads of black wool, then twenty threads of blue.

Magnus had left the bothy immediately after breaking the fast to snare a hare for their supper pot. A good thing, really. His presence wreaked havoc upon her concentration. Instead of carefully tracking the thread counts, she found herself dwelling on the faint curve of his smile, or the wondrous breadth of his muscular shoulders, or the rasp and rumble of his deep voice. But market day was fast approaching and a half-woven cloth would not buy them oats for their bannock or candles to burn after dark. Fortunately, with him gone, the cloth on her loom called to her, daring her to bring it to life.

Twenty threads of black, twenty-four of green, four of red.

Each spool of wool that fed her loom was dyed by her own hand, using the tinctures her father had developed, and watching the vivid pattern emerge sent a wave of pure joy washing over her. There was nothing so rewarding as seeing the image in her head take shape on the rack.

With a sigh of contentment, she threw herself wholeheartedly into her weaving.

But when the door to the bothy crashed open, Morag fell off her stool.

Heart pounding, she scrambled to her feet and faced her intruders. Two lean, hungry men stood in the doorway, garbed in the tunics and trews of Lowlanders. She'd spied many such men in the glen when Tormod MacPherson had held Dunstoras Castle for the king, but his mercenaries had departed weeks ago, replaced by Highlanders loyal to the new lady of the keep, Isabail Macintosh. Without taking her eyes off the intruders, she sent a quick prayer skyward. Now would be a fine time for Magnus to return.

"On what authority do you enter my home unbidden?" she demanded, doing her best to tame the quaver in her voice.

The larger of the two men answered, "My own."

Morag could see little of his features, just a halo of bright sunlight around the dark silhouette of his form. But there was no disguising the threat he posed. She tossed aside her shuttle and grabbed the long-handled broom leaning against the wall. Not the most intimidating of weapons, but it was the only thing in easy reach. "And who might you be?"

"My name matters not," he said. "Yield and your life will be spared."

Morag swallowed tightly, her throat suddenly dry. A cotter living off the land was rarely in possession of coin, so there was only one other thing these men might be seeking from a woman alone in the woods . . . and she wasn't willing to give it over. But her hopes of besting two armed men were slim.

She steadied her grip on the broom.

There was still a slight chance they could be persuaded to leave. "What is it you seek? I've no coin, but I'll willingly give all the food and water that I have."

The leader stepped closer, and she was able to see him more clearly. A pockmarked face, long tawny hair, and a finely woven dove gray cloak. Not the sort of cloak an ordinary mercenary would possess.

"We've no interest in your food," he said. Signaling to his cohort to go left, he advanced another step.

"Food is all I'm prepared to give," she said firmly. The bothy was small—a windowless one-room abode with a bed at one end and a small table at the other. The door was a mere four paces away, but the fire pit and a heavy iron cauldron lay between her and escape. "My husband will return anon. You'd best be away."

He grinned. "Your husband? You mean the strapping lad with the lame leg?"

Her heart flopped. Dear Lord. Had they already encountered Magnus? Laid him low in some shadowed part of the wood? "You won't want to vex him," she said, her palms suddenly cold with sweat. "His tolerance for lackwits is low."

A snort of laughter filled the bothy. "We watched him hobble up yon hill. He won't be so difficult to best."

Morag breathed a sigh of relief and banished the image of Magnus falling victim to a well-placed sword with the same determination with which she had built this bothy. Stone by stone. Thatch by thatch. Magnus had regained most of his strength these past four months. He was a far cry from the badly injured man she'd dragged home from the edge of the loch last October. While it was true that his left leg hadn't fully recovered, he was yet a formidable warrior.

"Give me the broom," the pockmarked man coaxed, stretching out his hand, palm open.

Morag slapped his fingertips. Hard.

"He'll be sore enough that you've given me a fright," she warned. She would not be able to keep them at bay for much longer. If only she knew when Magnus would return. How long had he been gone? One hour? Two? "But if you harm me, he'll not quit until he sees me avenged."

Morag jabbed her stick toward the leader, urging him to step back. He held his ground. His eyes were not on the broom, but on her face, and Morag knew he was gauging his best moment to snatch the broom from her hands. She pulled back sharply, terrified of losing her weapon.

"Get thee gone," she snarled.

Her only hope of escape was to run. Backward was not an option—the roof thatching was thick and firmly attached. Magnus had seen to that once he was on his feet. So it had to be forward. But was she sufficiently fleet of foot to round the fire pit and elude the two men?

And what would she do if she miraculously succeeded?

She had no plan for such an event. No hidden weapon, no place to hide.

Morag bit her lip. *Foolish lass.* She'd grown complacent under the protection of the MacCurrans. They'd had no tolerance for brigands and thieves and regularly patrolled her part of the forest. But Laird MacCurran was an outlaw himself now. An enemy of the king. Dunstoras had been seized, ransacked, and finally given into the hands of Lady Macintosh, but her men were too occupied with repairs to the keep and the village blackhouses to be riding regular patrols.

Her gaze flickered to the open door and back to the pockmarked man.

He smiled. "Too late for that, lass."

And without further warning, he stepped toward her, grabbed the broom, and yanked it from her hands. Tossing the stick aside, he thrust a hand into her long black hair, grabbing a sturdy hold. Then he pulled her to his chest with a forceful tug.

Tears sprang to her eyes, but she did not surrender her freedom willingly. Fighting with wild desperation, she raked her fingernails across his face and dug into his eyes with her thumbs. The mercenary loosened his hold on her. Morag bolted for the door.

Praying that Magnus was somewhere nearby, she screamed his name.

"Magnus!"

Magnus stared at his reflection in the calm, sunlit loch. It was a handsome enough face, pleasantly square. And it was familiar. But he struggled with the knowledge that it belonged to a man he didn't know. Wulf MacCurran was his true name, not Magnus. He was cousin to the laird and father to a fine lad, but five months after an attack that had left him near dead, he still could not remember one moment of the life he'd led before waking in Morag's bed.

Dipping a hand, he scattered the image and scooped up some water.

The water was icy cold as it slid down his throat, despite the hint of spring in the air.

He'd returned to Morag's bothy after being reunited with his kin at Candlemas because nothing else felt right. Chopping wood, hunting for food, and repairing her home gave him purpose—a purpose that seemed more in line with his beliefs about himself than living in a castle, even though he'd been assured by all that he and his family had roomed there before the fateful night that had stolen his life away.

Magnus abruptly pushed to his feet, his hands fisting. He attempted a smooth stand, but his left leg betrayed him, quivering in protest. The hare hanging from his belt swung wildly as he moved. It was a lean offering for Morag's stewpot, but he'd been lucky to snare anything this close to the bothy after MacPherson's mercenaries had decamped. The glen wildlife had scattered far and wide as the two hundred men trudged east toward MacPherson land a fortnight ago.

He stilled the swing of the hare and retraced his steps along the pebbled beach.

Normally, he would return promptly, eager to share his success with Morag and add the rabbit to the stew. But, of late, she'd begun to stare at her loom with wistful intent. If his presence caused to her to forgo her weaving, she'd come to resent him in time. And resentment was not the emotion he wished to cultivate in his lovely, dark-haired benefactress.

But how long should he stay away?

It was midday now, the sun high in the sky. Was the morning enough? It was hard to know. Although she sat at the loom infrequently while he was present, the moments she did spend displayed an incredible talent he could barely fathom. Changing colored threads without pause, moving sticks up and down, and sliding the shuttle from one side of the loom to the other at blurring speed clearly required a quick mind and nimble fingers. The cloth that developed at the bottom was a miracle of sorts.

His feet turned in the direction of the bothy.

He'd take a peek inside the hut, and if she was yet enthralled in her weaving, he'd grab a bannock and some cheese and head back into the wilds.

At the bottom of a woodland hill, about two furlongs from the bothy, he paused and frowned. In the soft mud of the path, the print of a bootheel was clearly outlined. The problem was, it was too small to be *his* bootheel and too big to be Morag's. Given the heavy downpour of last eve, a print this crisp must be fresh.

Magnus's gaze lifted.

There was no sign of movement in the trees, but his heartbeat quickened anyway. Morag was alone. And he'd left his sword hidden in the woodpile behind the bothy.

He set off a run.

Unfortunately, his lame leg proved uncooperative, wobbling weakly with every stride and sending shards of excruciating pain to his hip. He was forced to slow to a hobbled run, and even then the pain was biting. Still, he made it to the clearing in good time.

The door to the hut hung open, the interior cast in dark shadow.

The open door was not, of itself, a bad omen. Morag might simply have chosen to partake of the sunshine and the unusually warm day. But he could not hear the *clack-clack* of the loom in operation, nor could he hear her humming as she was wont to do when busy with a task.

He skirted the clearing until he reached the back of the bothy, then quietly dug between the stacked firewood for his long sword. Wrapped in several layers of burlap to protect it from the elements, the bronze-hilted weapon was exactly where he had left it. It settled into his palm with a familiarity that made his blood sing. Even in the absence of his memories, one thing remained true—he was born to be a warrior.

The sharp crack of wood on wood reverberated inside the bothy.

Magnus's grip tightened on the sword. 'Twas not the sound of something falling, but the sound of something thrown with great force. But as ominous as that sound was, it did not prepare him for what he heard next.

"Magnus!"

His heart sank into his boots. The raw desperation in Morag's voice could not be mistaken. She was in dire straits. Oblivious to the pain, Magnus ran for the cottage door at full speed. When he entered, it took precious long moments for his eyes to adjust to the dimness. Masking his inability to see well, he halted just inside the door, planted both feet wide, and challenged his opponent with cold, lethal intent.